family

and

other

accidents

family

and

other

accidents

A Novel

SHARI GOLDHAGEN

broadway books

New York

BROADWAY

PUBLISHED BY BROADWAY BOOKS

A hardcover edition of this book was originally published in 2006 by Doubleday.
It is here reprinted by arrangement with Doubleday.

"Stealing Condoms from Joe Jr.'s Room" originally appeared in the *Indiana Review*.

"By Being Young, By Being Nice" originally appeared in the *Wascana Review* under
the title "Things She Wants."

"The Next Generation of Dead Kennedys" originally appeared in *Confrontation*.

Published in the United States by Broadway Books, an imprint of The Doubleday
Broadway Publishing Group, a division of Random House, Inc., New York.
www.broadwaybooks.com

BROADWAY BOOKS and its logo, a letter B bisected on the diagonal,
are trademarks of Random House, Inc.

Book design by Caroline Cunningham

Cataloging-in-Publication Data is on file with the Library of Congress.

ISBN-13: 978-0-7679-2588-4
ISBN-10: 0-7679-2588-2

PRINTED IN THE UNITED STATES OF AMERICA

1 3 5 7 9 10 8 6 4 2

FIRST EDITION

To my family

contents

stealing condoms

from joe jr.'s

room

One hundred and ninety-eight hours before Jenny Greenspan's birth control pills should kick in, Connor is in juvenile traffic court explaining how he followed a pickup truck through a yellow light and slammed into the side of a minivan.

"It was raining and hard to see." He tries to sound apologetic, the way his brother suggested on the ride over. Really he just wants court to be over so he can use the bathroom; he's had a weird stomachache since Jenny told him about the pill last night. "I assumed it was okay, because the truck ahead of me made it through. I was only following."

"Your Honor, the conditions *were* treacherous." Next to him Jack pipes in self-assured and authoritative. "If you look at the accident report, the officer even made note of it."

Bored and gray-bearded, the judge looks at Jack and actually yawns, says Connor should be more careful next time and pay the seventy-five-dollar fine at the cashier's window. Connor thanks the judge because

Jack thanks the judge. Hurried as always, Jack pulls on his beige trench coat and fishes his wallet out of his briefcase before they've even left the courtroom. He rips out a blank check, hands it to Connor, tells him to wait in line while he calls his office. By the time Jack comes back Connor is forging his brother's signature and finishing with the clerk.

"Fucking ridiculous we had to come all the way down here," Jack says. At twenty-seven, he's ten years older, a second-year associate in their father's law firm, Connor's legal guardian for five and a half more months. "We could have just mailed that."

"Yeah, it would have been easier." Connor agrees to be polite; he's just glad his driver's license wasn't revoked. He's got his eyes on the men's room down the hall. "Can I run to the bathroom—"

"Aww come on, Conn." Shaking his head, Jack flips up his wrist and looks at his watch. "I have to drop you home before I can go back to work."

Connor starts to say he didn't enjoy spending Friday afternoon in court either, but changes his mind. Last month, while waiting for Jack at the Bagley Road Repair shop after the accident, the unsalvageable remains of his car bleeding oil and green fluid on the garage floor, Connor had felt oppressively guilty and had developed a laundry list of things he would do to make Jack's life better: learn to cook so Jack wouldn't eat greasy takeout every night; pick up Jack's dry cleaning; apply to Case Western and Ohio State and not just schools out west. So far he has done none of those things—he hasn't even thanked Jack for paying *his* traffic fine. Maybe not using the bathroom is a place to start.

"I can wait until I get home," Connor says, though he's not entirely sure. "Thanks for coming with me. I know you're crazy busy."

"Go ahead," Jack growls, as if it's truly a great concession. With the back of his hand, he waves Connor to the men's room. "Just don't take forever, okay?"

On the toilet stall walls, graffiti claims Pearl Jam sucks, the East

Side could kick the West Side's ass, and everyone should vote Clinton. Briefly Connor fantasizes these notes are from the mind of a serial murderer or a bank robber—infinitely more interesting than another juvenile traffic offender. But then he reads that Jill C. gives awesome head, and he's thinking about Jenny and the pill again. On the phone last night, she said they should have sex when it started working next weekend. "Sure," he'd said; he didn't think seventeen-year-old boys were allowed to turn down such offers. Even if the seventeen-year-old boy was almost certain he didn't love his girlfriend.

When Connor comes out of the men's room, Jack is down the hall by the water fountain, his hand on the shoulder of a girl. Connor can't see her well, but can tell she has great hair—long and red and curly. Her neck is tilted back, like she's laughing, like something Jack said is really fabulous—he probably didn't tell her there wasn't time to use the bathroom. Noticing Connor, Jack nods, leans in to say something to the girl, his fingers still on her arm. As they part, she turns to look at him again, but Jack doesn't look back.

"Who was that?" Connor asks.

"*That* was a reporter from the *Plain Dealer.*" Jack's mood has turned 180. He smiles, shoulders loose, coat draped over his arm, suit jacket unbuttoned. "She ran into me at the drinking fountain, and her stuff went everywhere. We're going for coffee tonight. Cute, isn't she?"

"Yeah," Connor says flatly. A girl from Penn's Young Alumni chapter spent the night twice last week, and the temp who organized files in Jack's office still calls their house constantly.

"You know, we've got to get cracking on teaching you stick," Jack says. "I'm going to work all weekend, so I can just skip out this afternoon. Let's go home, change, and you can practice for a couple hours."

Connor nods. Jack had used the accident as an excuse to get the BMW, saying he'd give Connor the Nissan Sentra he'd driven all through law school. But the Sentra is a manual transmission, and for weeks Jack has been promising to teach Connor how to drive it. Now, with Jack greased and happy from the encounter with another girl he doesn't need, is as good a time as any.

But an hour later (one hundred and ninety-six hours before Jenny Greenspan's birth control takes effect), on an empty service road in the business district, Jack is wound and tense as Connor tries to put the Sentra in second gear.

"Shift, shift." Jack slams his foot on an imaginary clutch on the passenger side, squeezes the utility hook overhead. "Now!"

But even as Connor switches the weight in his feet from one pedal to the other, the car shudders and dies.

"You can't just sit in the middle of the road," Jack says, as if they're on the interstate instead of a deserted alley. "Are you going to start the fucking car?"

Indignation percolates in Connor's throat. He restarts the Sentra. Downshifts. Stops at the stop sign—the engine trembles, stays running. Jack shakes his head, rubs eyebrows with his thumb and forefinger. Connor makes the easy left from the one-way onto the main road.

"What are you doing!" Jack yells as a Ford Taurus, bright yellow and angry, hurtles toward them. "Wrong side! Wrong side!"

Jack reaches for the wheel just as Connor starts to turn it. Hand on top of hand, they jerk the car across the double yellow line. The long blast of a horn dopplering by them.

"Pull in there." Unnaturally red, Jack points to a low-rise industrial complex with a squat sign offering the name "Cleveland Communications." "How did you ever get your license in the first place?"

"I made a mistake, okay?" In the worn vinyl driver's seat, Connor stares straight ahead as Jack gets out of the passenger door and comes around to the driver's side. When Jack opens the door, cold air rushes in, stinging his bitten lips.

"Get out." Jack bends down so they're eye level. "You're done driving today."

"It wasn't my fault."

"You decided we were in England." Jack drums long fingers on the car frame. "How is that not your fault?"

"You were making me nervous."

"Yeah, well, it makes me nervous when you drive into other cars. You're going to give me a fucking coronary." Their father's heart hadn't outlasted his fifties. Instead of exercising or eating vegetables, Jack makes lots of slightly off comments about having heart attacks. "Come on. If I have to take you out of the car, we're both going to feel really stupid."

Connor doesn't move, and Jack reaches in and unhooks the seat belt. Putting one hand on Connor's shoulder, Jack slides the other under the bend in his brother's knees. Maybe half an inch taller, Jack outweighs Connor by twenty-five pounds, could probably pick him up without much effort.

"Fine, I'm moving." Connor smacks Jack's hands away, climbs over the console into the passenger side, feet tangling with the gear shift and the cup holder.

Jack sighs, gets in, starts driving.

Cleveland rolls past, brown and crunchy in early November. Springsteen's *Born to Run* album is in the cassette deck, so low it's barely audible. As "Thunder Road" starts its whiny harmonica intro, Connor fiddles with the volume knob. But it's hard to adjust it blindly and he doesn't want to chance looking at his brother. So he stares out the window, tapping his fingers on the cold, cold glass in time with the music.

"Are you mad at me?" Jack asks.

"No," Connor tells the window.

A two-mile silence.

"Look, I don't think we can do this without killing each other," Jack says, turning onto their cul-de-sac. "Call the driving school you went to last year. Just give them a check."

It's the same kind of thing his parents did before they died—his father when Connor was ten; his mother of an aneurysm while showing a house in Shaker Heights two years ago. When Connor was born, his parents had been old enough to be his grandparents; there'd been lots of things they paid other people to do for their youngest son.

"I can't just go to the driving school," he says. "You're going to need to sign something."

"Have them fax me whatever I need to sign," Jack says. "Do you need a ride anywhere? I told the reporter I'd meet her at nine."

Waiting for the garage door to roll open, Connor can see into his bedroom window, where the shades are open, lights left on. Over his desk hangs the framed black-and-white poster of John Kennedy, hand under his chin, looking pensive and presidential.

"Jenny can pick me up," Connor says, out the door and in the house before Jack even puts the car in park.

One hundred and ninety-two hours before Jenny Greenspan's pills start working, Connor's head is between her thighs in a pile of dead leaves in Lakefront Park.

"Higher, higher." Jenny is on her back, jeans and panties bunched around hiking boots at her ankles. "Right there."

He and Jenny have been going down on each other every weekend for the past four months, but he still has no idea what she's asking for, what he's supposed to be doing. His friends offered bad metaphorical advice—like your tongue is a fine-point pen; not like you're trying to wallpaper a house. None of them warned it would taste very, very bad or that her pubic hairs would get caught in his throat. Jenny's orgasm— a series of uninspired "oh Gods"—seems largely faked, far too similar to that scene in *When Harry Met Sally*.

"Your turn." She pulls up her pants and runs fingers through her long ponytail. "But I don't see why we have to do this here. Your brother never cares if we're in your room."

"It's a nice night." Connor flips onto his back and unzips his jeans. "And the woods are romantic."

When he thought of it earlier in the day, it *had* seemed romantic—sort of rustic, a mountain man kind of thing. But it's about thirty-five degrees, and they're both freezing, having fashioned a makeshift blanket from their ski jackets and scarves. The leaves and crisp grass itch his ass, and a stick practically poked his eye out while he was going down on Jenny. They're *really* in the park because Connor wanted to get away from Jack, and the Sentra, and the new girl with the red hair.

Jenny curls her fingers around his dick, and he trembles—more because her hands are cold than because of anything she's doing. Then her hot mouth on his cock, going up and down, up and down. He props himself on his elbows and reaches for her breasts, malleable and firm like balled socks. Her cheeks are red from the breeze off the lake and her tan has almost completely faded.

They met as lifeguards at Euclid Beach last summer, peeling sheets of dead skin off each other's leathery brown shoulders and making out under the pier during breaks. She lives a few suburbs away in Solon and wanted to keep dating when school started. He likes the oval muscles in her calves, the dimples deep in her checks, how she says "soda" instead of "pop," is pretty sure he doesn't love her and often finds he has nothing to say in response to things she talks about when she calls.

As he feels himself starting to give, he taps her shoulder.

"Jen," he moans, "you should move."

She bobs out of the way and white jizz arcs into the air, landing on the sleeve of his coat. He just stares at it until he remembers to kiss her forehead through her knit ski hat; she likes that. Clothes and coats back on, they make their way to the car, branches and dying autumn things cracking under their feet. She threads her arm round his waist—always touching him, as if that could fill the awkward spaces between them.

Hand resting on Jenny's on the armrest, he drives her mother's station wagon back to his house. A Simon and Garfunkel song comes on the radio, and they both sing, quietly at first.

"Kathy, I'm lost, I said, though I knew she was sleeping. I'm empty and aching and I don't know why."

Squeezing his hand, Jenny smiles, and they sing louder. Her voice is thin but pretty—one more thing to like. On the high notes, his tenor splinters. Jenny laughs, and Connor forgets that they have to have sex in one hundred and ninety-one hours, that he can't drive stick, that Jack keeps pressuring him to apply to Case Western.

"Counting the cars on the New Jersey Turnpike, they've all come to look for Amer-i-ca—"

He stops singing when he sees the strange car in his driveway, realizing it must belong to Jack's reporter.

"Don't forget to get condoms before next weekend," Jenny says, as if she were reminding him to call ahead and find out movie times. "It's good to have a backup method, just to be on the safe side."

Connor gives a nod punctuated by the birth-control-announcement stomachache.

"I'll call you tomorrow," she says. She calls every day, even when they've just seen each other and she has nothing to say. Sometimes she'll call while watching reruns of *Three's Company* or *The Brady Bunch* and narrate the episodes to him scene by scene.

"Sure." He starts to get out of the car, but ducks back in to kiss her; she likes that kiss, too.

Her headlights cast his treelike shadow against the house as he fumbles through his pocket for the garage opener and waits for the door to rumble up. Side by side the M3 and the Sentra look like something from *Let's Make a Deal*. Through the laundry room and kitchen, Connor is at the stairs when Jack calls him from the family room.

"You didn't actually get a chance to meet Mona at the courthouse," Jack says. He's sitting on the floor next to the girl with good hair. The two appear to be playing Scrabble—board unfolded, letter tiles peppering the carpet. It's not the thing that pops to mind when Connor thinks about sex, but Jack gets laid on a regular basis. Jack points at her. "Mona Lockridge, general assignment reporter for the award-winning *Cleveland Plain Dealer*." Pointing at him: "Connor Reed, Beachwood High School senior."

"Hey." The reporter nods. She's cute in a pale way—an unfocused-eyes kind of way; a freckles-across-the-bridge-of-her-nose kind of way—very different from girls Jack usually dates, with their sleek page-boy haircuts and fitted skirts. "I'm sorry about your car accident."

"Thanks." Connor glares at Jack, who didn't need to tell the reporter about the accident, who didn't need to chastise him in the Sentra for an hour, who didn't need to be a cheeseball when introducing the reporter.

"Where's Jenny?" Jack asks, absolutely oblivious.

"She has a midnight curfew," Connor says, more accusatory than he intends.

"I can give you a curfew." Jack shrugs. He's wearing his uniform of khakis and a blue button-down. Since starting at Jones Day, all his clothes, even non–work clothes, look exactly the same. For Christmas, Connor decided to get him stock in Brooks Brothers. "You've got leaves in your hair."

"Yeah, it's fall." Connor tries not to sound sullen, not in front of the reporter with her amazing hair, who knows only that he gets into car accidents, is somehow mad about not having a curfew, must roll around outside. "That happens."

The reporter laughs, a little nervously, and the way her nose crinkles makes her beautiful, even though she probably isn't, is probably only pretty. It's funny she's a reporter because she looks like the character from the comic strip about the reporter he used to read at breakfast—Brenda Starr.

"Well, um, speaking of curfews, I should get going," she says. "I'm sorry. I've got work at seven tomorrow."

Pushing herself to her feet, she straightens her sweater, brushes palms across the front of her jeans. Connor knows she's leaving because she doesn't want to sleep with his brother, or she doesn't want to do it yet and doesn't trust herself to stay, and he likes her for that, likes her for wanting it to mean something.

Her hands are pale and chaffed, nails short and unpolished. They look cold, and he wants to warm them between his own hands. But it's Jack who reaches for her fingers.

"Don't go," Jack says. "Not so soon."

"I'm sorry." She squeezes Jack's fingers—neither one of them particularly interested in Connor or his lack of a curfew anymore. Then Jack smiles his Jack smile, and Connor takes that as his cue to leave.

He and Jack may look alike, have the same black hair and eyes, but when Jack smiles he looks like such a yearbook-handsome, all-around good guy. Last weekend Jenny gave Connor doubles of photos her parents took before homecoming, and he noticed his own smile looked not only forced but pained—more like he was squinting from a migraine than genuinely happy.

Upstairs Connor's bedroom door is closed, and he wonders if that means Jack brought Brenda Starr upstairs or planned to and didn't want her to see the mess—sheets and comforter on the floor, college application parts scattered across the quilted mattress, clothes and shoes and school stuff blanketing every square inch of the carpet, skis and poles creating a dangerous obstacle in the middle of it all. When the maid service came last week, the uniformed girl just shook her head and said she wouldn't touch the room. There was nothing she could do. He'll have to make them clean it next Saturday so he and Jenny can have sex; the dull stomachache.

Connor's bedroom is really Jack's old room. But Jack had been staying in their parents' room since he came back from Philadelphia after their mother died. Last year Connor had switched to Jack's room because it was bigger and had a double bed. But he never got around to taking Jack's old stuff off the walls—an Indians poster with a home game schedule from eleven seasons before, framed photos of Chagrin Falls Jack's high school girlfriend gave him for Christmas a decade ago, and the huge JFK poster over the desk. At first Connor had hated the poster with its intense eyes, but he grew used to being watched by someone with more authority and experience. Now he finds Kennedy oddly reassuring. With Jack hardly ever home, Connor has started running things by Kennedy, just to get a second opinion. Generally the poster doesn't say much. Though Kennedy didn't object when Connor said he wanted to leave flat Ohio, with its strip malls and burger chains.

Downstairs, the front door opens and closes, and Connor watches through the window. Jack is holding Brenda Starr's hand, walking her to her car. Looking around to make sure nobody is watching, Jack leans in to kiss her, and their faces disappear behind her hair. Body contouring to fit the car, back arched, she has one hand on the metal frame for support, the other against Jack's chest. Still holding her hand, Jack starts to walk away but then they're kissing again, then apart, together, apart, together, like scissor blades. Connor looks away. From the wall, Kennedy suggests Connor need only watch and learn.

Thirty-three hours before the scheduled sex, Connor finds a box of condoms in Jack's nightstand drawer, exactly where he thought they'd be. Pocketing two square packets, he puts the box back in the drawer on top of coffeemaker instructions, a broken watchband, cellophane-wrapped restaurant mints, and a picture from Jack's college graduation that Connor must have taken because Jack and their mother have no heads: tall bodies (their mother's in some turquoise wrap dress, Jack's in a black gown) against a redbrick building somewhere in Philly.

Picking it up, Connor wonders why Jack kept the photo; they have better pictures from Jack's commencement—a good one of the three of them is in a silver frame downstairs. Yet there *is* something interesting about this shot, where the hands have become the focus. Both sets of fingers long and tapering—Jack's hold the box with his diploma, while their mother's clutch her leather handbag. She had used her hands when she'd talked, and his mother had talked a lot, always exaggerated and fast.

She'd been a member of Coldwell Banker's Five Million Dollar Club for fifteen years. Other than constantly telling Connor he needed a haircut, his mother had hardly been around to offer sitcom-mom witticisms. But a few months before she died, the two of them had been in a booth at Slyman's, quickly eating sandwiches before she had to show a house. "You know about sex and love, and all of that, right?" she'd asked from nowhere, reaching out to put her hand on his. He'd looked down at his corned beef and nodded, anticipating the horrible conversation he'd seen in movies. "Good," she said, focusing again on her turkey sandwich. "Just try not to be careless with people, okay?" That had been the extent of his sex talk. He wonders now if she meant careless with girls like Jenny. Careless the way Jack is careless.

Lying back on the bed, Connor stares at the ceiling and thinks about the girls Jack has brought home who've shared the view. Other young Jones Day associates, an MBA student at Case, his married high school sweetheart, other childhood "friends" who live in more exciting places but come home to Cleveland for Thanksgiving and Christmas. He wonders what they thought looking at the ceiling, what they expected—if they knew they were just there for a little while. Wonders if the reporter has seen Jack's ceiling yet. Since meeting her the other night, Connor started reading Brenda Starr again—not a whole lot has changed for Brenda: she's still chasing Basil, still wandering into zany situations. He hopes Jack's reporter hasn't looked at the ceiling, hopes she really is different than the sleek-skirted girls, and that the nervous laugh and freckles across her nose are real. He wonders how Jenny *really* feels about him, why she wants to have sex with him, why she wants him to be her first.

A car chugs down the cul-de-sac, but Connor is certain it's not his brother. Some company Jack isn't allowed to name is being bought this week; and he has been getting home after midnight. Congested and cranky with some flu, Jack just grumbles up the stairs and goes to bed when he does come home. Connor has barely spoken with him since last Friday's driving debacle. Still Connor puts the photo back in the drawer and goes to his room, where he puts the rubbers in his own nightstand drawer next to mix tapes Jenny made him, his less-than-stellar SAT results, and *Penthouse* magazines he and some friends stole from the Little Professor in Beachwood Place a few years ago. From the wall over the desk, Kennedy makes a snide comment about how he never stole condoms from Joe Jr.'s room.

"I don't have a car," Connor says.

Five hours before Jenny Greenspan's pills should start working, Connor draws a face with squiggly hair on the cover page of a University of Colorado application. He's having trouble concentrating because the pre-sex stomachache he's been having has been bad all day and because Jack, who's in denial about being sick, has ratcheted the heat up to ninety.

"I'm taking Mona to dinner at nine." Across the kitchen table, Jack is wearing all kinds of clothes—another pair of generic pants, another blue button-down (business casual acceptable on weekends), a University of Pennsylvania sweatshirt, and a stocking cap Connor is sure is his. Even though it's Saturday and he just got home from his office, he's going through a mammoth box of contracts, highlighting the word "buyer" with a fat yellow marker. His job is absolutely nothing like lawyers' on TV; Connor can't believe Jack went to seven years of school to be such a minuscule cog in the workings of the Man. "Do you need a ride anywhere?"

"Jenny can pick me up," Connor says.

It's been snowing all afternoon, but half an hour ago he gave up trying to convince Jack it was too hot in the house and so he just stripped to boxers. He shifts to unstick his sweaty thighs from the wooden chair. Jack starts coughing, keeps coughing, and continues coughing while Connor wonders if someone can die from coughing. Getting up, he has the impulse to smack Jack's back, the way their mother used to. Instead he runs the faucet, fills a glass of water.

"You should go to bed." Connor hands Jack the drink. "You sound like you're choking on a cat."

Jack nods, takes a sip. Connor thinks he should tell Jack about the sex—discussing that with older brothers is industry standard, even older bothers who tell you there's no time to use the bathroom. He's about to say something when Jack winces, rubs his chest, points to Connor's applications.

"Those things would look a lot better if you typed them," he says.

Connor shrugs; Jack highlights more words, starts coughing again. Something yellow-green and unpleasant flies from his mouth and lands next to Connor's drawing on the manila paper. Connor just stares at it; he hadn't realized he was drawing Brenda Starr.

"Does the reporter want to write novels?" Connor asks, looking at the sketch with its linked circles for hair. "I feel like most journalists I know really want to write books."

"How would I know; we've been on one date." Jack cocks his head. "And what other journalists do you know?"

"I just think it's funny she's a reporter, because she looks like Brenda Starr."

"The woman who sings 'Total Eclipse of the Heart'?"

"That's Bonnie Tyler," Connor says. "Brenda Starr is the comic strip; it's in the *Plain Dealer.*"

"You've thought about this an awful lot." Jack smiles, eyes narrowing into something between a shared joke and ridicule. "Do *you* like her?"

"No." Connor looks at the squiggle next to the drying snot. "I just thought she seemed nice."

Jack nods. "Did you call the driving school?"

Connor says nothing.

"Good to see you're really on top of this." Jack coughs again. He winces and rubs his chest again. "You might think about doing that Monday."

But Connor doesn't want to think about Monday because that's after tomorrow, which is after tonight, which he's still thinking of as something distant and abstract—something happening to him that he has no control over, like turning into a werewolf or the Incredible Hulk. Blood vibrates in his temples; the dull stomachache. Maybe he's getting sick.

"Do you think what you have is contagious?" he asks.

Jenny's pills are probably working, but instead of having sex, Connor is picking globs of melted cheese from waffle fries and celery out of a tuna melt in a booth at Yours Truly. Across from him, Jenny is playing with bread crusts she cut off her BLT.

"I had a really big lunch," he apologizes to the defeated sandwich.

Actually he had half a bowl of Frosted Mini-Wheats and a couple cups of coffee, but his stomachache has progressed to the point of distraction. Gesturing toward the dishes between them, he asks if Jenny is finished.

"Yeah." She smiles, dimples popping into creamy cheeks. "We don't want to get too full and prevent other activities."

He takes the check to the register and surveys the display of gum, mints, and antacid tablets. Growing up, Connor rarely saw his father, but one of his few distinct memories he has is of his dad eating Tums the way other people chain-smoked—a heftier, grumpier version of Jack popping them off the roll and into his mouth with a smooth, practiced motion. Connor buys a package and chews the first three. Putting the change in his wallet, he looks at his long fingers—cuticles shredded, knuckles scabbed and red from rock climbing at Headlands before it got too cold—and wonders what his mother would have thought of Jenny. The Tums have an odd peppermint flavor; he's pretty sure he doesn't love her.

"Ready?" Jenny comes up behind him and takes his hand, leads him to the station wagon in the lot.

Lake-effect snow is still falling—each dandruff flake turning to water as it hits the pavement. She gives him the keys, assuming he'll drive her mother's car, which he does without question, even though it's snowing and dark and he has been trying not to drive in bad weather since the accident. But he makes it home safely and kills the engine in the driveway. As the car loses heat, he stares at the big brick colonial where he has lived his entire life—the giant elm in the front lawn almost completely bare.

"Come on, Conn." Jenny squeezes his fingers. "You still want to do this, right?"

From his bedroom window, where he left the lights on, Kennedy says it shouldn't be a question.

"The torch has been passed to a new generation," Connor says, and Jenny laughs, tells him he's weird.

When the garage door rolls open, the BMW is gone, and the Sentra is in the same place it has been for a week.

"Why is it like three hundred degrees in here?" Jenny asks as they kick slushy snow off hiking boots, shimmy out of down coats, scarves, and gloves.

Explaining about Jack being sick, Connor spins the thermostat down twenty degrees, and the heat chugs to a stop. Jenny leads him upstairs to his room, which has been vacuumed and straightened—blue sheets tucked into crisp corners, pillows fluffed. Even though Jack isn't home and would never come in without knocking, Connor locks the door behind them. They sit on the edge of his bed, and he looks at their feet, then at Kennedy on the wall, puts his hand on Jenny's thigh.

"I made a mix." She grabs her backpack, unzips the front pocket, and puts the tape in the bookshelf stereo.

Other tapes she gave him have themed names—"Fourth of July Mix," "Three Month Anniversary Mix," "Road Trip Mix"—all written in her curly, girlie handwriting, and he wonders if she called this one "Sex Mix." The first song is Dylan's "Tangled Up in Blue," which is reassuring. Relaxing, he brushes her long hair behind her shoulder, kisses her, tasting bacon and tomato.

"You taste like Tums." She licks her lips; he stops kissing her.

"I'm sorry." He wants Jenny to say she's nervous, too, that her guts are knotted and clenched, legs and arms distant and tingly.

"My mom takes them for calcium," she says.

Kennedy probably never had sex that started this way. Kissing again, his hands on her waist, hers on his shoulders. He notices a faint blond mustache above her lip, realizes he doesn't know her father's first name or if she believes in God.

"We should take off our clothes," she says.

Sweaters and turtlenecks are wrestled overhead and jeans are wiggled from slim hips. Bra and boxers are removed with quick, deliberate motions. Finally they take off their socks, because they look dumb wearing nothing but socks. He met Jenny in a red bathing suit and flip-flops, but being naked with her embarrasses him, especially with the light from the overhead fixture, especially with Kennedy watching.

"You'd make a good junkie." She points to the thick blue-green vein running from the underside of his wrist to his elbow. Another one of those things she says that he isn't sure there's a good response to.

But it doesn't seem to matter, because she's easing herself down on his bed (Jack's old bed), pulling him close. Two fingers in her panties, he kneads the folds of flesh, waits for her to moisten. Below them the garage door opens and closes; footsteps and muted voices—Jack and a girl, probably Brenda Starr. By the closet, the vent sputters to life, spewing additional hot air into the sauna of his bedroom, where the window is already fogged.

"That's good," Jenny says. "Are *you* ready?"

And he is ready, physically, he's ready.

Touching his lips to the bones in her knee, he's flushed and sweaty because he wants to be inside her, and because he feels guilty wanting that when he doesn't love her, and because it's too hot in the house and he might be coming down with the Jack flu. Two sets of feet sound on the stairs along with the laughter that makes Brenda Starr beautiful. Jack's door closes across the hall.

"Maybe now?" Jenny says.

Finding the condoms in his drawer, Connor slides one on, climbs on top of her. Trying to line his cock up with her pussy, he thinks of it in terms of a puzzle piece or a finger in a glove. Only it's not working like that—more like forcing a plastic spoon into a block of cheddar cheese. Beneath him her face screws up—certainly more like pain than happiness. She gasps and jerks her body away from his. Pulling out, he looms over her on hands and knees, casting shadows on her smooth belly.

"Why'd you stop?" she asks.

"I thought I was hurting you."

"It's supposed to hurt the first time."

"I don't want to do it if it hurts you," he says, and means it. He wonders about Jack next door who does this all the time with all kinds of girls, girls he hasn't known half as long as Connor has known Jenny. "Maybe we should wait?"

On the wall, Kennedy rubs his eyebrows with his thumb and forefinger and shakes his head—just like Jack does—but Connor might just be delusional from the heat.

"No, I want to," Jenny says. "Maybe you should go down on me a little? Make things wetter?"

So he's back under her raised knees, where things never tasted all that great to begin with. But now she's bleeding, the metal mixed with a strange rubbery taste from the condom. George Michael's "I Want Your Sex" comes from the mix tape on the stereo, which is just stupid. Connor's digestive tract digests itself; he might get sick, is rapidly losing his erection.

Across the hall, Jack is coughing again over Brenda Starr's soft voice, her words indecipherable. And even though he doesn't want to, even though it's not fair, Connor closes his eyes and imagines the reporter—her hair, the freckles across the bridge of her nose, her cold hands. Things stir again. He thinks about Brenda Starr staring at the smooth plaster of the ceiling in Jack's room, about her pale skin on Jack's gray sheets. About Jack reaching into his nightstand drawer for the box of condoms.

"I think I'm ready now," Jenny says, but she's not Jenny anymore, she's Brenda Starr, and maybe he's not Connor, but Jack.

Silky and sure, he swings his leg over her, pressing himself inside. Things tear, and he feels her become stiff and rigid underneath him.

"Stop," she says, pushing on his chest with open palms. But he can't stop because he's finally inside, and it's not really something he can control anymore—he truly has become the Incredible Hulk. "Connor, you're hurting me. Stop, please!"

"I can't yet," he mumbles, kisses her tear-streaked cheek. "All I need is a minute, Brenda."

Trying to soothe her, he smoothes her hair from her face. He expects red curls, and is surprised when his hands connect with fine long strands. Still it's enough; everything in his lower body tightens to loosen.

"I'm not Brenda," she says. "Stop, please."

Then it's done. Panting and drained, he tumbles off of her, feeling relief not unlike the feeling that comes immediately after puking.

Jenny looks as if she has no idea who or what he is—the mild-mannered professor turned green and massive. She inches against the wall, as far away from him as she can get. Underneath her there's a circular stain that looks almost brown on the blue flannel, and Connor winces, realizing it's her blood.

"I asked you to stop, and you didn't stop," she says. "And you called me Brenda."

"I did?" He tries to wrap arms around her shoulders, but she squirms away. "I'm sorry, Jen. I was just thinking about the comic strip."

She's out of bed, looking for her clothes on the floor—stabbing legs into the holes of her panties; working her arms through a lacy bra.

"You didn't stop."

"Please, Jenny." Sitting up, he takes off the oozy condom, but can't find anywhere to put it so he just holds it. "I'm sorry."

She shakes her head, pulls on her sweater, backs into the hall. Condom still in hand, he puts on boxers and goes after her.

"Jen, wait," he calls from the upstairs landing. At the front door she turns around, dark hair fanning behind her. "You know I'm not like that."

"I don't know *what* I know."

"I'm so sorry, Jenny," he says. "Come back. You can stay for a half hour and still get back in time."

"Call me tomorrow. Maybe things will be different." And then she's gone.

On his way back to his own room, Connor pauses outside Jack's door, listens to the muffled sounds—Jack hacking, saying something about South Euclid; the reporter's soft laughter; rustling that might be sheets or clothes or skin. Connor squats, resting his head against the wood to listen. Things become almost rhythmic—the reporter's small moans; Jack's voice gentle, asking if everything is okay, if there's anything he can do. Closing his eyes, Connor strains to hear the difference between what's going on inside and what happened in his room.

Then everything is quite, then shuffling, then the door opens and Brenda Starr stumbles over him, her bare feet cold against his calf. Yelping, she scurries down the hall. Too stunned to move, Connor just sits there.

"What's wrong?" Jack races out of the bedroom in undershorts and a crumpled blue button-down. Caterpillar eyebrows raised with panic, he kneels next to his brother. "Are you sick?"

"No."

Breathing wet and heavy, Jack sighs, sits back on his ankles. "Then why are you outside my door in your underwear?"

Brenda Starr makes brief eye contact—her eyes aren't darty and unfocused anymore. Gone is the light laugh that made her beautiful; she's one more girl in one more of Jack's T-shirts. Turning away, she looks at the white wall.

In unison Connor and Jack notice the used condom crusting in Connor's left hand, and Jack's face twists in a way Connor is pretty sure he'll remember the rest of his life—the way people remember where they were when Kennedy was shot.

"Jesus, what is with you?" Jack asks as Connor closes his hand and pulls knees to his chest. "I feel like shit. I'm having the worst week at work"—he rolls his eyes to the reporter—"do you have to have this meltdown right now?"

Jack looks sick and sallow, his skin looser than that of a normal twenty-seven-year-old. Pebbled guilt in Connor's rib cage expands to a grapefruit, because Jack probably didn't want to live in Ohio and do monumentally boring things in their father's law firm where he has worked two years and senior partners still call him "Reed's kid." Because Connor hasn't done anything he promised himself he would do at the repair shop after the accident. Because Brenda Starr's dislike radiates like gamma rays. Because Jenny says "soda" instead of "pop" and deserved better.

"I had sex with Jenny," he finally says, because that might give some sense of purpose to Jack's sacrifices. But Jack looks at him, blank as oatmeal, things going on behind his black eyes that Connor can't read.

Sighing again, Jack reaches out and lays his palm on top of Connor's fist. "You still need to throw that away," he says.

The two of them don't have the kind of relationship where they touch often, and in this brief exchange of flesh on flesh, Connor thinks he understands, a little, about the girls who come in and out of Jack's life like cheap pens. About how those girls mean something to Jack at the time. About how they feel when they're with him or sleeping smashed against his side afterward.

"Go to bed, kid," Jack says, and then he's up, taking Brenda Starr's hand, shaking his head, and inventing an explanation that makes more sense than the truth as he shows her to whatever it was she needed in the bathroom. Connor goes back to his bedroom and folds the condom in a piece of notebook paper on his desk. Kennedy stares at him with disapproval.

"What?" Connor asks.

The poster says nothing.

Picking up the phone, Connor dials Jenny's number, but hangs up when her mother answers—groggy and mad. He showers, gets dressed, and takes the keys to the Sentra from the hook in the laundry room. Maybe he's going to drive twenty minutes to Jenny's and apologize, or maybe he's going to the twenty-four-hour market for bagels and soup so there's food in the house. Maybe he'll only make it to the end of the cul-de-sac. It all depends how much gas is in the tank, if they've plowed the roads, and how badly things go when he gets behind the wheel.

cold without

snow

Jack asks Mona to move in the day the Ronco food dehydrator arrives in the mail. It makes sense—she sleeps over four or five nights a week, she's been dropping hints about her lease expiring for months, and her panties are overrunning his sock drawer. Then there's the disturbing discovery he made last fall when his brother left for college: Jack doesn't like being alone. The nights Mona doesn't stay, he can't sleep in the echoey house that had belonged to his parents, so he watches infomercials into obscene hours of the morning, showing up at the firm the next day with eggplant blotches under his eyes. The moment of clarity comes when he opens the food dehydrator box, the first of five $19.95 installments already charged to his American Express card, and looks absently at the machine in his kitchen where nothing but coffee was made even before his mother dropped dead three years ago. No good is coming from solitude.

So the weekend before Christmas Jack rents a cargo van to move Mona's clothes and books and CDs; they leave behind the semi-disposable furniture from Value City she got when she started at the

Plain Dealer after college. Loading boxes, Mona's tennis shoes slide on water frozen in the gutters. Her fat red ponytail bouncing behind her, she's just so clean, like girls in douche commercials. And Jack feels good about her move-in until she suggests they get a Christmas tree while they have the van.

"I'm not really a tree kind of guy," Jack says. "I'm more of a pretending-to-be-Jewish kind of guy."

"Are you serious?"

"I'm an attorney, I live in Beachwood." Jack smiles. "I've been getting Hanukkah cards from my neighbors for years."

Amber eyes wide, Mona looks bewildered and adorable, much younger than twenty three, and he feels obliged to say more even though he has already explained that major holidays for him usually involve exchanging unwrapped gifts with his brother over Chinese takeout.

"I'm not Scrooge," Jack sighs. "It's just bad timing; we've got work and my brother's in town."

"I know, I'm sorry." Mona apologizes because she apologizes for everything—the horrible alarm clock gong on mornings she has to wake up first, traffic jams on 271, paper cuts he gets at work. "But it hasn't snowed, and there's no tree, so it doesn't really feel like Christmas to me yet."

Jack shakes his head; that drummer boy song is playing on the radio for the nine-billionth time, and every store window in the greater Cleveland area has a frosting of spray-can snow.

"We'll be at your parents' house in a few days." He puts his hand on the knee of her jeans. "Won't they have a tree?"

"My parents have a great tree." Mona lays an always-cold hand on top of his. "But, I don't know, I thought it might be nice to have one of our own."

Suddenly Jack has a weird vision of what might happen if he let the van drift into the crowded right lane of the highway. It's so clear he can hear the glass and metal bust up all around Mona.

. . .

Two days later he's trying to push her off a balcony. His hands on her pale throat, her eyes wide and confused. Even as it happens, Jack is pretty sure it's a dream—he's not crazy about heights, the balcony looks suspiciously like the one from *Rear Window*, and he can't think of a reason he'd try to kill Mona. Still he jerks awake, heart knocking against his ribs. Her head is on his chest, arms draped across his stomach, throat seemingly unmarred.

Sliding out from under her, he goes downstairs to the living room and flips through channels—sitcom holiday episodes on Nick at Nite, soft-core porn on Cinemax, *Jaws*, which he has seen half a dozen times because it's always on TNT late-night—until he gets to paid programming. He's watching a show about a sit-up machine shaped like a miniature fighter jet when Connor gets back from his high school girlfriend's.

"Jenny says hi," Connor says, black hair a mess, lipstick smudges on thin cheeks.

Jack nods and gestures to the television, where an enormous man, round muscles ready to pop through oiled skin, presses the fighter jet against his midsection and does crunches. "Think that thing actually works?"

"Aren't you going to work at some ungodly hour?" Connor tosses Jack the car keys. Still in his red ski jacket, he moves an overstuffed pillow and sits next to Jack on the couch. "Shouldn't you go to bed?"

"I was asleep, I had a nightmare."

"About what?"

Mona's confused eyes, his blue shirt cuffs on her neck. "I don't remember." Jack looks for a place to put his keys, but he's in his underwear, no pockets anywhere.

On TV there's a series of impossible before-and-after photos and a phone number. Slouching into the couch, Connor puts his feet on the coffee table, folds hands across his abdomen, looks at Jack like he wants to say something, but doesn't.

A new program starts; Ron Popeil, in his butcher's apron with the Ronco monogram across the front, shows a rapt audience the dehydrator.

"That's what you and I are giving Mona's parents for Christmas." He points to the screen.

Connor rolls his eyes, and guilt tickles Jack's guts. He can't remember a single conversation his brother had with Mona in the past year, both of them becoming awkward and quiet, almost sullen, when in the same room. Still, Mona's parents had specifically invited Connor.

"If you don't want to go, you don't have to. If you'd rather go to Jenny's mom's or—"

"I don't have anything else to do." Connor yawns. "Besides, I've always wondered what real people did for holidays. It's like research for a soc class or something."

"Are you taking sociology?"

"My roommate is."

It occurs to Jack that he doesn't even know this roommate's name, what he looks like. Doesn't know his brother's major, doesn't know who Connor fucks or watches Indians games with.

On the TV, Ron gives the blond cohost a piece of turkey jerky, and she discusses its virtues without irony—it's fresher and lower in fat than what you buy in stores. Having seen the program eight times, Jack knows Ron's lines by heart.

"So you're going to stay in Cleveland?" Connor asks.

"Where would I go?"

"I just kind of thought once I left for school you might go to D.C. or something. You used to talk about stuff like that."

Jack does have vague memories of such talk, in the days before he took the associate position at the firm where his father had been managing partner, but now that seems part of another life, the one from the time before he ordered new living room furniture to replace the beige stuff his mother bought in the early eighties.

"You're going to stay with Jones Day?" Connor is asking.

"Yeah, I should make partner in a few years."

"That's cool." Connor nods, even though Jack knows he probably thinks that it is the absolute antithesis of cool. "I guess you've got your reasons."

Ron and Blonde make trail mix from dried fruit, and Jack wants to explain that staying in Cleveland has nothing to do with Mona, that it doesn't mean he's going to get married or buy a dog, that it's simply practical.

"If you drive me to work, you can have my car tomorrow," Jack says instead. Connor nods and yawns.

Maybe Jack senses the change in his brother's breathing or catches a glimpse of Connor's head, arched at an odd angle against the top of the couch, but he doesn't expect any answer when he asks, "Do you think it's weird we never had a Christmas tree?"

The tree in Mona's parents' house is huge. Even as he's pulling the car into the driveway, Jack sees it through the living room's full-length window, its star squashed against the ceiling. He visited her parents' place before and found it nice, if a bit quaint, with all the dark wood and heavy furniture. Now it's barely recognizable, every cubic foot of the wood and brick two-story blinking with colored bulbs, a life-size manger scene in the front yard and plastic Santa in a plastic sleigh with plastic reindeer mounted on the roof. Parking the car, he looks at Mona and waits for her to apologize for the house like she apologizes for everything else.

"Wouldn't it be great if it snowed tonight?" She smiles, pats his knee, and bounces out of the car.

Reaching into the back, he shakes his brother awake.

"Welcome to Jesusland," Jack says.

Mona's parents, like their house, have undergone a bizarre holiday transformation. Her father, a professor of Civil War history at OU, is wearing a corduroy jacket with elbow patches, while Mrs. Lockridge, thick through the hips and thighs, is in one of those seasonal sweaters—this one depicts the twelve days of Christmas with gold thread and sequins. Instantly Jack is uncomfortable in a way he hasn't been since sophomore year at Penn when a girl he was dating dragged him to a "Take Back the Night" rally.

"Good to see you, son." Mona's father extends his hand, while her mother hugs Connor, whom she's never met.

Three years younger, Mona's sister Frankie shivers in the doorway, wearing a skintight T-shirt and lots of purple lipstick. Red curls cropped at her jawline, five silver studs dotting the curl of her right ear, body firm like only the bodies of twenty-year-old girls are firm—Frankie could be the ghost of Mona past.

"Thank God you guys are finally here," she says, though she's looking exclusively at Connor, who's still wobbly with sleep like a newborn calf. "Mom's making us all crazy. Maybe now she'll chill."

Mona's mother mock swats Frankie's shoulder, and the six of them carry three overnight bags and boxes of presents (including the food dehydrator, which Mona wrapped the night before) into the house, where holiday music oozes from every room. Upstairs, Mrs. Lockridge assigns bedrooms with exaggerated gestures. Jack and Connor can sleep in Frankie's room; Frankie can bunk with Mona's older sister, Melanie; Mona gets her childhood bedroom, aggressively pink, with bookcases of worn stuffed bears and dolls in costumes from around the world.

Setting Mona's duffel bag on the lacy bedspread, Jack tugs Mona's hand, pulls her back in the room when everyone else has left, and somewhere in the house Eartha Kitt is crooning that Santa Baby shouldn't keep her waiting.

"You told your parents you moved in with me, right?" he asks. "And they're okay with that?"

"Yes." She laughs lightly. "You can sleep with me tonight. Mom just put you and Connor together for Frankie—it's one of those things my parents do. They pretend she's still a virgin."

"She's not?" Jack smiles, raises eyebrows in fake astonishment. Frankie's jeans were tight and low enough on the hips to showcase two inches of pale, flat belly.

"No-oo." Mona slips a hand between his dress shirt buttons; even through his undershirt, he can feel her hands are freezing. "Frankie's like a total sexual predator."

"You're *sure* your parents are cool with you moving in?"

Mona looks up at him, pupils blotting out the color from her eyes.

"Sure," she says. "My parents lived together before they were married."

On her wrist sticking out of his shirt, Mona wears the tennis bracelet he gave her when they exchanged gifts last night. He got it the week before at a Chagrin Falls jewelry store owned by the father of his first girlfriend. Anna, the ex-girlfriend who had married an area doctor, was working behind the counter, stomach swollen with her first child. When he said he needed a gift for his girlfriend, she'd laughed deep and from the back of her throat. "A ring, perhaps?" she'd asked.

"No," he had told Anna. "Anything but a ring."

Jack hears himself saying something to Mona—maybe "Okay," or "I just wanted to make sure they knew."

"Don't worry." She grabs his ass. "If you're a good boy, you'll get some tonight."

But her room is so oppressively girlie with its dust ruffle and throw pillows, the collection of Sweet Valley High paperbacks stacked above the desk. It's the last place in the world he wants to have sex.

"Sure," he says, brushing her long hairs out of his face.

• • •

Long red hair in thick braids, Melanie—the ghost of Mona future—is reading from a very fat book at the kitchen table, seemingly oblivious to trays of iced wreath- and present-shaped cookies drying around her.

Jack has never met Mona's older sister before, but knows she's getting a Ph.D. in Russian literature at Johns Hopkins, that she's slept with more than one married professor, and she'd made Mona feel stupid when they were kids, which Mona isn't over yet.

"You must be Jack and Jack's brother," Melanie says without getting up. In her cat-eyed black glasses, she comes from central casting to play a role: embittered intellectual in her late twenties.

"'Jack's brother' *is* what it says on his birth certificate." Jack smiles, shoulders loosening; he's known girls like Melanie all his life—in advanced placement calculus classes, at law school, at Jones Day—her he can handle.

"His name is Connor," Frankie says with more authority than the eight minutes she's known his brother should warrant. "My sister Melanie."

Melanie nods, and Frankie ladles eggnog from a giant copper pot on the stove into green plastic cups for her and Connor. She offers Jack a glass, but he shakes his head.

"So what is your drink then, son?" Mona's father has one hand on Jack's back, the other around a tumbler of amber alcohol the same color as his daughters' eyes. "Scotch? Brandy?"

The closest thing Jack has to "a drink" would be the gin and tonics he orders at business lunches if clients are drinking. "Coffee?" he asks, noticing the half-full pot in the machine next to bottles of red and white wine for the post-dinner party Mona warned about.

"Baileys and coffee?" Mona's father asks hopefully.

When Jack agrees, her father actually winks at him. But in the Lockridge house, there's an incredibly skewed ratio of Baileys to coffee—a strange upper-downer combination. It warms his lungs and chest as he sits in the empty chair next to Melanie. Mona rests her butt against his knee, a display of affection Jack isn't sure about, not with Mona's father, round and red and Santa-like, hovering and topping off everyone's drink; not with Connor so close to the Total Sexual Predator.

Mona's mother balances on tiptoes to grab an upside-down shoe box lid from the top of the refrigerator.

"Everyone who spends Christmas Eve in our house has to hang an ornament on the tree," she says, and Jack realizes the things on the box lid are little crafty projects fashioned from pipe cleaners, glitter, and molded plastic: things likely learned from the home and garden channel, a channel he always skips. "Usually we insist everyone make their own ornament, but Mo thought you boys wouldn't want to. So with you all getting here so close to dinner anyway, the girls and I went ahead and made ornaments for you."

Jack looks at Melanie with her Dostoevsky; he can't imagine she had much to do with the ornament making.

"We weren't sure what your major was," Mrs. Lockridge says to Connor. "But Mo said you loved skiing, so Frankie and I came up with this."

She hands Connor a pair of Popsicle stick skis with poles fashioned from mini-marshmallows and toothpicks, everything painted and shellacked. Holding the wire hook between his long thumb and forefinger, Connor thanks Mona's mother with so much sincerity he may actually mean it.

"The poles were my idea." Frankie winks at Connor, and Jack is pretty sure the *Jaws* theme plays somewhere.

The ornament they've made for Jack is a palm-size, construction-paper Constitution—a document he hasn't had much use for since passing Con Law six years ago, certainly nothing he needs at the lawyer factory. A more fitting representation of his life would be a mini-carton of sesame beef from the twenty-four-hour Chinese place across from his office.

"This is great," Jack says. "I've never had my own ornament before."

"The joys of Christmas at Chez Lockridge," Melanie offers, but even she shuffles with the rest of them to the living room, where the massive tree narrows into the ceiling plaster.

There's a weird moment when Jack, Connor, and Mona are supposed to find spots on the tree not already occupied by lights, figurines, popcorn and cereal chains, to hang their ornaments. Mona easily makes a place for hers—a pair of pink ceramic ballet slippers, remnants of some long-extinguished dancer fantasy she has never mentioned. Connor, likewise, threads the wire over a green branch and silver foil slivers. With seven sets of eyes on his back, Jack tries twice to hook his Constitution, but it keeps falling onto the packages stacked at the tree's base. Finally, Mona puts her small, cold hand on top of his and helps.

"There you go," Mona's father says. "You make a good team."

Jack nods and worries about Mona's family, who have a better understanding of Connor, who likes to ski and doesn't have a major, than they do of him.

Four hours later Mona is shuffling Jack from one cluster of wine-drinking guests to the next. Some are colleagues of her father, others additional carrot-topped family, but they all have questions. It's as though he's on a never-ending job interview. So many "what kind of law?"s, and "where abouts are you from?"s, and a bunch of "you went to school where?"s.

Making things all the more challenging, he's lapsing into a turkey coma from the multicourse dinner, and Mona's father keeps freshening Jack's mug of Baileys and coffee. If that weren't enough to contend with, his brother, fresh glass of eggnog in hand, dances somewhere between fast and slow with Frankie to "It's a Wonderful World." In April Connor will turn nineteen, but with his dental-floss frame and too-long-in-the-front black hair, he could pass for fourteen—far too young to be drunk at his brother's girlfriend's house on Christmas Eve, to be dancing so close with his brother's girlfriend's sister.

Easing away from Mona and the mini-circles of mingling professors and redheads, Jack puts a hand on Connor's shoulder, bony even through a thick cable-knit sweater. The song has stopped, but Frankie stands close enough to Connor that the dun dun dun dun of the *Jaws* music is blaring.

"Can I talk to you for a sec?" Jack asks, and leads his brother to the kitchen, where dozens of dirty dishes fill the sink and there are enough empty wine bottles for a three-lane bowling alley. Jack had been legally in charge of his brother until Connor turned eighteen, but he hadn't thought to make any rules other than common-sense understandings: *Don't block each other in the driveway. Buy more coffee if you use the last of the beans. If doors are closed, knock before entering.* Now Jack realizes there should have been all kinds of things Connor shouldn't have been allowed to do.

"Hey, lamppost, whatcha knowin'?" Connor asks. "I'm about to barf from all those cookies; you?"

"You'd feel better if you took it easy on the eggnog." Jack takes the cup from Connor's hand and sets it on the counter. "And can you *not* fuck around with my girlfriend's sister in her parents' house, as like a Christmas present to me?"

Blood rushes to the hollows under Connor's cheekbones.

"I'm only here because of you," he says, voice suddenly hard. "The only reason I even came home for break was because of you. And you know what would be a great Christmas present? If you could at least pretend to have the teeniest bit of faith in me."

"It's not that—" Jack says, but of course that *is* exactly what it is. "It's just, Mo says Frankie is a total sexual predator."

Eyes blank, Connor stares at him. "She's a hundred-and-ten-pound girl," he says, brushing Jack's hand off his shoulder. "I think I can handle her." Taking his glass, he's through the swinging doors before Jack can say anything else.

The continuous job interview in the living room is such an unappealing prospect that Jack doesn't follow. Despite being sickeningly full, he opens the pantry and looks inside at boxes and cans—Chunky soup, Rice-A-Roni, dry pasta, an all-purpose cleaner he recognizes from one of the infomercials on overnight programming, cling wrap, foil, five different kinds of cereal—things he never had growing up. His mother had been anorexic before it was fashionable, and his father had made it home by dinnertime maybe once a week. There'd been lots of ten-dollar bills and notes taped to the freezer—*Jack, showing a house at seven, pick something up for you and The Kid, XOXO, Mom*—not many turkeys with homemade dressing; no mixed nuts and red and green M&M's in cut-glass candy dishes.

"Hey, you." From behind, Mona laces arms around his hips. "Hungry?"

He shakes his head, turns to face her. "Your mother made me eat enough for three weeks."

"You're being so good about this family stuff," she says. "I'm sorry."

"It's no big deal."

"Sure it is." They're alone with the dirty dishes and canned goods, but she still stands on tiptoes to whisper in his ear. "Certainly worth a blow job."

"Re-ea-lly?"

She gives him a quick kiss, and he taps her nose with his finger. "That is *not* what you said you were going to do."

Laughing, she reaches for the back of his neck. "*Later,*" she says, words muffled as her tongue flirts with his lips. "My family really likes you."

Her mouth tastes like bubble gum, and he chews the meat of her lower lip, harder and harder, until she pushes him away. Her hand flutters to her mouth, and she smears the small blood drop. Together they stare at the thin red stain on her fingertip; her eyes are the eyes from his dream. Finally she shakes her head.

"That is *not* the way to get me to do *that* other thing," she says, but it seems forced.

In his mouth he tastes her blood.

Because her parents passed out on the sunken couch, mother's head on the shoulder of father's corduroy jacket, father's head stacked on mother's, Mona sees out the last professors and redhead. She's the one who gets down on hands and knees to scrub a circle of red wine spilled on the cream carpet.

"Here, try this," Jack whispers, getting the bottle of cleaner from the kitchen cabinet. "I saw this infomercial where it worked miracles on grape Kool-Aid."

Kneeling beside Mona, he sprays the product on the carpet, takes her dish towel, and begins to rub.

"No wonder my parents love you," Mona says. "Frankie and Mel never bring home guys who wash our floors."

Though he has no memory of ever cleaning anything, Jack scrubs the carpet as if the fate of the Western world depended on it, as if he's trying to prove something to someone. Finally Mona puts her hands over his—the nurse on *ER* telling the handsome surgeon he has to give up, that the patient is lost, that he can stop shocking the body with those paddles. Jack hopes the food dehydrator does a better job living up to its "as seen on TV" promise.

"Come on." Mona takes his hand. "Everyone's outside."

She leads him past the tree in the living room, through the kitchen, to the deck with its patio furniture and gas grill covered with a fitted tarp.

Connor and Mona's sisters sit against the wood slats with their legs jutting out in front of them, passing a joint. The phone number of his own college dealer is probably still in Jack's address book, but he's furious at his brother. Not getting high at his girlfriend's parent's house is another rule he should have made. He glares at Connor, but his brother's eyes are downcast and dull.

"Where have you guys been all night?" Frankie asks from between Connor and Melanie, her elbow resting on Connor's thigh. Melanie hands Frankie the joint, and she takes a long drag, closing eyelids dusted with sparkly purple shadow.

"We've been around," Mona says, an edge in her voice Jack isn't sure he's heard before. "Someone had to put Mom and Dad to bed."

Frankie hands the joint to Mona, who brings it halfway to her lips, then stops and looks at Jack for approval. Shrugging, Jack tells her to go ahead.

"You don't have to ask him," Connor says, words lubed by alcohol—one of the first things he has said directly to Mona since Jack introduced the two of them last year. "Jack may have decided he's Dad, but you don't have to ask his permission."

"Conn—"

"What?" Connor's eyes narrow to coffee beans. "You live in Dad's house, you work Dad's job, you periodically show up and tell me all the crap I'm doing wrong. But she shouldn't have to ask you what she can and can't do."

"Don't—" Jack says, but Mona speaks at the same time.

"Don't worry," she says to Connor. "I know it's good to piss him off every once in a while. You know, keep the big guy in line."

Connor nods, but Jack just looks at Mona. He thought she would apologize, but instead she turned Connor's anger in a way he wouldn't have thought her capable of. Conspiratorially, she bumps Jack's hip with hers and passes him the joint.

Jack wants to get high at Mona's parents' house with his brother like he wants major dental work, but Connor is looking at him, and Frankie's and Melanie's mouths curl in the same curious way. Even Mona's lips (lower one still puffy) purse into a question. For the first time in his twenty-eight years, Jack understands what junior high health teachers meant during peer pressure lectures. Still, this is a test, and from opening doors on first dates to the SAT, Jack always aces tests. It smolders his lungs, and he wrestles back a cough, but everyone's shoulders relax. Connor offers the truce of a shy smile.

"I like the Reed boys," Frankie says. "You guys are okay."

And maybe it is okay. Jack straddles a patio chair, Mona between his thighs, her back pressed against him. She shivers; it's thirty degrees and she's wearing a silk shirt. He rubs her arms, moves her hair off the back of her neck.

"I hate it when it's cold without snow," she says. "It's like, I don't know, pizza without cheese."

"Doughnuts without holes?" Connor's eyes and voice droop again.

"Sex without love?" Melanie looks up from tapping weed out of a film canister.

"Naw." Frankie smiles a naughty, practiced smile. "See, Mel, that one can be okay."

They pass the new joint until it's spent, while Jack contemplates sex without love. He thinks about Mona moving into his house, about whether or not he *is* becoming his father. But, God, pot is stronger than he remembers. His head weighs more than the turkey Mona's mother served, and his lips feel as though they're made of rubber.

"As we have no more weed and Jack has no more brothers, I'm going to bed," Melanie says, pushing herself to her feet. She's not really heavy, but she moves as though she has the extra thirty pounds her mother does. "Merry Christmas and all of that."

Jack wonders if Mona will walk that way in a few years, wonders if her refusal to get tangled with academia will keep her gait light as Frankie's. Wonders if wondering means he'll be around to see it, wonders if he wants to be.

After Melanie is through the glass doors, the rest of them become aware of the cold. Frankie suggests a game of pool, and they tiptoe inside so they won't wake the parents. Even the basement has been Christmasified—cardboard cutouts of reindeer and paper snowflakes the girls probably made in grade school Scotch-taped to the wood paneling; Santa figurines crowding the tables.

"Reeds versus Lockridges?" Mona suggests as she orders the balls on the table and Frankie gets cues and chalk from the wall-mounted rack.

"Who knows." Frankie winks, and Jack has no idea who the intended receiver is. "We might all be Reeds one day."

"You're going to scare away the Reed boys," Mona says. "Ladies versus gentlemen?"

"Normally, I'd say you're on." Connor rubs blue chalk on his stick. "But you're girls with a pool table in the basement."

"You have a pool table in your house," Mona says, and Jack notices she doesn't say "our house" or "the house" or any other phrase implying residence, even though she lives there now and technically could. He also notices that she and his brother seem awful chummy, or at least more comfortable around each other than they've been for the past year. He can't decide if that makes him happy or if he'd prefer to keep the parts of his life compartmentalized.

"Yes, but you girls actually have balls and cues." It's hard to be charming when his head feels only loosely associated with his body.

They end up with the obvious teams of Jack and Mona against Frankie and Connor. Jack was in high school when his father had his first heart attack and his parents refinished the basement with the pool and Ping-Pong tables—"recreational therapy," the doctors had called it. Though his father never used them, Jack and his friends played lots of pool, and he's still pretty good, even stoned. By the time Connor was old enough to play, though, the table was a storage area for boxes of unused things. He's decent with straight shots, but every time he tries to angle a ball off the rim, Jack is reminded of the C his brother got in high school geometry. For reasons Mona explains with only a smile, she's the best of them all, taking trick shots with the cue behind her back. And Frankie is awful, or maybe she pretends to be awful so Connor can guide her hands on the wood pole, position her slim hips against the table's varnished curves. They play three games, Jack and Mona winning all of them easily.

"You hungry, Conn?" Frankie asks, running her pale hands up and down her cue so gratuitously it's laughable. "Jack and Mo can play a winner's tournament, and you and I can check out the leftover cookie situation."

Connor nods, follows Frankie upstairs. Watching them leave, Jack sits on the end of the pool table and realizes he isn't mad at his brother anymore—not for drinking too much, or getting high, or screwing around with the total sexual predator, not for almost starting a fight or for being disappointed in Jack for becoming their father. But Jack *does* feel as though he might cry, which is strange because he can't remember the last time he cried—when his mother died? the end of *Hoosiers*? He tosses his cue from hand to hand, stares at the cheap carpeting.

"Jack?" Mona's voice is like cotton gauze. Sitting next to him, she runs fingertips through his dark hair. "What's wrong?"

Shaking his head, he touches his lips to her cheek, whispers, "I like your family."

"But?"

"No, there's no 'but,' I really like them." It's true. There's something charming about her mother's horrible sweater and the fact that her father is the fun kind of alcoholic. Even the ghosts of Mona Past and Mona Future are amusing—Melanie because she has given up trying and Frankie because she tries so fucking hard.

"Does my family make you miss your parents?" she asks.

"Maybe." But he doesn't think that's it; there is a "but," but he's not sure what it is.

"I'm sorry," she says. He turns his face to hers, and she kisses his forehead, both eyebrows. He closes his eyes, and she kisses the lids. "I wish I could have met them."

When Jack thinks about his parents, he thinks about how he wanted his father there when he got his bar results or how he would have liked his mother to yell at the doctors when he was hospitalized with bronchitis last year. Never once in the thirteen months he has been with Mona has Jack ever lamented her not knowing them. That is as close to the "but" as he can get, but he doesn't say anything because a launch sequence has been initiated. He's kissing her harder as she fiddles with his belt; then he's got her on her back on the green felt table. Pulling off her gray pants, he licks her ankle, her calf, her knee, her thigh. He slides down her panties and licks the folds of skin—the only part of her body that's ever warm. She chews her lower lip, and a bead of blood swells at the spot where he bit her in the kitchen. As she comes, her arms fly up, knocking around all the stripes Connor and Frankie couldn't sink.

When they finish and Jack goes upstairs to Frankie's room, Connor is already sprawled across the bed, long legs and arms everywhere, Frankie nowhere in sight. In the dark, Jack puts on the cotton pajamas Mona gave him as part of his Christmas gift and moves his brother's hot body to one side.

"Hey." Connor smacks Jack's hands. "Go sleep with your girlfriend. As sort of your Christmas present to me, let me have the whole bed."

"I'd rather sleep with you. You don't warm your feet on my stomach."

"Is that the way to get rid of you?" Connor rolls over and looks at the clock glowing two fifteen. "It's after midnight. Merry Christmas, Jack."

"So you're Tiny Fucking Tim, now?"

"God bless us, everyone."

An hour later Jack wakes with the dead weight of Connor's arm across his throat. Pushing him away, Jack remembers the strangling-Mona dream. Connor moans, flops to his front, mumbles something about Beth, who may be someone at school or might be a dream creation. Jack doesn't get to know those things anymore.

He goes to the bathroom and finds Santa figurines even there, in a neat row across the toilet top. Instead of getting back into bed with his brother, Jack goes downstairs. Mona's parents are still sleeping, but they've shifted, solidified into each other. The CD changer shuffles back to Bing Crosby, who, like Mona, dreams of an unrealized white Christmas. Mammoth and bright, the tree glows like trees in movies, the biggest box underneath it is the food dehydrator wrapped in red foil. A blue light sizzles and slowly loses its brightness. Jack worries a short might ignite the dry branches, bends over to unplug the tree, changes his mind and leaves it glowing.

In her bedroom, Mona sleeps on her back. Eyes closed, freckles across her nose, and all that red hair strewn across the pink pillow-case—*a girl from a douche commercial*. For a split second, he imagines smothering her with a pink throw pillow—how her body would shudder, arms fighting him. He climbs into the bed, lays his head on her breasts.

"Jack?" she murmurs, touching his forehead with drowsy fingers.

"Shhh, go back to sleep."

"Christmas kisses?" she asks, sleepy and childlike.

"Okay." Inching up so they're at eye level, he lightly presses his lips to hers. Turning on her side, she pulls him closer, kisses more urgently.

"I love you," she whispers in his ear.

"I love you, too," he says, and means it, loves warming her hands, loves the way she sleeps on him. Still, he has figured out the "but" from earlier. "But I'm not a Christmas-tree kind of guy."

"I know, you're a pretending-to-be-Jewish kind of guy."

Her heated breath raises hairs on his neck. Maybe she does know that her family likes him for the wrong reasons; that she's only in his house to fill the emptiness; that in a parallel universe, he keeps trying to kill her. But he doubts it.

"I'm freezing," she says, slides frigid hands under his pajama top, then looks at him, suddenly wide awake. "Did it snow?"

"No," he says without looking through the window.

all those
girlie-girl
things

For almost four years Mona has been living with Jack, but she's still "and guest," still an accessory. Thumbing the parchment place card with Jack's name written in calligraphy, Mona nods when the waiter comes by and offers to refill her chardonnay. She can't decide if she's sad because she's drunk or just sad. She does know she's annoyed Jack won't dance with her at *his* friend's wedding—annoyed that Jack has spent most of the reception talking with his very pregnant, very married ex-girlfriend; with the ex's parents, who've apparently known Jack for almost three decades; with the ex's cousin, who happens to be an appellate court judge.

"What's wrong, Mo?" It's not Jack who asks, but Connor, seated on the other side of Jack. "You look like you can't keep your shoelaces tied."

Jack doesn't notice because he's busy being charming and easy. Left foot balanced on his right knee, he trades billable-hour stories with the appellate cousin and the cousin's husband.

"Nothing's wrong, I'm just tired," Mona says, flattening her cake to a paste with a heavy silver spoon. "I filed a late story last night."

Connor nods and scrapes fondant frosting from his plate with a fork. Licking the edge, he seems closer to twelve than twenty-two.

"How's school going?" Mona leans forward to talk to him better. A few years ago, she used to hate Jack's brother, seeing him as bizarre competition for Jack's affections. But she likes him now, and Jack is ignoring him, too.

"Same old, same old," Connor says, too quickly.

If he were her responsibility, she'd pry, but he isn't. For almost three years after their mother died, he was legally Jack's ward, but tonight Connor is drinking wine, reminding them he's old enough now, that he belongs to no one.

"How come the only time anyone ever eats phyllo dough is at a wedding?" he asks.

"Because phyllo dough isn't very good." Jack eases back in his chair, back into her conversation with his brother. It's as if he finally remembered they were there, remembered the appellate cousin made a comment about Mona's hair not being natural, remembered Connor has been dodging questions about his post-graduation plans all night.

"No, phyllo dough actually sucks," Connor says. "We should order a pizza later."

In nearly identical black suits, Jack and Connor are a matched pair. If Mona had to give a police artist details to make sketches of them, she's not sure the descriptions would be very different—bushy eyebrows, black eyes, cheekbones high and broad. But Jack's nose is straighter, and Connor is thinner. They have the same dark hair, cut almost the same way—longer in the front—but Connor's doesn't part evenly in the middle, and he's not nearly as comfortable with his long arms and legs.

"Pizza's fine," Jack says. "Whatever you want, kid."

"You in on the pizza action?" Connor asks Mona.

"Sure," she says, distracted by Jack's ex-girlfriend swaying in the arms of her doctor husband on the dance floor.

Anna—"AnnaFram," as Connor calls her, squishing together her first and maiden name as if it were one word—is the rare woman who looks good pregnant, olive skin flawless, shiny dark hair piled on her head in a way that's somehow casual and elegant. Looking at Anna's swollen round breasts, Mona yanks up the front of her own dress, wonders what possessed her to think her B-cup boobs could support the black strapless.

Anna's sister is the bride. A cute girl, Carrie has wilted since the ceremony—without the veil, her updo looks weird and her lips have paled from reception-line kisses and chicken in puff pastry. Still, she and her groom look happy, dancing and giving warm nods to each new pair to join them on the floor. The song is familiar, yet Mona can't quite place it—something from crepe-paper-covered OU formals.

"Please dance with me." Mona reaches for Jack's fingers on the table. "Just this one song."

"I really can't dance." He clasps her hand between his and smiles at Mona, but also at the couple across the table. "Best just to accept it as a character flaw."

"Jack." Even as she whines his name, she realizes she's whining and that she probably shouldn't. She probably *is* drunk. "It's just your friends."

"Happy or sad?" Jack asks.

It's a game they play, based on a bookmark they saw at the University Hospital gift shop when Jack's brother broke his shoulder in a biking accident four summers before. The bookmark offered a series of questions, the first one being "Are you happy or sad?" If you answered happy, it proclaimed you had nothing to worry about. At the time they laughed at the simplicity of it—no qualifiers, ifs, ands, or buts—happy or sad. Now they use it as a way out of arguments not worth fighting over.

"Sad not to be dancing," Mona says to her smushed cake.

"Conn will dance with you." Jack lets go of Mona's hand, nods toward his brother. "And he's actually good at it."

"Yeah, I've been taking swing lessons." Connor swallows his wine. Standing, he takes Mona's fingers and bends into a strangely formal bow. "Ms. Lockridge, may I have this dance?"

At that very moment, AnnaFram appears and floats into Connor's chair, even though she's assigned to the head table with her sister.

"You're doing better than I ever did." Anna winks at Mona in a way that is annoying because it seems sincere. "Jack and I spent senior prom by the punch bowl."

Feeling blood rush to her cheeks, Mona can't think of a way to get out of it, so she allows Connor to lead her out to the raised center of the ballroom.

Dancing with Jack's brother is embarrassing. Not because Connor is that much younger, only five years, no younger than she is younger than Jack. What's humiliating is that Jack saw her, and probably Connor, as a problem easily fixed—send the kids off to go play, let the grown-ups talk. Still, after the first song, she relaxes against Connor's chest, feels the bones of his torso through his jacket. Drakkar Noir haunts his collar, and she remembers giving him a bottle as a Christmas present last year, wonders if he wore it tonight specifically because he knew he would see her or if he liked it so much that he wears it every day.

"So you guys and the Frams grew up together?" Mona asks. Until the fine-grained linen invitation arrived, she'd heard virtually nothing about these Frams, was aghast and unsettled to find out they had been a huge part of Jack's youth.

"Yeah, they lived next door," Connor says. "Mrs. Fram spent all this money redecorating, and she wouldn't even let you go into certain rooms. AnnaFram and Carrie practically lived with us."

In the years Mona has lived in Jack's house, she's seen no signs of any of it, and she wonders about the artifacts. Where are the pictures of Jack and Anna at high school dances? Shots of the girls dressing Connor up like a cowboy? Where are the stuffed animals won at Cedar Point? Love letters Anna wrote Jack during college?

"Did Anna and Jack break up when she met her husband?" Mona asks, and Connor's shoulders tighten under her arms.

"I guess they just wanted different things," he says, hesitantly. "I mean she's already working on her second kid, and Jack, well, you know."

"Sure," Mona says, and Connor loosens, drums along with the song, tapping the rhythm where he holds her at the waist. But she wonders if she does know.

"And then she asks me," Connor sings the words in her ear in a way that's both spooky and oddly endearing—something Jack would never do. *"Do I look all right? And I say yes, you look wonderful tonight."*

"You're drunk, aren't you?" she asks.

"I think I am, milady."

"Good," she says, because it seems like something Jack wouldn't say.

She thinks about this thing Connor assumes she knows. In theory Jack *should* be good with children. When Mona started dating Jack, she'd been vision-blurring jealous of the time and effort Jack put into his orphaned brother—chauffeuring Connor all around Cleveland's suburbs, sitting through swim meets and parent-teacher conferences. Secretly, Mona had been thrilled when Connor packed his Nissan Sentra and headed off to school in Boulder instead of Case Western where Jack had wanted him to go.

Now she feels guilty and embarrassed for having felt that way. Now she *does* like Connor, as he hums in her ear, *"It's time to go home now, and I've got an aching head. So I give her the car keys, and she helps me to bed."*

"Yep." Connor stops humming. "I'm definitely drunk."

"Me, too." She laughs, rich and throaty, even though she doesn't feel that way, even though she's still annoyed, still hurt. "Tell me a secret."

"Like what?"

"I don't know, something you haven't even told Jack."

"It's not like I tell him *everything*." Connor stretches out the word, making it luxurious.

"So tell me something he doesn't know."

"Okay, it's fitting for today," he whispers. "Beth and I were engaged for five weeks."

Mona remembers the petite brunette Connor brought home two Easters ago.

"Really?" She looks over at Jack; he's talking to the Fram uncle. She wishes he were jealous—jealous she's dancing close with someone else, jealous she's sharing secrets with his brother.

"Yeah, I went out and got a ring and got down on one knee and everything," Connor says. "And she did all those girlie-girl things—crying and kissing and saying yes. But then she got into Stanford med school, and things just fell apart. I told her I'd go with her, but she said no. I haven't talked to her in a month."

"Oh, that's so sad," Mona says. And it does seem horribly tragic in an adolescent way. "I'm really sorry."

"Ehh." Connor shrugs against her. "I guess it's better it happened now rather than five years from now."

The next song starts—a watered-down version of "Brick House," and she doesn't want to try it in high heels.

"I'm sorry," she says again.

Disengaging herself from Connor's arms, Mona turns him over to Anna's three-year-old daughter. Curly-haired and cherubic in a frilly blue dress, the girl swings Connor's hands back and forth, flashing ruffled panties.

Starting back to the table, Mona thinks about the cute slope of

Anna's nose, the way her dress lays over her changing body, and walks out of the ballroom to the ladies' lounge to check her makeup.

Any question concerning her sobriety is answered in one of the stalls, when Mona rolls down her panty hose and flops onto the toilet seat. The world is hot and wiggly, her lips thick and dumb. It's nothing short of rocket science to work her tights back up her legs, wash her hands at one of the mirrored vanities, and apply lip gloss. She's trying to snap into some sort of clarity when a toilet flushes and AnnaFram appears at one of the sinks, rummages through her purse.

"One of the things they don't tell you about being pregnant is that you have to pee all the time." Anna smiles as she runs her hands under the faucet. "It's a giant pain in the ass."

"I can imagine." Mona nods, wonders if Anna is making some slight, an implication that Mona will never know the hassles of pregnancy peeing because she's with a man whom Anna already tried and discarded.

"You and Conn looked cute out there." AnnaFram dusts her face with a fat powder brush. "It's freaky to see him all grown up; he was kind of like my little brother, too."

And then Mona *does* feel guilty for knowing a secret about Connor that Jack doesn't, for leaving him alone at table fourteen with the uncle who makes sexist jokes and has endless questions about a malpractice suit.

"Yeah, Conn turned out okay," Mona says, and then goes back to her table in the ballroom and stands next to Jack's chair.

The Fram uncle is leaning in, gesturing broadly as he talks. Jack doesn't look up, but his arm snakes around Mona's waist. Finally the uncle's story ends, and Jack smiles at her. With his free arm he grabs her middle, and she falls into his lap, despite her cocktail-length skirt.

"Hey," he says.

"Hey yourself," she giggles. Public affection is rare from Jack, and Mona checks to see if he's looking around; he isn't.

"You look good." Jack runs his thumb along the top of her dress. "I like this."

"Dance with me," she whispers in his ear. Bold from the wine, she lets her tongue linger over the lobe, traces the C curve.

"I can't—" His breath catches as she slithers in his lap, feels his cock swell through his suit pants. "Mona," he says her name in a way that means yes and no at the same time.

On the dance floor, the bride and groom bend to the music. And Mona wants to ask if she and Jack will get married, will have children, wants to ask if she, like AnnaFram, could be erased from his house and his life. But she's not ready to hear the answer to that yet. So she asks the question she knows he'll answer right.

"Happy or sad?"

by being young,
by being nice

It's already too late.

Another involuntary flinch of his stomach, like a CD skipping in a changer, and Jack knows it's just a matter of time before he throws up again. Watching the rise, crest, and fall of champagne in the glasses, he puts his palms on the linen tablecloth and wills the Dramamine tablets to kick in, wills the boat to stop rocking, wills his girlfriend and the older couple at their table to stop trying to include him in the conversation.

"George and I take this cruise every year for our anniversary." The white-haired woman nods at Jack and Mona. A few minutes ago she introduced herself as Helen Stein. "And we were wondering if it's your anniversary, too."

"Nope, just a vacation." Mona finishes her second glass of champagne. A semicircle of mauve lipstick stains the rim—when Jack met her, she wore only bubblegum-scented Chap Stick.

"We've actually avoided the altar thus far," Mona continues. "But we've been together for a long time. Five years, right?"

"Right." Jack looks up. He runs through witty things to say, but can't think of anything other than the motion; he wishes he were any-where else in the world, as long as it wasn't rocking. The Steins smile, and he tries smiling back. George Stein looks a little like Jack's father might have if he hadn't died thirteen years earlier.

Their waiter brings a dimpled dish of escargot. Jack's stomach shudders again, and he's on his feet, excusing himself.

"Do you need help—" Mona is up, too, setting her napkin on her chair, reaching for Jack's lower arm. In the five hours since the ship left port, her hands and soothing words have gone from gentle to bored.

"No, please, just have din—" Guts spinning and whirling, he gags, waves her away. "Please, I just want to be alone."

He turns away from Mona's look of sympathy and annoyance and stumbles through the narrow halls back to their tiny cabin just in time to vomit in their tiny toilet with its enormous flush. Then he crashes into their tiny double bed.

Three hours later the Dramamine is finally working; instead of feeling sick, Jack feels sick and very, very sleepy. He's drifting in and out under the stiff sheets when Mona stumbles in and flips on the overhead light.

"Were you sleeping?" Her words are bleary from alcohol. "Do you feel any better?"

"Not really," he answers both questions. "How was dinner?"

"Fabulous." Kicking off her shoes, she opens the efficient closet and takes out a silk nightgown. Her voice trails off as she goes to the bathroom. "We all had lobster. The waiter said he'd have room service send you some crackers, if you want."

Mona left the closet open, and her dresses sway back and forth on wooden hangers. Ten dresses for a seven-night cruise. The first winter they dated, he bought her a green velvet cocktail dress so she would have something to wear for his firm's holiday party. With her hair down at the party, she'd looked like a sexy elf—something found on a naughty Christmas card.

"You know that couple at our table got married three weeks after they met?" Mona says. In the full-length mirror on the open bathroom door, Jack sees her reflection, naked and pale. "Isn't that crazy?"

"It seems to have worked out okay for them." Jack sighs. "Are you coming to bed?"

Sucking in her stomach and straightening her spine, Mona tries to pinch an inch of flesh from her thigh.

"I've put on ten pounds already," she says. "If you keep hurling, at least you won't fatten up too much on this trip."

Jack rolls his eyes; he's weighed 175 since he was nineteen, and he doubts she's gained two pounds since he met her.

"I guess three weeks isn't that strange. Craig and his ex-wife got married after dating only a month or something." Mona pulls the nightgown over her head, studies some blemish on her chin and frowns into the mirror.

"Who's Craig?" Jack mumbles.

"God, *Jack*. He's the other council reporter. I've introduced you to him at every *Plain Dealer* party for five years. Do you ever pay attention to anything I tell you?"

"Blond boy?"

"Yes."

"Oh, yeah. I don't like him."

"Why not, because he looks like Brad Pitt?"

"I dunno, he seemed like a space case." Jack can't remember if this is true, he only knows he doesn't like the way Mona says Craig's name—as if this Craig were developing a cure for cancer or reading to the blind on his days off from the paper. "Come on. I'm tired."

Closing his eyes, he tries to let his body become one with the rocking. Eighteen years ago, one month before his fifteenth birthday, he'd lost his virginity to Anna Fram on her parents' heavy oak bed. He'd felt sick then, too—wanting everything to be perfect because he loved Anna, or thought he did. He'd assumed it was love because when she would go home after finishing necking and schoolwork, Jack would lie awake and smell her on the sheets. Hundreds of years seemed to cram themselves into those hours before he would see her on the way to school the next morning. As Mona brushes her teeth and washes her face, he tries to remember if he ever felt that way about her and why he stopped feeling that way about Anna once he was at college.

Finally he senses the change in light, feels Mona pull down the bedspread and get in. Her hair, full from the salty, humid air, tickles his face and throat. The first few times they messed around (she wouldn't sleep with him until they'd been seeing each other nearly a month) he hadn't been able to keep his hands out of her curls. Now it occurs to him that they haven't had sex since they left for vacation. He tries to think of the last time they had sex at all; he'd been working late to bill enough hours so he wouldn't feel guilty for the time off, and she'd covered all those early city council meetings. Maybe two weeks, maybe three?

Letting his palm linger over her head, he flexes fingers, but retracts his hand at the last minute.

"So, are we *ever* going to get married?" Mona asks.

It's something she brought up last May at Carrie Fram's wedding. Then he'd flipped it around, asked if she wanted to get married—she'd just shrugged. Tonight he's so close to sleep, he doesn't feel guilty not giving her any answer.

"Come on," he says, doubling a pillow under his head. "Are you happy or sad?"

"I don't know," she says. Their room hums with something mechanical, perhaps the engine. "Happy you stopped puking."

• • •

Mona is not a particularly fast runner, but she likes the thing that happens when she hits her stride, the click when her thoughts become clear. But because Helen Stein wants to jog with her, Mona knows it will take longer for the click to happen today.

Helen diligently follows Mona's lead, stretching her right leg against the deck's wood railing, then her left. There's no way Helen presses hard enough to warm her muscles, but Mona says nothing. She "ran" with Helen yesterday, knows the older woman will only walk around the track once or twice before calling it quits. Still it's hard for Mona to be annoyed as the water beyond them shimmers with phantom flecks of gold and silver.

"Jack looked good today," Helen says. "I hope the two of you are having better time now."

"Yeah, much better," Mona says; but last night, even though Jack wasn't sick, they hadn't made love. After the ship's subpar presentation of *42nd Street*, they'd gone back to their cabin, where she'd skimmed glossy island shopping magazines and he'd tried to figure out how to check his messages remotely using their cabin phone.

"Well, we're in St. John tomorrow, and the beach is the most beautiful you've ever seen," Helen says. They start around the track, Helen keeping their pace at a casual hop. "And then there's the big ball on Friday night. I know it's silly, but people here get so dressed up. Oh, and, the dancing. Do you like dancing, dear?"

Mona says Jack doesn't dance, and Helen reaches for Mona's arm, suddenly serious. There's a trace of Rita Hayworth in Helen's eyes, and Mona realizes Helen was once a very beautiful woman. "We've taken this cruise for years, and every time we take the ballroom classes," she says. "You and Jack should join us. It makes everyone so happy to see nice young people."

"I'll ask him," Mona says, finding it strange she and Jack could make people happy by being young, by being nice—by being anything.

As Helen aborts the run to sunbathe, Mona jogs ahead, pushing for the click, when it becomes automatic, when she doesn't think about the ache in her left knee, forgets the gnawing headache from too much wine the night before. Her thoughts become clear and she can line up all the things she wants—the investigative piece she's writing about Ameritech, what she would say if she won a Pulitzer prize, names she might give children starting with Arrabella and Alexander and working down the alphabet. Today she also thinks of dancing in the full-skirted black dress she got at Saks for the trip, spinning, round and round, with a faceless partner.

Drinking a dry martini and watching the whisked white peaks of the waves from the Admiral's Deck with George, Jack actually feels a little like an admiral, or at least someone of moderate importance.

"What kind of law do you practice anyway?" George asks, and Jack says he does mainly corporate litigation without going into much detail. Generally it's a question people ask without any real desire to know the answer.

"Ah, I bet you never go to trial," George says warmly.

"Twice in seven years."

"You know," Frank says, "I'm only two semesters shy of a law degree myself."

"Really?" Jack asks, shifting in his deck chair, the plastic straps eating into his thighs. "What saved you?"

"After the war, I wanted to take advantage of the G.I. Bill, but I already had an engineering degree. So I started law school. Helen got pregnant during the start of my third year, and I took a job at G.E., thinking I'd go back and finish up later."

Nodding, Jack drains the inverted-cone glass, the alcohol hot in his chest. Generally he doesn't drink other than an occasional gin and tonic with clients. Today, however, it seems right to have these James

Bond–esque martinis with George, like a moment of maturity Jack never got with his own father—most of their conversations had ended with his father asking rhetorical questions.

Catching the eye of a blond server, Jack raises a finger, signaling they need another round. The waitress, a college-aged girl in short shorts and a red and purple bikini top, appears with a martini in each hand. She gives Jack a plastic pen and charge slip. He signs it to his cabin number—an imaginary account he assumes will be settled at the end of the trip.

"So you never went back?" Jack asks, pinching an olive off the miniature sword.

"I thought about it," George says. "But I liked my life; it was just too much to give up for something I didn't want that badly."

"A fine decision," Jack says.

He starts to crumple his copy of the receipt, but notices that the waitress wrote a note—*If you want a friend*—followed by a cabin number. Looking up at her, Jack remembers a girl at Penn who handcuffed him to the frame of the bunk bed in her dorm room when they fucked. He can't recall that girl's name, and wonders whatever happened to those nameless girlfriends who drifted in and out of his life like the changing of the weather. When the blond waitress sees him seeing her, she motions him to the bar with a jerk of her ponytailed head. Telling George he'll be back in a minute, Jack goes over, smile ready.

"So I hear you're in the market for friends," he says. He hasn't cheated on Mona since the early days in their relationship (when she probably wasn't seeing other guys but he kept on with a few other girls until it became too much work). Still, he knows the drill, when to nod, when to touch his chin with the back of his thumb.

The waitress introduces herself as Alix-something. Telling him she's taking a year off UNLV to get some "real life experience," her voice is full of good-natured exaggeration. Jack laughs along with the stories about the leak in the staff lounge and how she'll change her major to hotel management when she returns to school. She leans in, grazing his shoulder with her hand, asks if he'd like to tour the staff quarters, see how the other half lives.

"Your father can come, too," she says, nodding at George, then winks. "Or he doesn't have to."

Mona is two decks below tanning with Helen; it would be so easy for Jack to have Alix-something—a fun, pretty girl who works on a boat to get a tan and get laid. He imagines his hand at the small of her back, and her lips tasting of sea salt and coconut rum. But then the achiness sets in, just like trying to work with the flu, that feeling he should have just stayed home because nothing's getting done.

Jack didn't tell Mona, but two months ago he went in for a physical, certain he had leukemia or a grapefruit-size tumor growing in his guts. It wasn't even that he felt sick, just drained all the time. Jack's doctor told him to get more rest and exercise—the prescription for all hypochondriacs. But over the past few weeks, Jack has been wondering if it's simply his life catching up to him. All those years of working hard for things—writing a thesis as an undergraduate, law review, taking care of his brother after their parents died, billing eighty hours a week to make partner. Perhaps there's a finite amount of what someone can work toward, what someone can want.

"I'm flattered," he tells Alix-something, "but I'm here with my girl-friend, so it's probably not the best idea."

Alix-something shrugs and walks away, wiggling her perfect heart of an ass to showcase what Jack is missing.

"I'm going to go check on the girls," Jack tells George back at their chairs. "We'll see you at dinner?"

"Al-right-y then." George gives a good-natured salute. "Good to see you're finally getting your sea legs."

Downstairs, the sunning deck has all the trimmings of the community pools from Jack's youth—skinny kids chilled from frigid water, grilled hot dogs, hopelessly suburban women in hot pink bikinis darkening like bread sticks in the oven, everything slippery and wet. With three empty daiquiri glasses on the table next to her, Mona is on her stomach in a modest one-piece. Her rice-white skin is already the color of a fast car.

"You're burning, Mo," Jack says. There's a book in the cabin he thinks about getting—some enormous David Foster Wallace thing everybody's reading.

"What?"

"You're getting sunburned." Loosening into the chair next to her, he abandons all thoughts of his book.

"Shhh. It'll turn to tan," she murmurs, words drowsy. "Happy or sad?"

"Happy not to be puking anymore." He closes his eyes, but the sun is so bright, it's still light through the skin of his eyelids. "You should put on some sunscreen."

Hovering in that place right before sleep, he wonders if turning down Alix-something means that he loves Mona or that he's tired of sex.

Maybe he's just tired.

Slumped on the bed against the wall of their cabin, Mona stares at Jack's dress shirts—initials "J.A.R." stitched on the cuffs, swaying in the closet. She's wearing only gauzy drawstring pants and a silk bra; anything form fitting is an absolute impossibility. In twenty-seven years, she can't recall being this burned, every inch of her skin a sore, tight casing.

"Your initials spell 'jar,' " she says.

"That traumatized me as a child." Jack comes out of the shower shrouded in steam, towel knotted around his waist. "Thanks for bringing it up."

He smiles and Mona recognizes it as the same smile he gave her five years ago when he literally bumped into her at the water fountain of the Cuyahoga County Courthouse. Then she melted like tar in the sun, fiddling nervously with her press pass, trying to stammer out her

name while he helped her gather her notepads and pens. His confi-
dence had dazzled her—she had slept with a couple guys at college,
but when Jack smiled at her she'd finally understood the kind of desire
her younger sister always bragged about. He'd radiated the same thing
she'd felt when she and Joey had driven to Cincinnati from Athens and
waited around the Suspension Bridge to see Tom Cruise filming *Rain-
man*. Now the smile makes her sad, and she looks away. Suddenly, the
brass and glass pseudo-splendor of the dining room is a horribly unappealing prospect.

"I don't think I can go to dinner tonight," she says to his shirts.

"Don't worry, Tarzan will bring food to Jane," Jack says in the
movie icon's stilted voice. Letting the towel drop from narrow hips, he
smacks his penis back and forth against his thighs. Mouth rounded into
an exaggerated O shape, he makes ape noises until she looks at him.

"Jack." Her smile dies before it actually becomes a smile, even
though she knows that this is supposed to be funny and sweet, that this
is why she's supposed to love him. "I'm serious. Look at me."

"Do you want me to put aloe on your back?" He points to the
bottle next to her on the bed.

"Would you?" Her burned skin makes her feel gross and stupid in
a way she hasn't felt in years, since she started dating Jack and began
meeting him for lunch downtown. Back then she noticed that Jack, and
everyone he knew, had a crisp, contoured look. Until she got her job at
the *Plain Dealer*, she'd lived her whole life in Athens, Ohio—a college
town, where bushy eyebrows and sweatshirts were fine.

Before Jack's fingers even make contact, before he even starts to
smooth the goo onto her shoulders, she draws in her breath in pain,
anticipating.

"Does that hurt?" he asks.

"Yeah, you're hurting me," she says, bowing her head forward,
curls spilling over her face.

"I didn't mean to hurt you, Mo," he mumbles. "I'm sorry."

"What?" She heard what he said, but wants him to say it again. It seems important, because Jack has never apologized to her for anything and because she doesn't think they're talking about sunburns anymore.

"I love you," he says instead.

"I love you, too."

And she remembers how the walls of her stomach were ready to cave in the first time she told him she loved him. Six months into the relationship, after sex, the words came out in a high-pitched squeak, like a hiccup stuck in her throat. She froze in his arms after she said it, paralyzed to even breathe until he said something, because it was *that* important, meaning so much more than when she'd said it to those guys at OU.

"I think we should go to the infirmary," he says. "You probably have sun poisoning."

"Maybe." With her thumb, she pushes on the red flesh of her arm. For a moment the spot turns white, then blood rushes under her skin to fill in the thumbprint. "They already know you so well. Don't we make a great pair?"

"Let's just skip dinner," he says, more to his shirts than to her. "We've still got all those crackers from the other night, and if we're up to it later, we'll go to the midnight buffet."

Letting the shirts sway in response, she remembers the day before she left for vacation, how Craig rubbed her head, static electricity on his fingers sending her long hairs everywhere. "Wear lots of sunscreen, Red," he warned her. "Pale folks don't do so well in the tropics."

From a wooden bench in St. Thomas's shopping district, Jack watches a grimy unattractive bird spastically peck a groove in the worn cobblestone streets—like a desk ornament his father had kept in his office. Up and down, up and down, stupid but fascinating.

And, all at once, Jack recalls the last time he spoke to his father about anything consequential. It had been winter break when Jack was a high school senior and working at the firm. Jack had been proofing a memo in his father's big leathery office when, apropos of nothing, he'd asked: "Should I go to Penn?"

"It's the best school you got into." His father had looked at him as if Jack had suggested the world was flat or the Indians would win the pennant. "Why would you go anywhere else?"

Jack had meant to say something then about Anna Fram and how the two of them had talked about going to Carnegie Mellon together, but realized that if it was something he really wanted, he wouldn't have mentioned it to his father in the first place, he would have just done it. He'd also realized that over the past few summers and holiday breaks he'd grown to like working with his father, to like his father's life.

But now Jack wonders if his father was happy. Happy in that big leathery office just like the one Jack has now, in the big brick colonial that Jack lives in now, with a pretty woman to warm the bed and take to functions—like the woman Jack has now.

And then Mona is standing in front of his bench on the streets of St. Thomas, removing yards of lacy white material from a shopping bag. Because the ship's doctor—who actually sighed when she saw Mona and Jack again—insisted Mona not expose her charred skin to more sun, they'd had to pass on the postcard-beautiful Magens Bay with the Steins. And despite the mercury kissing ninety-five degrees, Mona is wearing jeans and a long-sleeved T-shirt with the ship's logo that Jack got her from the gift shop.

"Isn't it beautiful?" she asks, and Jack folds the upper corner of a page in the book he wasn't reading.

"What is it?" He sets the book on the bench next to the things Mona's already bought—perfume for her mother, a marble hunting knife for her father, polished rocks she picked out for *his* brother, rolled tubes of prints by some island artist that they will never hang on the walls of his house—all "duty free," all charged to his American Express.

"It's a tablecloth." Holding one end to her sternum with her chin, Mona unfolds layer after layer of seemingly endless delicate fabric. "St. Thomas is famous for its lace."

"According to the guy who sold it to you?"

"No, Craig lived here for two years after college."

"Can we *not* talk about Craig?" Something dark rumbles in his chest. "How much was it?"

"I told you I was going to get one earlier, and you said it was fine." There's an edge in Mona's voice that wasn't there five years ago. It makes Jack very tired. "You never listen to anything I tell you."

"How much was it?" he asks again, blankly eyeing the material.

"It's not like we can't afford it."

"*I* can afford it."

"What's that supposed to mean?"

"It means the paper pays you like ten bucks an hour." Jack watches her face fall and can't believe that some crucial filter between his brain and mouth failed and he actually said it. So much will have to be done to get things back to normal.

"I'm sorry I'm not a corporate whore." Bunching the cloth back into the bag, she throws it at his feet.

He picks up the bag and thinks about telling her a giant corporation owns the paper she works for, but decides against it.

"You're right, we need a tablecloth," he says, even though he can't remember a single time they used the dining room table as anything other than a place to put mail.

"No. I'll just take it back."

She looks so defeated and so red and so ridiculous that he just wants to hold her. But he can't because she's sunburned, because he doesn't hold her anymore. In the distance their ship is anchored to the ocean floor, and Jack is overwhelmed by the desire to go back to the cabin for a nap before the boat leaves port and starts rocking again. Standing up, he tries to take her hand, but she shakes him away. Still, she follows when he picks up her packages and starts walking.

"This is a great tablecloth." Looking in the bag, he feigns interest. "Now we just need to make some friends so they can come over and eat things off our tablecloth. And you can start cooking so we can serve things on our tablecloth."

A sound between a laugh and a sigh comes out of her nose. "We *can* return it. And we can return the one we got for Helen and George."

"We got them a tablecloth, too?" Jack smiles. "For their anniversary?"

"I'm sorry."

"It's fine. I love you," he says, because it's easier than apologizing.

"I love you, too."

The first night she told him she loved him, he hadn't felt ready to say it back. He said it anyway. Her body had been soft and comfortable in his arms; he didn't want to discuss it. Looking back, he was too much of a coward to tell her the truth. But he wonders if he really feels any differently now than he did five years ago, wonders if he ever did or ever could, flashes back to the fall fifteen years earlier, when his father helped him pack a U-Haul for college. Anna Fram had crossed the cul-de-sac to say good-bye, her eyes dry but her voice holding all the gravel and hurt of the truly betrayed.

And then Jack sees the jewelry store. The kind of overpriced place littering every island where they've docked, it's designed to prey on tourists looking to create memories. Like everything else in town, the store is pink, as if it were dunked in Pepto-Bismol. In its window, earrings and chains are propped against glossy shells, driftwood, and draped velvet, a tennis bracelet spills out of a large conch shell. Above a display of engagement rings, square-shaped, pear-shaped, and emerald-cut diamonds in little red boxes, a sign, in decadent cursive writing, offers the slogan *When the islands make you realize it's right.* And maybe it *is* right with Mona, at least as right as it is ever going to be with her or anyone. In Cleveland Anna's father could give him a deal, but Jack can't remember why things like that matter—it's not as though his parents won a prize for dying with money in the bank.

"Is this what you want?" he asks, gesturing to the store. "Do you want to get married?" Even as he says the words, he knows that that isn't what she wants. She wants candles and roses and a bended knee. She wants poetry and love songs and dancing.

It must be close enough, though, because her whole face rises in a way he hasn't seen in the past year.

"Are you asking?" The rushed excitement in her words makes him think of their first date at the coffee shop, after the courthouse, when she spilled her hot chocolate.

Because he can't think of a reason not to, he nods.

"Are you serious?"

"Sure."

And she's on tiptoes, arms knotted around his neck like the life jackets on the ship.

Happy or sad? he asks himself as she braids his fingers with hers and leads him into the store.

When they get back to Ohio, the ring they got in St. Thomas won't fit and will have to be resized. Mona realizes this at the ball on the Promenade Deck, as she leans against the ship's railing, the Atlantic at her back. Here her fingers are swollen from sea salt, but in Cleveland, the two-carat solitaire will be too big.

The deck chairs have been cleared from the floor, and in their place three dozen couples make slow circles in time to melodies from a band comprised of three middle-aged men in tuxes and a woman singer in gold sequins. Christmas lights shaped like stars and moons dangle from the railings and flaming torches, while the real moon looms overhead, full and pocked like greasy skin.

A tuxedo-clad waiter comes by with a tray of champagne flutes. Mona takes two and hands one to Jack. He looks at it hesitantly before clinking his glass against hers.

"Cheers," Jack says. "To the most beautiful woman on the ship."

She looks down at the full-skirted black dress from Saks, tries to remember the last time he told her she was attractive. The first time was at the coffee shop on their first date, when she spilled hot chocolate in his lap. She said she was a klutz, and he said she was a beautiful klutz. The next day at work she tried typing "Mona Reed" as her byline.

Murmuring a fat thank-you that gets caught in her throat, tears burn her eyes, and she's not sure why. "You look nice, too." It isn't a lie. But then, she always thought so, from that first day at the courthouse when she noticed his dark eyes arched like crescent moons when he smiled and that the bones of his face were almost fragile, too pretty for someone like her. Suddenly she can't look at him anymore.

"I guess if we're here, we should dance?" he says uncertainly.

Even as she nods, she realizes something is horribly wrong, so wrong Jack is trying everything he can to fix it. They make their way onto the floor with cautious steps. His palms go to her hips, and she encircles his neck with bare arms, her skin shuddering with the faint echo of the electricity she used to get when he touched her. She tries to let him lead, but he's not very good, and they're really just rocking, her own feet following haplessly behind his. Jack feels and smells so familiar as she rests her head against his suit jacket, it makes her want to cry, but then there's a tap on her shoulder, and Mona sniffles back a sob.

"You kids look great," says Helen Stein, in a pink chiffon dress, smiling as though she'll never stop. "I don't know what you were afraid of."

"Yeah, we're okay, when we try," Jack says, and Mona realizes she and Jack haven't told the Steins or anyone else about their engagement; that she hasn't called her parents or her sisters.

"Would you like to see what we learned in the ballroom classes?" Helen asks; Mona nods absently.

With a grace that seems impossible for their sagging bodies, Helen and George swirl and step in perfect time with the music. Like something from an old movie with Ginger Rogers, Helen's skirt billows out as she follows George's steps. And then Mona can't look at them, because she and Jack are nothing like them. Burying her head in the silk fabric of Jack's jacket, Mona cries, no longer caring if her eyeliner smudges or if Helen and George see.

"What's wrong?" Jack's hands caress her hair.

"I don't know," she murmurs into his chest. "I want something."

"Whatever you want, I'll get it for you. Just, just don't cry, okay?"

"I'm sad." She gasps for air, salt from tears and the ocean biting her eyes and nose.

"Mona." There's all the tragedy of Shakespeare or Bosnia in the way he says her name. "Don't cry, please."

"Jack, I want to be happy," she says, and feels more than sees his face crumble as he pulls her body tight against his.

They've stopped dancing, but their hips still sway to the song. Jack makes cooing sounds into her hair. When she looks up, his brow is creased and his eyes, eyes that aren't crinkled into confident half-moons, are full of something closer to understanding than pain. His dark hair has fallen into his face, and he looks very, very young, years younger than she is—so young it makes her stomach shudder to know she's hurting him. Jack's fingertips press hard against her skull, and he grips her so tightly she can feel all the contractions of his torso muscles. The wood deck is slippery and her black heels so high, she isn't sure she could stand on her own if he let her go now. So she clings to his lapels, which smell faintly of shrimp scampi, even though she knows that she should let go, that if this were a book or a movie, she would let go. But it's not, so she doesn't. The boat continues to rock, and they continue to shuffle, out of time, with the music.

the next
generation of
dead kennedys

Jumping out of an airplane is the best way for Jack to get over Mona, according to his brother.

"When you're up there, you can just let everything go," Connor says, right hand easy on the Sentra's steering wheel, left arm, disproportionately tan, resting on the open window. "Everything's quiet and loud at the same time. Skydiving will clear your head right up."

"I don't know." Jack leans back into the worn vinyl passenger seat. His flight from Cleveland got into Logan ninety minutes ago, and, since finding Connor at passenger pickup, the two have been stuck in rush-hour traffic en route to a vegetarian restaurant in Cambridge, where they were supposed to have met Connor's girlfriend a half hour ago. "I'm not so great with moving recreation. I don't get along so well with boats and roller coasters."

"Naw, it's free-fall, totally different experience." Connor inches the car up and turns down a less crowded side street, cutting off a minivan with the license plate "It's Bev" and receiving the long blast of a horn. "Those giant cars should be illegal."

Not since trying to teach Connor to drive six years earlier can Jack remember being in a car his brother was driving. Nostalgia, like a too-sweet cake, leaves a film on the back of his throat, even though teaching Connor to drive had truly been one of the most miserable experiences in his life—one of the few times they ever *really* fought, one of the few times he may have come close to death—nothing to get choked up about. But then everything has made Jack choked up and nostalgic since Mona moved to Chicago three weeks ago.

Boston rolls past, gray and soggy, just how Jack envisioned it would look. It's his first time there, having shunned the city fifteen years earlier when he got the skinny letter from Harvard—something he credits with ending his delusions of doing anything remotely noble (politics, public defense, ACLU) and starting his descent into the smarmy lucrative world of corporate litigation. Now his brother is at Harvard for graduate school in government—his brother who got a C in high school geometry and scored two hundred points lower than Jack did on the SAT.

"Anyway, I'm too old to skydive," Jack says. "They'll check my driver's license, see I'm over thirty, and won't let me. I'll have to find some sixteen-year-old kid to buy my jump for me."

Connor laughs. To Jack, he always seemed skinny and young. Connor still looks skinny—thin legs lost in corduroy pants, torso broad and flat in layers of long- and short-sleeved T-shirts—but he looks his age. At twenty-three, he's no younger than the BU and Emerson students shuffling through puddles with backpacks and raincoats.

"You'll love it," Connor says, scanning the narrow street for a spot. "I've got a pilot friend who flies for one of the schools. He'll probably let you jump with me, so you won't have to hold on to a total stranger."

Lurching the car backward into a space, Connor kills the engine and checks his watch as they speed-walk down the streets. "Laine is gonna be pissed," he says.

The words are still hanging in the air when a tall blonde, presumably Connor's girlfriend, steps out from under a green awning with lettering designed to look like vegetables.

"You're fucking forty-five minutes late," she says, rolling bored gray eyes at Connor, who mumbles an apology and something about traffic, rain, and the Big Dig. Then, easy as sleep, the blonde smiles at Jack, extends her hand for him to shake, and introduces herself as Laine Rosen.

"Laine" is probably really "Elaine." Jack is willing to bet she shortened it to create mystery, make her seem more unusual and important than she is. But she's the kind of girl who can get away with it. The kind of rope-thin Harvard girl who can get away with lots of things, like messy pigtails, not wearing a bra, raunchy language.

She just seems like such a type to Jack. Like girls he knew at Penn, and even some lawyerettes at his firm. She's the kind of girl who makes him tired, tired for Connor and tired at the prospect of dating again. And, like words to a catchy pop song or a prayer drilled through repetition at Sunday school, Jack finds Mona's name on his lips, and bites his tongue to keep from saying it out loud.

Nothing on the World's Harvest menu looked particularly appealing when the three of them made small talk in the tapering rain while they waited for a table, nor does it look particularly appealing twenty minutes later in an uncomfortable wooden booth—Jack on one side, Laine and Connor, thighs touching, on the other. About half the dishes are foods Jack has never heard of, the other half involve tofu, which he knows about but doesn't want to eat.

"Don't worry," Connor says, setting down his menu and nodding at Jack. "Tomorrow Lainey's gonna visit her ma, and I'll take you to Union Oyster House for chowder, the real Beantown experience."

"No, this is great." Jack smiles. Of course Laine is a vegetarian, they all are. "Should we get wine?"

He doesn't even like wine. When he and Mona ordered a bottle at restaurants, he'd sniff the cork, taste the sample, and then leave his own glass half full so the waiters wouldn't ask to refill it. Jack raises the question to be polite more than anything, because wine gives you something to do.

"Wine sounds good," Connor says, and both men turn to Laine.

"I probably shouldn't." She blinks and briefly looks at Connor under lowered eyelids. The exchange takes a hair-fracture of a second, but it's enough for Jack to realize three things: first, that Laine is pregnant; second, that Connor knows Laine is pregnant; finally, that Connor and Laine have discussed said pregnancy and were waiting for a good time to tell him, and the present is not the time.

"Oh, God," Jack says before he even realizes he's saying it. Once it has been said, there's no taking it back. Laine and Connor look at him, then back at each other, their faces dotty as if they're in a Seurat painting. "I'll be right back."

Because he can't think of anywhere else to go, he wanders through the tables to the bathroom—another adventure in uncomfortable wood. And because he can't think of anything else to do, he reaches into his pants pocket for his cell phone and calls Chicago information for the listing of Mona's new job.

"*Sun-Times*, Mona Lockridge," she says in her professional voice. Not the way she normally speaks, it sounds more like someone who might ask what you're wearing rather than interview you about local weather trends.

"Mo," Jack says. In the six years they dated, he rarely called her randomly. She would call him several times a day, at the office or on his cell, often with some mini-crisis or question. He'd learned to balance the phone between his chin and shoulder, listening to her while still checking things online, still editing memos. But he has no idea how to start a random conversation. "It's me," he says. "Connor's pregnant."

"Jack?" Her phone voice is gone; she's Mona again. "Where are you? Are you drunk?"

"No," he says. It seems Chicago has made her a better journalist already, concerned about the who, what, where, why, and how. "I'm in Boston. This girl he's living with is pregnant."

"Oh, what's he going to do?"

"I don't know; we haven't really talked about it."

"Jack." She says his name in a way that makes him feel silly, as if he'd missed the obvious choice. But something in her voice softens, and she relaxes into the conversation.

"I'm actually hiding in the bathroom of a vegetarian restaurant."

"What are *you* doing in a vegetarian restaurant?" Mona laughs, and he almost forgets Connor and lanky Laine, has to restrain himself from asking her to hop a plane and meet him. "Don't tell me Connor is a vegan now?"

"God, I hope not."

The men's room door swings open, and Connor comes in, shrugs. "Dude," he says, "what's going on?"

"Go talk to him." In his ear, Mona's voice attached to Mona's body (a body he's no longer allowed to touch) in a low-rise building on the Chicago River: "Call me later."

To Connor, Jack holds up his pointer, indicating he needs a minute, mouths the word "Mona."

Nodding, Connor turns away, stares at the urinals.

"Okay?" Mona asks on the phone. "Do you have the number for my apartment?"

"Yeah, I think," Jack says. "I'll call you tonight. I love . . . fuck, it's habit." He holds out his hands as if he can wave the word away, as if Mona were standing there to him to see.

"I know." Mona, somewhere not in the bathroom. "Don't worry about it. Just call me tonight and let me know how it goes."

The click of the phone, and she's gone.

"You okay?" Connor asks.

"Were you going to tell me that girl is pregnant?" Even as he asks the question, Jack hopes he's wrong, that maybe he just misread things, that maybe Laine is embarrassed that she's allergic to grapes.

Instead Connor grins, thin cheeks reddening.

"Oh, yeah." He buries his hands into pockets of baggy pants. "We would have told you earlier, but the day I called was when you told me about the Mona-leaving thing. It just didn't seem cool then. You're still the first person I'm telling. So, Laine and I are gonna have a baby."

"Conn." Jack rubs his eyebrows, realizes he's rubbing his eyebrows, stops. "Have you thought about this at all?"

"Not in the men's room," Connor says evenly. "You can yell at me all you want later, but can we not do it here?"

"It's just—" Jack starts but gets distracted by a yellow stain on the ceiling. "We can talk about it later."

Dinner feels as though it takes place underwater. A pink-haired twenty-something takes their order; Jack gets eggplant lasagna because it seems safest. Both Connor and Laine order some kind of spiced tofu and black bean burrito, but Connor slathers his in Tabasco sauce—at least Laine hasn't changed everything about him. No one gets any wine or mentions the baby. Laine talks about business school, working for a not-for-profit the summer after undergrad, and asks uninspired questions about corporate law in Ohio. Jack answers with nebulous authority.

"I'm going to take Jack skydiving," Connor says at a pained break in the conversation. "Laine loved it when I got her up there. Totally freeing, wasn't it?"

"Yeah." Laine nods, eager to have a new subject. "And I practically had to be dragged on the plane. I was like, 'If we don't die, we're breaking up.' But then I just adored it, really adored it. Such a fucking rush."

The food arrives, hot and gooey with melted soy cheese, and Jack stabs the purple eggplant without any real intention of eating it. He hasn't felt like eating much of anything since Mona left, and he certainly doesn't want to start with this.

"We'll see," he says.

After dinner the three shuffle around the damp grass and muddy pavement of Cambridge. Everything is as Jack thought it would be with all the bronze plaques and the engraved stone. It's been a decade and a half since high school Latin, but he translates the school's motto, *Veritas*, on sight.

"Truth," he says to no one in particular.

They walk down JFK Street, passing the redbrick John F. Kennedy School of Government complex where Connor reports daily.

"I remember being a kid and getting totally freaked out by that Kennedy poster you used to have over your desk," Connor says, so sincere Jack feels the post-Mona-nostalgia phenomenon well in his throat. "That used to be your thing, right? You were going to be president?"

Jack stares at the brown-green water of the Charles and thinks about the Cuyahoga, his river.

"Something like that," he says, feeling old and stodgy in business-casual khakis and a button-down. Everyone looks about nineteen—girls with pierced navels peeking out of baby tees, guys with too-big jeans. It's not as though he's the oldest person tromping through the rain-softened ground, but he's definitely in the latter half. And he wonders where that line of youth resides and how he stumbled across to the other side, a place where the stars of sitcoms and romantic comedies are now a few years his junior instead of his senior.

"What happened?" Laine asks, and Jack can't tell if she's being polite or if she's genuinely interested.

"Sometime in law school, I guess I decided I wanted a Porsche instead." Jack smiles now because he does plan to yell at Connor later.

"Sounds reasonable." Laine's gray eyes flash something.

"I could still go for the whole Jack Kennedy image," Jack says.

"Would that make me Bobby?" Connor asks.

"Hey, I don't want to be Ethel," Laine says, swollen lips in a pout. "She looks like a horse. I want to be Jackie."

"Fine with me." Jack puts his arm around Laine and gives her a good-natured squeeze. In some parallel universe in his head, he lets his hand linger too long on her shoulder, maybe taps her ass when Connor isn't looking—shags her for the sport of it, because she goes by a stupid name, and she'll end up hurting his brother eventually anyway. In this universe he lets her go. "You can be my Jackie anytime."

"All girls want to be Jackie," Laine says. "It's one of the things we're taught when we're growing up—be elegant, be loyal, wear really nice clothes."

Jack thinks Laine means girls other than her, not the smart, sexually aggressive ones getting their MBAs from Harvard. It's the girls like Mona who want to be Jackie, demure and pretty, good with children and the elderly. Or at least, that's what he thought Mona wanted.

"Naw, Lainey," Connor says. "You're not Jackie or Ethel, you're Carolyn Bessette and I'm John-John. We're the next generation of dead Kennedys."

"I like it." Laine reaches for Connor's hand and braids her long fingers with his long fingers. "I like it a lot. Doomed, but doomed in new and different ways."

Letting Connor and Laine walk ahead, Jack kicks stones at the chunky soles of their Dr. Martens.

"Still doomed," he mumbles.

It's after midnight when they get to Connor and Laine's minuscule apartment—the apartment Jack sends Connor seven hundred dollars a month for.

Everything looks three-quarter scale—a narrow stove and half-size refrigerator, a sink that could hold no more than a few dishes. Though the paint is peeling in a few places and the hardwood floors are hopelessly cracked, everything is surgical-ward clean, which has to be Laine's doing.

"I made the futon for you," Laine says, pointing toward the mattress and wooden frame against one wall of the living room, more accurately the room in the apartment that isn't the bedroom. "I slept on it all through undergrad, it's actually more comfortable than the bed."

"That's great," Jack says. He'd wanted to stay at a hotel, but Connor had sounded hurt when he'd suggested it. "I'm so tired, I could sleep on the floor." And he is tired, tired from the flight, and Laine, and the post-Mona nostalgia, and the fight he still plans to have with his brother.

Then they all just stand there, Jack with his leather travel bag still on his shoulder, until Laine announces her train leaves early the next morning, and disappears into the bedroom.

Setting his bag on the floor, Jack sits heavily on the futon. Connor follows.

"Are you okay? Really?" Connor asks. "I know I was loony tunes for months after Beth and I broke up."

"Is Laine short for Elaine?" Jack asks instead of answering.

"I don't think so."

"You don't know?"

"*Jack.*"

"You're going to have a baby with this girl, and you don't know her name."

"Jack, don't."

"How long have you even known her? Five, six months?"

"Her name is Laine, okay?" Connor bows his head and kneads black hair that's too long in the front. "It's not as though there's a set amount of time you need to spend with someone before you know them."

Jack exhales, tries not to get too frustrated too quickly. "I just want to know why you think this is a good idea."

"It's not an idea," Connor says. "It's something that's happening. I've always wanted to have my kids when I was still young enough to play with them—"

"What's the fucking hurry? You're still in school."

"I just don't want to be the kind of dad Dad was to me, okay?"

"Jesus, Conn, the man's been dead thirteen years—"

"That's not what I mean." The muscles in Connor's face shift. "It's just that maybe some of that stuff is more important to me than maybe it was to him."

"Fine," Jack sighs, "then wait a year, see how you feel then."

"Jack, I'm not asking for money or—"

"You can have any money you need, this isn't about money." But on some level it is. Jack had told Connor not to think about money, to just go when Connor called from his AmeriCorps station in Arizona to say he'd gotten into the Kennedy School last summer. Four months ago, Connor had called to say he only needed half the rent because he was moving in with his girlfriend. Jack continued to send the seven hundred; the checks still got cashed.

"I don't want any more of your money." Connor's cheeks redden, his nose twitches.

"I just don't want you to have your whole life decided because you accidentally got some girl pregnant."

"Jack." There's a weight, an authority, to the way Connor says his name that Jack isn't sure he has heard before. "Don't you think I was an accident?"

And Jack starts to say no, but remembers his mother pregnant at the age of forty-two, how she spent the whole nine months annoyed and angry, how his father was grumpier than usual, around even less.

"You didn't come here to fight with me about this." Connor sighs.

"We're not fighting, we're discussing," Jack says, but he tries to remember why he is here—in his brother's world of futons, lanky blondes, vegetarian restaurants, and bad life choices. It has something to do with Mona's leaving. She said he'd be okay, that he didn't need anyone. And he's here to prove that he does need people, people like Connor—the only living person in the entire world required to love him.

"Then can we discuss tomorrow?" Connor asks. "It's like two in the morning."

"Whatever you want, kid."

"I'm gonna crash." Standing up, Connor backs toward the bedroom. "We have toothpaste and towels and stuff in the bathroom. Red Sox tomorrow at one; I'll talk to my friend about skydiving on Sunday."

And then Connor is in the bedroom with Laine, who may be snoring, angled features softened by sleep. Or maybe she stayed up to wrap long, long legs around Connor and whisper dirty things in his ear. Jack hasn't worried about his brother's sex life since Connor was in high school, when Jack wondered if he was supposed to say something about condoms. But the way Connor fucks Laine seems important, the power dynamic of the thing. Does Connor spend hours with his tongue between her thighs or does he enter her hard, not caring if her head bumps against the wall?

In the bathroom Jack pees, studying the Warhol soup cans poster hanging over the toilet. Looking for the promised toothpaste, he opens the mirrored cabinet above the sink, but gets distracted by the contents: a clamshell of birth control Laine apparently hadn't thought much about, MAC compacts, sunscreen, a lipstick, shaving cream and razors, contact case and solution (does Connor wear contacts? are they Laine's?), an amber prescription bottle from CVS—*Connor Reed*, it says, *take once daily for seasonal allergies*.

The bottle brings the post-Mona-nostalgia phenomenon to the back of Jack's throat. Apart from the years Jack was at Penn and those Connor was in school in Boulder, Connor has lived in the same house with Jack since he was born, easily the person Jack should know the most about, but he finds himself wondering what he does know about his brother. That Connor lost both parents by age fifteen, that he once broke his shoulder, is allergic to strawberries, likes to jump out of airplanes, chose his undergraduate university based on skiing, spends three hundred and fifty bucks a month on something that isn't rent, apparently has allergies, says he likes kids, might wear contacts?

And what about Mona? For six years Jack slept with his arms and legs woven with hers, passed her salt across the table of hundreds of restaurants, got annoyed listening to details of her days, knew and grew bored with every inch of her body. But what does he really know of her? That she made the bed every morning? That she was always on time? He was sure he'd be the one to tire of her, the one who needed to find someone more challenging. Never did he think she'd really leave. Not when she nervously spilled hot chocolate on him on their first date, not when she hung her dresses in his closet. Not even when she interviewed for the job in Chicago. But last week, the engagement ring she'd been wearing for six months came back to him via FedEx. It was currently sitting in a coffee cup on his kitchen counter, an extremely expensive souvenir from a different life. Maybe that's why he wants her back, because her leaving proved he was wrong.

The drip of the coffeemaker wakes him, and Jack realizes that, even with the futon frame poking through the thin mattress, he must have fallen asleep. All his body parts feel stiff and bunched. He tests them out as he reaches for the balled heap of yesterday's khakis. In the kitchen, which is really just the wall of the living room where appliances purr, Laine, long and lean in low-rise jeans and a tight sweater, pours coffee, spreads tofu cream cheese on a bagel, and hums some song Jack knows but can't place.

"Hey," he says, "can I have some of that coffee?"

She jumps, probably scared she has to deal with him without the buffer of Connor. "Did I wake you?"

He shakes his head no, but she apologizes anyway.

"Do you want a bagel or cereal or something?" she asks, reaching for a mug from the cupboard. "We might even have some meat-type things."

Her nervousness greases his resistance to her. Jack sips the coffee she pours and straddles one of two chairs at a card table he assumes they use for meals.

"Are you from Boston originally?" he asks.

She's from Providence—her father owns a Volkswagen dealership; her mother is a teacher—but she always thought she wanted to live in Boston. Now she's not sure.

"It's weird, you know, like no one here seems really committed to staying for a long time." She sits lightly on the other chair. "Something like one in four people in the area is a college student, and everyone just feels transitory."

"Yeah," Jack says. Though he isn't thinking about Boston, but Cleveland, where he lived at first by necessity, because of his parents, because of Connor, because of Mona. But somehow he's the one who got stuck there, in his parents' house, in his father's law firm. So stuck that when Mona suggested he move to Chicago with her, he'd refused to even discuss it; he told her just to go.

"I mean I still love this city." Laine finishes her bagel, checks her watch. "I just don't really want my kids to grow up here."

Jack wonders if this is her way of saying she's taking Connor to Rhode Island after the baby is born and they've racked up a hundred and twenty thousand dollars' worth of advanced degrees. He wonders if he's supposed to argue with her.

"I'm taking the train to my mom's," she says. "But I think I'll be back before you leave tomorrow."

"I'll take you to the train." Jack gets up and sets his coffee mug in the sink.

She protests that it's just a short ride on the T, that traffic will be bad and he'll never find another parking spot in the neighborhood, but Jack offers until she accepts. Laine hands him the keys to Connor's Sentra, and he picks up her duffel bag.

"I could get that." She gestures toward the bag.

"I know," he says, and then neither one of them mentions it again.

In fact it is a short ride to South Station, and they talk briefly about the Red Sox tickets Connor has for the afternoon and how the day looks nicer than the last. With her long, long fingers, Laine pauses to indicate the turns. The wheel of the car feels cheap and plastic, the brakes not nearly as responsive as they should be. Jack makes a mental note to remind Connor to take the car in. At the station, Laine gathers her bag from the trunk and comes around to the driver's-side window to say thank you.

"Like I said, I'm pretty sure I'll be back before you leave." And then she leans in through the open window to give him a clumsy hug, made clumsier by the fact that he isn't expecting it. "But just in case I don't see you again, I'm glad I got the chance to finally meet you."

On her way through the crowd—those pierced-navel girls and big-jeaned guys—she turns and smiles a small smile, or maybe she's just squinting against the sun. With her thick sunglasses it's hard to tell, but in that moment she looks a little like Jackie Kennedy.

• • •

By the time Jack thumbs through the keys and opens the front door to Connor's apartment after forty-five minutes of circling the one-way streets for a spot, Connor is up and drinking coffee from a crimson mug and reading the *Herald*'s sports section.

"You run off with my girl?" he asks.

"I took her to the train. Your brakes don't feel right."

"So you ran off with my girl *and* my car?" Connor smiles, naked except for plaid boxers. "My brakes just don't feel right to you, because my car is cheap. You left your cell phone here; Mona called."

"What'd she say?" Jack asks, heartbeat quickening at the mention of Mona's name in a way it hasn't done since he had a crush on Anna Fram in seventh grade—a way that seems absolutely ridiculous considering during the whole last year he lived with Mona, he was constantly coming up with reasons to stay late at work so he wouldn't have to talk to her.

"You were supposed to call her back last night."

"Fuck, did she sound mad?"

"Not at me." Connor sips coffee. "You guys sure talk a lot for people who broke up."

"It wasn't the cleanest of breaks."

The pink scar from a biking accident five years ago snakes around Connor's left shoulder. That also had been a messy break, and the surgeon had to insert a pin to keep things in place.

"Remember when you broke your shoulder?" Jack asks.

"Every time I go through a metal detector." Connor taps his arm. "Why?"

Jack remembers the cold aluminum of the chairs where he sat and waited for Connor to come out of anesthesia. How he stayed in the hospital for close to fourteen hours, long after Connor, groggy and drugged, told Jack to go home. Surely that's a sign he needs people, that Mona is wrong.

"I don't know. Did Mona say she was at work?"

Connor nods, and Jack picks up the phone from the coffee table and starts to dial. Taking the paper, Connor shakes his head, goes into the bedroom.

First her phone voice, then her real voice.

"Hey," Mona says. "You never called me last night. I just wanted to make sure everything was okay."

"Yeah, I fell asleep."

"I was a little worried, you don't usually call me from bathrooms in Boston," she says, and Jack imagines her propping the phone between her neck and chin, doodling spirals on her reporter's notebooks—everything always curly, like her hair. "It sounds as if everything is under control now."

"Something like that."

"That's good," she says, and he can tell she's going to hang up unless something changes, unless there's something else they need to talk about.

"So everything's okay out there?" Jack asks. "You have enough money?"

"I'm not your little sister." She sounds angry. "You don't have to take care of me because our parents are dead. I should go, I've got edit board in a minute."

"Do all women want to be Jackie Kennedy?" he asks, because it's the first thing that comes to mind.

"What does that have to do with anything?" She sighs. "I've got a meeting. I'll just talk to you when I talk to you, okay?"

Jack stays on the phone until the beeping ends, and the canned voice of the operator suggests that if he would like to make a call, he should hang up and try again.

During a wave at Fenway, Jack's cell phone rings. Rummaging in his pocket, he checks the number on the caller ID, sees it starts 312.

"Hey, Mo."

"So all morning I've been thinking about what you said about every woman wanting to be Jackie Kennedy," she says, "and I think that's not right. I think it's men who want women to be like Jackie Kennedy."

"I hadn't really thought about it that way," Jack says, struggling to hear Mona over the crowd and the rubber-band voice of the announcer. "But that sounds about right."

"What woman wants a philandering husband who gets his head blown off?"

"I guess not too many."

"I mean, think about all the diseases that poor woman probably got. And it must have been so embarrassing."

"You're definitely onto something. Maybe you could even suggest a feature on it."

"I don't know, I'd just been thinking about it all morning, so I figured I'd call."

A pause that goes on and on.

"Are you happier without me?" Jack finally asks. "Honestly?"

Another titanic silence.

"Maybe we shouldn't talk for a while, you know?" she says. "Certain things aren't going to change, and I'm not sure we're making things any easier, you know?"

Jack doesn't know, but he agrees and hangs up.

Something important has happened on the field, people around them stand up to clap and shout encouragement.

"Mona?" Connor asks.

"Yep."

"It's weird to see you like this," Connor says, and Jack sees his brother wants to pat him on the back or hug him, to make some sort of contact, but for whatever reason—the hot dog in Connor's hand, something about friendships between men, the inapproachability of being Jack—Connor doesn't. "It's like you're walking through soup."

"Are you going to marry her? Laine, I mean."

"We've talked about it." Connor shrugs. "I want to."

"She doesn't?"

"Naw, I think she does. She just wants to be sure it's her and not the baby."

"Is it?"

"Of course," Connor says, too easily. *Doomed in new and different ways.* "Maybe you should just move to Chicago. It's like Cleveland. It's cold and gray; it's got a lake."

"I don't know," Jack says, thinking about how everything felt wrong with Mona for a long time, long before she interviewed with the paper. How they almost broke up on vacation six months earlier, and they could never set a date to get married. "It might be kind of like taking spoiled milk to a new place to see if it will freshen up."

"Spoiled milk?" Connor shakes his head. "That's a terrible metaphor."

Jack shrugs and thinks about reaching out to touch Connor, but doesn't. They don't have that kind of relationship, and it's easier to send rent checks.

"Don't worry," Connor says. "I talked to my friend about skydiving, and he can take us tomorrow before you leave. I'm telling you, it will fix you right up. You can just let everything go."

From the backseat of the Sentra, Jack can't really hear what Laine and Connor are talking about, but he can see their fingers touch on a to-go coffee cup in the console between the bucket seats. Jack and Connor have just picked her up from the train station, and the three are headed for the airfield so Jack and Connor can jump out of an airplane before Jack has to get on one that takes him back to his house in Cleveland— the house that Mona and Connor don't live in anymore.

He dials Mona on the cell.

"I can see this not talking thing is going to work great," she says, but he can tell she isn't angry, might be relieved. "What's up?"

"I'm going to skydive."

Over the headrest of the driver's seat, Connor's head swivels around. With raised eyebrows, he asks if it's Mona. Jack nods.

"Are you nuts?" Mona asks. "You get sick on merry-go-rounds."

"I've been told that it's free-fall," Jack says. "That it's a totally different experience."

"I can't believe your brother talked you into this. Put him on."

Turning the phone over to his brother, Jack can only guess at what Mona is saying. All he hears are Connor's lines—"Hey, Mo, whatcha knowin'. Yeah, good. Nope. Would I lie to you? I know, I promise. Good to talk to you, too. Here's the big guy."

And then the phone is back under his ear, carrying Mona's voice, which is attached to Mona's body in a low-rise on the Chicago River.

"Don't break your neck," she says.

"I'm going to call you when I get on the ground."

"I'll be here," she says and hangs up.

They park the car and file out. Connor tells Jack to give Laine the contents of his pockets—wallet, keys, spare change, cell phone.

"Mona will probably call, because they talk every fifteen minutes even though they broke up." Connor makes quotation marks in the air when he says "broke up." "Just explain who you are so she doesn't mistake you for some floozy Jack picked up."

"Right." Laine winks a gray eye at Jack. "Not a floozy." Running fingers on the back of Connor's neck, she leans against him, whispers in his ear, but Jack hears. "Be careful, baby, we're going to need you around here."

Connor ropes his arms around Laine, presses her body against his, kisses her cheek, then lets her go.

Spreading out her jacket on the grassy area by the parking lot, Laine sits down, opens her backpack, and takes out a giant book. The sun makes her dirty blond hair a halo, her skin the same color of the golden dry grasses around her. For the first time since meeting her two days ago, Jack realizes just how impossibly beautiful she really is—maybe the most beautiful real woman he has ever seen. Holding one hand to shield her eyes, she uses the other to salute them as they walk toward the skydiving school where they'll get their Mylar suits and chutes.

"See you on the ground," she says.

As Connor opens the door to the building, Jack kicks pebbles in the gravel of the parking lot.

"So I just grab onto you when we jump?" he asks, even though Connor has explained it a half-dozen times—*"Hold on, let your legs fly back."*

"Pretty much." Connor smiles, and Jack recognizes it as his own smile. "Don't worry. I promised Mo I wouldn't let you die."

And Jack realizes that Connor has been wrong about one thing. For Jack, skydiving is not going to be about free-fall or about letting go. It's going to be about holding on as tightly as he can, about trusting that Connor knows when to pull the cord.

in the middle
of nowhere, dying
# of salmonella

After watching some of the grossest shit he's ever seen (literally shit, and blood, and other icky substances between liquid and solid), Connor leaves the delivery room and calls his brother from the hospital pay phone. Jack is hurried, emphatic, and impersonal—*A girl? Great! Laine and the kid are both fine? Great!*

"I've got a conference call in a minute, kid," Jack says. "I'll call you tonight."

Jack doesn't call that night, but Connor tries calling him. He tries him the next night, and the night after that, but the voice mail picks up at Jack's house, at his office, even on his cell. A check comes in an envelope from Jack's law firm with a note inside. Not a card, but a note written on company letterhead. It simply reads, *Let me know if you need more.* Jack hadn't even bothered to sign it. Connor is so hurt, he doesn't want to cash it. But he and Laine both have crappy grad-student health insurance and big papers to finish before getting real jobs. Laine writes a thank-you note, and Connor leaves more messages on all Jack's voice mails.

A week rolls into a month, one month into four, and Connor's hurt and anger bunches into an unpleasant knot in his throat that surfaces in the rare moments when he and Laine aren't busy trying to keep the baby clean and alive. Then the phone finally does ring, when Connor has Jorie on the changing table, plastic-tipped diaper pins balanced between his lips.

"It's your brother." Laine pulls back the bedsheet she hung to make a nursery in the bedroom. "It sounds important."

"And all my phone calls weren't?" Connor says, words muffled by the pins.

Laine shrugs bony shoulders; already she's long and lean again. Her flaxen hair that curled from prenatal vitamins is back to being straight.

"He wants to sell the house and move to Chicago," she says.

"What?" One of the pins slips, pokes the skin under his thumbnail. He shakes off the blood dots. "It's my house, too. He can't just sell it."

Coming behind him, Laine touches Connor's bicep in a way that's both condescending and comforting—a way that reminds him she's a lot smarter than he is.

"Go talk to him." She takes the pins and cloth, licks his nose. "I've got this one."

So Connor goes into the apartment's other room and picks up the phone.

"You want to sell the house?" he says as way of a greeting.

"Yeah, Mona and I got back together, and she wants me to move. I called Mom's old assistant, just to get an idea, and she brought this couple by from New York. They made an amazing offer, right on the spot."

Five hundred miles away in Ohio Jack pauses, but Connor isn't sure how to respond.

"It's a really good offer," Jack says.

"It's our house."

"Conn, you haven't been here to visit in like two years." Jack sighs. "I thought you'd be excited about the money. It's more than enough for you to buy your own place."

Connor looks around the five-hundred-square-foot space he shares with his wife and daughter. The plastic milk crates that still serve as sock drawers, bookshelves they've fashioned from concrete blocks and plywood, Kmart's finest futon.

"I guess . . . I don't know . . . I guess."

"We have to act sort of quickly if we want to take their offer," Jack says.

"I guess," Connor says again. But he feels his anger shifting into something else. When Jack had come out to visit in August, Connor had thought they'd almost connected, but that had been a year ago. Now Connor has a hard time even remembering what Jack looks like. Rationally he knows Jack looks a lot like him, tall and limby, thick black eyebrows and hair, but he finds himself slipping back to the default picture he had a decade ago, when Jack, ten years older than him, loomed over Connor's adolescence like another species, one that knew how to talk to girls, drive a manual transmission, and figure out restaurant tips. "So you and Mo got back together?"

Jack explains how Mona called from Chicago and about the job offer he got from a giant Chicago firm, but Connor senses it's a tidy revision of some larger story his brother won't share.

"Studying for another bar is a bitch," he says, "but I've got a couple of months."

"Maybe you could come out here for a few days with your time off," Connor says. "It would be swell if you got out to see Jorie before she's driving."

"We'll see," Jack says in a way that means no, then haphazardly asks how things are going. "I would have called, but I figured you'd be busy with the kid and all."

Because he's annoyed and hurt and Jorie is crying in the space be-yond the curtain, Connor tells the kind of story Jack just told. The kind where you say all the expected things when talking about a newborn—he and Laine are tired because they don't sleep much, he can't believe how long it takes them to go anywhere because of all of the baby crap they need to bring. He says nothing about how everything in his life since Jorie has felt charmed and important, about the hours he spends looking at her fingers and toes. Nothing about how her birth has made him rethink almost everything about his own childhood.

"Sounds like you have it under control," Jack says, then tacks on the first sincere thing since picking up the phone. "I just can't believe my kid brother has a kid."

In bed later, Connor finds himself distracted as Laine crisscrosses her legs with his. "It's weird, you and Jor will probably never get to see where I grew up," he says quietly. They say everything quietly with Jorie asleep so close by. "You'll never see this weird poster of John Ken-nedy I had over my desk or these ridiculous Jane Fonda exercise videos my mother had."

Laine stops running her fingers down his thigh, suggests he go to Cleveland and see if there's anything in the house he wants Jorie to have.

"I can handle Jor for few days," she says.

"It's not just the house."

"It will be good for you to see him, too, before this gets bigger and stupider," she says. "Jack strikes me as someone who'd be uncomfort-able around children. Honestly, he's probably just freaked out."

"Jack's too self-centered to be freaked out," Connor says, but Laine clicks her tongue.

Eighteen months ago, on their first real date (Laine had picked him up in a bar and taken him to her place two nights before), Connor and Laine ended up at his apartment where she asked about a family pho-tograph from Jack's high school graduation. Connor explained both his parents were dead, and Laine had lowered gray eyes and said she was sorry. "It's been a really long time," Connor told her. "I don't even think about them every day anymore." It had been true then, but it had become less true. When Laine got pregnant, Connor had thought a lot about his parents retroactively. He would be the exact opposite of them: young, energetic, and involved—he would potty train, coach Little League, make peanut-butter sandwiches and cut off the bread crusts. But over the past few months, while he rocked Jorie to sleep or fed her bottles of Laine's breast milk, he started thinking of them more and more, not in terms of the kind of parents they'd been, but simply that they had been his parents. Of course that started him thinking of Jack, too, willing his brother to want to be a part of things.

Laine's parents had gone through the world's longest, messiest divorce, but they'd been able to pull it together for their grandchild. They'd driven up to Newport and watched Connor and Laine's last-minute nuptials on Easton Beach, eaten fried clams at Flo's afterward. Three weeks later, for Laine's entire twelve-hour delivery, her parents managed to put aside the things that made them crazy long enough to feed their daughter ice chips and go over potential names. Connor's only living relative, on the other hand, took four months to pick up the phone because children made him uncomfortable. And it didn't seem fair, because Connor had chosen Jack years ago.

When his mother died almost ten years earlier, Connor spent a good chunk of time feeling sorry for himself. He had nightmares where he bolted awake screaming and cold, friends who'd fallen out of his life because they didn't know what to say to him, and he was forever waiting in the freezing northern Ohio dusk for Jack or Jack's ex-girlfriend to pick him up from swim practice. But he'd felt sorry for Jack, too, stuck in a city he'd tried to leave, working a billion hours a week at a law firm where the partners called him "Reed's kid." Connor didn't feel sorry for himself *because* of Jack until they'd been orphans for four months and Connor woke up at three in the morning with a headache so intense he couldn't see straight.

He'd heard Anna Fram (Anna Fram Levine since the previous spring) pull her car into the driveway a few hours before. It was supposed to be a big secret that she was sleeping with Jack again. On nights when her husband worked the graveyard shift at the Cleveland Clinic, Anna came over after Connor went to bed and left in the morning before he woke up. Connor had been playing along, but his mother had died of aneurysm and his own head felt like it was in a vice, so Connor went into Jack's room without much thought about the situation's etiquette.

Still, there *was* something startling and horrific about seeing Anna in his brother's bed. In all the years Anna and Jack had dated in high school, Connor had never so much as seen them kiss. But there she was, a swatch of brown hair and an olive-skinned arm across Jack's chest. If Connor hadn't been convinced his brain was going to blow up, he would have left.

"Jack." Connor nudged his brother's shoulder, lightly at first, then more demanding. "Wake up."

"Wha—" Jack blinked, sleepy and unfocused. In jerky motions, he propped himself on his elbow, glanced at Anna, who was wearing one of his undershirts and squirming awake beside him. His features tightened. "Jesus Christ, you can't just come—"

"My head is killing me—"

"—in here without knock—"

"I'm really sick." Connor felt his face crumbling, eyes pooling.

"Your head?" Jack didn't look angry then, but truly terrified. Sitting up he rubbed his own forehead, pressed his lips together until the color changed from pink to white. "Like sick enough to go to the hospital?"

"I'm sorry," Connor said, though he wasn't clear why he was apologizing.

"It's okay." Jack reached for his discarded boxers and pants. "Lemme get dressed and I'll take you."

Sitting up, Anna took Connor's hand as if there weren't a reason for her not to be there, as if the three of them hadn't eaten her buttercream frosted wedding cake at the Ritz-Carlton Ballroom.

"Sweetie, it's probably just a migraine," she said, and Connor loved her for saying everything would be all right.

"I'm going to take him to Deaconess." Jack buttoned up a wrinkled button-down. "I'll call you?"

"I'm coming with you, and we should go to the clinic." Anna was up and putting on jeans. She turned her back to Connor and slid her arms into a bra, pulled a sweater over her head. "We'll tell Eddie you called me. If I weren't here, you would have called me anyway."

It was true. Jack had called Anna for everything since he moved back. She'd made all the funeral arrangements for their mother, hired the cleaning lady to go through their mother's stuff. And she was always threatening to do more—pick up groceries, have Connor over for dinner when Jack worked late. As far as Connor could tell, Jack was letting her because it was easy and familiar, and she was married, so she wasn't allowed to ask all those questions about the future that Jack had never wanted to answer when he was her boyfriend.

"Come on, Ann." Jack shook his head. "Going there is a really bad idea."

The pain in his head was no less than epic, and there was panic rattling around Connor's chest. Leaning on the mattress, he realized it had been their parents' bed and he wondered how the scene would have played out if his parents were alive. One thing he knew was that he wouldn't have to be worried about Jack getting into a fight at the hospital because he was sleeping with a resident's wife. It wasn't fair, and life already wasn't fair enough.

Anna Fram said Jack's name in a way that made Jack close his eyes and nod and Connor sure that he had only seconds left to live. So they got in the Sentra and Jack drove to Eddie's hospital because it was a better hospital, and it was closer, and Jack and Anna both knew Eddie Levine would take good care of Connor, even if he might murder Jack. But no one said anything until they got to the emergency room, when Anna asked the receptionist to get her husband.

"What's the emergency, Ann?" Eddie was a former college tennis player, tall and full of lean muscles. He had one of those jutting jaws, and it jutted further when he saw Jack, who had the decency to look down.

Anna Fram went to Eddie's side, put her arm around the back of his white coat, spoke to him in the quiet way she used to speak to Jack when the two of them were in high school watching movies or playing pool in the basement.

"So you've got a headache?" Eddie smiled at Connor. "Sounds like a migraine. We'll fix you right up."

"You know about our mother?" Jack's head was up, alert and flush. "That she died—"

"Yeah." Eddie nodded. "So we'll do a CAT scan, just to be on the safe side."

Eddie led them to an examining area behind the front desk, where Anna helped Connor onto a gurney covered with uncomfortable paper. A nurse took his temperature and what seemed like a lot of blood. Eddie asked Connor a bunch of questions about when he started to feel sick, what he'd eaten that day.

"You're allergic to pencillin, right?" Jack was filling out a clipboard of paperwork and studying the back of his insurance card. Still piqued, he hadn't looked at Anna once since they left the waiting room.

"And strawberries," Connor said. Perhaps it was the thought of strawberries, or the blood leaving his arm through the plastic tube, more likely the way Eddie's eyes narrowed every time he looked at Jack. "I think I'm gonna be sick," Connor mumbled.

The nurse stopped stabbing him long enough to hand him a plastic basin, and Connor threw up, apologized, threw up again.

"Oh God." Jack bit his lower lip, exhaled, looked as though he might barf, too. "Is that bad? That can't be good—"

Anna's fingers twitched, and Connor knew she wanted to touch Jack, to take his arm, hold his hand. But she was standing next to Eddie, his hip against hers.

"Jack, why don't you go get some coffee in the lobby," Eddie said.

Jack shook his head, "No, he's really sick. Look at him."

"You're making things worse, Jack." Eddie was suddenly icy, and it was a weird moment in which everyone knew everyone knew everything. "Go get coffee."

Jack finally looked at Anna, who looked at Eddie, who suggested that they both go to the waiting area while he took Connor to run some tests.

With Jack and Anna gone, Connor felt his guts shuffle again, half-expecting Eddie to ask about what had really happened, about what had been happening since Jack came back after law school. But Eddie became friendly again, making jokes as he wheeled Connor's gurney down the hall to the lab, where the giant white CAT scan hummed. It looked like the slab in a TV morgue, and when the technician rolled his gurney into the cave, Connor instantly thought of his parents, of their grave sites that he hadn't been to since their funerals.

Eddie was searching for pulsating blobs of blood, but Connor wondered about all the other things inside his head the scan wouldn't show. Pulsating blobs of anger and self-pity because he was probably dying and Jack was making it worse. Blobs of guilt because he would lie if Eddie asked about Anna and Jack, more guilt blobs for never telling Anna about the other women who slept over nights when Eddie Levine didn't work late. Blobs of a secret fear that he didn't miss his mother as much as he should and didn't miss his father at all.

Eddie didn't find pulsating blobs of anything, though. He told Connor everything looked fine and rolled his gurney back to the examining area where Jack and Anna looked nervous, their heads down. "A classic migraine," Eddie said, and the nurse gave Connor a shot, dabbed his arm with a cotton ball, and warned him that he might feel drowsy.

"You'll be okay, Conn." Eddie wrote Connor a prescription and clapped him on the shoulder, something Jack would never do. "Just take it easy. These things are sometimes brought on by stress."

"I know you've had kind of a rough time lately." Anna tried too hard to sound light. "And if Jack's ever too busy or whatever, you know you're welcome at our house—"

"Thanks, but he's okay," Jack cut her off, then looked at his polished black shoes. Eddie and Anna looked at each other, then at Connor.

"We're okay," Connor said, even though it probably wasn't true, even though he was still mad, and self-pitying, and mildly panicked. Jack was his family, fair or not.

Eddie's shift at the hospital was almost over, and Anna said she would leave with him, come by later to get her car. After that, Anna didn't invite him over for dinner anymore or pick him up from practice. Connor ordered delivery and stood out in the cold, his hair freezing to spikes while he waited for Jack. As far as Connor knew, she never slept over again.

Now, almost a decade later, it's Mona, a different girlfriend Jack makes crazy and won't marry, who meets Connor at the gate of Cleveland Hopkins Airport. In a burgundy leather jacket, she's sleeker than he remembers, lipstick a deeper brown, gold highlighting the swirls of her red hair. When she hugs him, she smells the same as she did when he was seventeen and she started dating Jack, and Connor remembers exactly how it felt to fantasize about her in the next bedroom.

"I go away for a year and you're married with a kid." Mona holds him at arm's length when the embrace ends. "Even on soap operas these things take more time."

"Yeah, it's like Bizzaro World." Connor looks over her shoulder. "So where's the big guy?"

Stepping away from his chest, Mona looks up at him, eyes apologetic.

"They needed him in Chicago." She tries to sound like it's not a big deal. "Isn't that crazy? He can't even practice in Illinois yet and already they have him working weekends."

Connor shakes his head.

"He promised he'll be back late tonight," she says. "He didn't think he was going to have to go, and then he thought it was something he could handle over faxes, but he really needed to meet with people. I *do* have specific instructions to take you out for dinner."

Mona reaches for his forearm, and he feels a gut-balling sorrow for her. She's apologizing for Jack not being there like all of Jack's girlfriends have apologized for his not being there—Anna Fram's Camry pulling in front his school forty-five minutes after swim practice, *Jack just called and asked if I could get you, he's running late.* A part of him wants to warn Mona that Jack's going to Chicago will only move their problems a few hours west. But he says nothing, nods and smiles because it's kind.

Again she mentions she's supposed to take him to dinner, but Connor says they don't have to do anything fancy. So they get carryout from Corky & Lenny's.

It's been almost two years since Connor's been back to the sprawling brick colonial, and when Mona turns onto the cul-de-sac and the house comes into view, it takes a few seconds to register that it's even his house. The big elm in the front yard has been cut, new pear trees in its place, the shutters a different shade of cream. If the Frams' old house weren't next door, looking exactly like it always had, Connor isn't sure he would be able to place it at all.

In a way it's more Mona's house than his—she left only a year ago, while he hasn't lived here in six. She is the one with the garage door opener, the one who knows where to find soupspoons and napkins. Over pastrami sandwiches and steaming bowls of matzo ball soup at the kitchen table, Mona asks to see photos. He shows her pictures of Jorie at the hospital, with the Easter Bunny at Copeland Mall, in her baby swing in the apartment.

"Laine and Jorie are both so beautiful," Mona sighs. "I can't believe how much I've missed."

And Connor believes her, wonders why it's so easy for her to care about him and the things he loves, while Jack refuses to be a part of his life in any real way.

By the time they put the dishes in the washer, it's after eleven, and Mona says she has to drive to Chicago the next morning, says she should go to bed and disappears upstairs. Connor wanders the levels of the house, trying to find something sentimental, but he can't shake the feeling that he's snooping in someone else's home.

Since he left for college, his brother has changed the sofas; installed a series of bigger, flatter televisions and stereos throughout—nice furniture Connor has no associations with. The heavy cherry set in the dining room is the one they always had, but the lack of memories attached to it overwhelms him. His mother never cooked; his father never made it home for dinner. Growing up, they'd used the dining room table as a place to put mail and keys and other items easily lost.

Boxes in the basement are full of discarded, broken things from his youth—hiking boots missing laces, cracked skis, concert T-shirts of bands he no longer likes, yearbooks signed by people he's forgotten. A more recent box offers grammatically challenged term papers from the University of Colorado and assignments he must have forgotten to return to his students when he taught with AmeriCorps. There's a set of child's golf clubs his father gave him for his ninth birthday, but Connor's father had been too busy and then too dead to ever take him to the course.

Upstairs Jack's old bedroom is exactly how Connor left it, the black-and-white poster of John Kennedy still looming over the desk. Pensive and presidential, Kennedy looks at him now, and Connor squints at the poster, to see if there's any judgment left in its eyes. He can't tell.

The alarm clock on the table (he does have distinct memories of hating its clanking and bitching on weekday mornings) glows midnight, Jorie's final feeding time, so Connor calls Laine in Boston.

"How's it going?" she asks. "Bridged any gaps yet?"

He tells her that Jack isn't even back yet. "I just feel like this is one more thing that he needs to apologize for," Connor says. "One more way he's sucking."

"Baby," Laine sighs. "Just promise me you won't expect some big dramatic moment. Okay? It's not as though everything in his world changed because you knocked me up."

When he hangs up the phone, he looks out the window at the Frams' old house, feels the same rush of self-pity he did at the hospital when he was fifteen. Unsure what to do, he gets into his old bed, still wearing his jeans and sweater, and thumbs through old comic books until the images blend into dreams. Three hours later, he wakes up to Kennedy staring at him again, and for a moment remembers exactly how it felt to live in this house with his brother and the women in his brother's life. Hearing the garage door rumble, he runs down the stairs and through the kitchen to the garage like a dog excited to meet its owner.

"Hey, kid, what are you still doing up?" Jack asks, pulling a shoulder bag and laptop case from the passenger side of a Porsche. Jack had always talked about getting one, but Connor had assumed he was fantasizing—like when people talked about moving to an island or starting their own business. But there it is, shiny and dark. Jack is also shiny and dark, his jawline cleaner than Connor remembered.

"When did you get the car?"

"You like it?" Jack smiles his Jack smile, and Connor starts to think that maybe his default mental picture is true, that his brother is some other breed from a land of TV people where everyone is sleek and manicured and self-contained. "It's my midlife crisis mobile, I got it when Mo and I broke up. I'm keeping it now that we're back together."

And then Connor remembers that he's mad.

"I want to take some of the furniture and my stuff back with me, so Laine and I can have some sentimental things when we get our own place," Connor says, the idea forming as he talks through it. "I can rent a U-Haul and drive it back. I'd really like it if you came with me. Just for a day or two."

"Conn, I'm just walking in the door. It's like four in the morn—"

"You could see Jorie, and we could switch the return part of my ticket, so you fly home from Logan."

"I don't know," Jack begins, but Mona appears in the doorway, arms folded across her chest from the cold.

"You should go," she says, winks at Connor. "You can *not* study for the bar in Boston just as well as you can *not* study for the bar here."

"I might have to go back to Chicago—"

"It's like one day." Connor realizes he's bordering on whining.

Jack looks at Mona, who nods.

"I can drive with you," Jack finally says. "But I have to be back Monday."

So the next morning they rent a van. Without any discussion about who is going to pay, Jack clicks his credit card down on the counter. Without any discussion about who's going to drive, Jack gets behind the wheel of the truck. Mona meets them at the front door, her hair pulled back into a thick ponytail, the Mona of Connor's youth. The three of them load the dining room set, the golf clubs, the framed poster of Kennedy, and the boxes. Jack insists that since they're already schlepping crap to a storage space in Boston that Connor at least take one of the TVs and the couch. So they load those, too. Connor rolls down the rear door and starts to lock the chain, but Jack stops him.

"Lemme do it." Jack says, taking the lock and chain from Connor's hands. "These things are tricky, and you usually end up just locking the lock to itself."

Connor shrugs and Mona hugs him, whispers in his ear, "Good luck."

"You, too," he whispers back.

When Mona leans in to say good-bye to Jack, Connor starts to look away, but can't help noticing the awkward way his brother kisses the crown of Mona's head, glancing around with darting eyes—the best Jack can do for her after almost seven years.

For a while, Jack and Connor ride along trying to listen to a staticky NPR broadcast. Connor asks about the project Jack was working on in Chicago.

"Honestly, it's even boring for me to talk about it," Jack says. "Plus, it's illegal, until it goes through."

Connor shrugs. He's never really understood what Jack does, or what his father did for that matter. He knows only that their names sometimes appear in the business section of the newspaper.

"Mo seems happy," he says. "Are you guys gonna get married?"

"Conn, we just got back together. Not everyone is on your accelerated family plan." Jack pauses. "You and Laine and everything all right?"

Through small towns in upstate New York, Connor talks a bit about Jorie, but can sense Jack's disinterest, suspects he's listening to the flickering radio. By Buffalo, they're both just starring at the billboards along the highway boasting mile countdowns to McDonald's and Burger Kings and British Petroleums.

"Let's get steaks," Jack says, after they pass a sign for CattleHand's Steak House. "I worry Laine's got you eating tofu all the time. Your arteries are probably all clean and confused. You realize you have a legacy of heart disease to maintain."

CattleHand's is perhaps the most masculine place Connor has

ever seen. Everything inside is dark wood and brown leather, with bad Western artwork and heavy metal horse-related objects mounted on the wall. A cute waitress with pigtails smiles a lot, touches both their shoulders while taking their order, and convinces them to start with a deep-fried onion appetizer. The meat comes out, tender and bloody, french fries crisp, iceberg lettuce drowning in blue cheese dressing. They talk about which one of them the waitress is flirting with, how good the food is, and if the Indians will be contenders next season. And Connor can feel the two of them relaxing into familiar roles—they've always been able to talk about red meat and a baseball team with a politically incorrect name, it's the real things that give them trouble.

"Chicago is like the steak capital of the world," Jack says. "And Wrigley Field is amazing. You have to come out and visit."

"Jorie makes it kind of hard to travel right now," Connor says.

"Oh." Jack nods, as if remembering his niece for the first time. "Yeah, of course."

Without discussing it, Jack pays the bill and gets back behind the wheel of the truck. Two hours later Connor's digestive system is twisting in all kinds of unpleasant ways. He thinks his stomach has simply forgotten how to deal with that kind of food, but then he notices Jack squirming in his seat, eyes winced.

At a truck stop called Granny's they pull over and get the key to the men's room.

"Go ahead." Jack waves Connor to the bathroom. But when he comes out fifteen minutes later, Jack is antsy, like a circling vulture.

Thumbing through a metal rack of bumper stickers waiting for Jack, Connor's guts churn with a new urgency and he has to argue with the attendant to get the key to the women's bathroom. Green and uncomfortable, Jack is waiting for him when he comes out. "We must have food poisoning," he says, grimacing.

There's a line of customers waiting for the restrooms, and the clerk behind the counter gives them a look. So they drive the van across the street to a downscale motel, one of those chains with a number in its name, six, eight, ten. Connor isn't sure which it is because while Jack checks in, he pukes in the crabgrass separating the building from the highway.

He gets their bags from the back of the truck and brings them to the dank room. Jack is in the mildewy bathroom (no complimentary shampoo bottles or cakes of soap), so Connor calls Laine, who tells him about chamomile tea. Jack calls Mona on his cell phone, and she tells them to go to the emergency room. The front desk attendant doesn't seem the kind to know much about teas, and he tells them the nearest hospital is a good forty minutes away. Neither one of them wants to leave the haven of the room with its functioning toilet and mushy but inviting mattress, so they drink canned ginger ale from the soda machine and try not to disrupt the universe by moving too much. When it's Jack's turn in the bathroom, Connor flips on the TV and finds an *All in the Family* marathon on the channel getting good reception.

"Dad used to watch this," Jack says when he comes out, one hand draped loosely over his belly.

"Really?" Connor asks. His father had been the managing partner of one of the biggest law firms in the country; it seems unlikely that he'd have had much in common with Archie Bunker.

"Yeah, he loved it. Mom and I weren't allowed to talk when it was on."

They watch an episode Connor doesn't get. His bowels turn liquid again and he staggers back to the bathroom. When he comes out, the TV is off and Jack is on the bed, propped against the wall (of course there's no headboard), reading a huge workbook entitled *Barbri Bar Review*. Connor sits on the bed, cups his forehead with his palm, feels hot blood coursing under his skin.

"I think I'm running a fever," he says. "Check my head."

"If you have a fever I do, too," Jack says. "You won't feel warm to me."

"Jor's got this thermometer we stick in her ear, and it gives you a reading in like three seconds. Maybe we should go get a thermometer."

"Why? You could have a fever of one hundred and fifty degrees, but there's nothing I can do about it."

"I'd just like to know." Connor shrugs, and then the two of them don't say anything. From his backpack Connor takes out heavy books on social policy written in heavy language. He contemplates working on his thesis, but since Laine started editing it, she's been making useful suggestions and he figures he should just wait for her input. He calls her again.

"Feeling any better, baby?" she asks, and he complains a little more. Then she puts the phone to Jorie's ear, and he coos and giggles in a language of response to his daughter's gurgles.

"It's crazy how much I miss her," Connor says when Laine is back on the line. "It feels like I've been gone for years."

When Connor hangs up the green plastic phone, he feels Jack looking at him. He looks back, wondering if this is the moment where something important is going to be said, the moment Laine warned wouldn't happen.

"You could have used my cell," Jack says. "They charge you like two dollars a minute to make calls from a hotel room."

There had been a moment, once, the night of the migraine when Connor was fifteen. It was after the CAT scan came back clean and Eddie didn't punch Jack. Connor got dressed, Jack put on his coat, and Anna Fram stayed to go home with her husband. The brothers Reed wandered into the dingy morning light full of chirping animal sounds. Jack unlocked Connor's door first, walked around to the driver's side and got in, but made no attempt to start the car. Even though the key wasn't in the ignition, he put his hands on the steering wheel and extended his arms, pressing his back against the leather.

"Anna and I, it isn't what you think." Jack breathed deeply. "I guess it is what you think, but it's not like I don't care about her. There are times when the light hits her hair or when she smiles . . ."

"It's your life," Connor said.

Jack rubbed his forehead, swallowed and looked like there was something bubbling inside of his throat that he wanted to smush back down.

"I know, but it's . . . it's not only my life, is it?" Jack's voice wavered. Connor looked out the window at the traffic light leading out of the parking lot, because Jack falling apart was a whole lot scarier than Jack being awful and selfish. "I'm doing the best I can."

"I know," Connor said to the window.

"But I'm not doing a very good job," Jack said. "I'm sorry."

And Connor didn't say anything while the light changed from yellow to red, then back to green. That was the only time in his life Connor had ever heard Jack apologize for anything, and he didn't know what he was supposed to say. He was fifteen years old, tired, and drugged. He was fifteen years old and had just been through yet another traumatic experience. The anger and self-pity in his throat dissolved like sugar in coffee, and Connor knew he was supposed to turn around and tell Jack it was okay, that he was doing just fine. But it was too earnest, too real. He was only fifteen and it was too much.

"I'm sorry," Jack said again.

Connor wakes up not knowing where he is or why he's there. All he knows is that light screaming through a window might as well be serrated knives in his eye sockets. There's a pain in his temples, a soreness in his guts, and his throat feels as though it's been sanded. Seeing Jack in the room's lone and questionable chair, reading the enormous book of Illinois law, Connor remembers the steaks, the U-Haul.

"I think I'm dying." He sits up, feels the world rock and shift.

"You're not dying," Jack says.

"Oh God." Connor swallows against fresh nausea. "Do you feel this awful?"

"You're dehydrated." Jack folds down the corner of a page, sets the book on the nightstand. "I drank a thing of Gatorade, and it really helped. I'll get you a bottle." Sliding a Penn sweatshirt over his oxford, he takes his wallet from the table and plants it in his back pocket. "There's Advil on the counter."

When Jack leaves, Connor slips back under pilled sheets, but the horrible light leaks through the thin skin of his eyelids. On his way to shut the blinds, he notices a twisted metal rod on the asphalt parking lot, then another. Golf clubs—the golf clubs his father gave him fifteen years ago. The rolling door on the back of their truck is open, the chairs, table, TV, and couch are all gone; a sad, solo sofa cushion is all they've left behind. Finding his shoes, Connor goes to inspect the damage. It's crisp and bright, and he shivers against the cold air as he yanks the strap of the truck door until it closes halfway. The padlock is still locked, only it's hooked to the chain, just as Jack warned. Most of the stuff has been left in the boxes, but the papers are scattered and pruned. The framed Kennedy poster is facedown, huge footprints on the brown backing. Picking it up with both hands, Connor holds it at arms' length, examines the spiderweb of broken glass. The print itself seems okay, although Kennedy seems so much older than he remembers, or maybe it's simply that Kennedy seems exactly the same age and looks more dated. Sitting on the stoop of the truck, Connor pulls the jigsawed glass with the tips of his fingernails. A shard pierces the flesh between his nail and the pad of his thumb. Dots of blood pimple up and he sucks them off.

"What happened here?" Back from the convenience store, Jack looks over the scene and smiles a crooked smile. "You locked the chain to itself, didn't you?"

"No, someone jimmied the lock," Connor says unconvincingly.

"Well, I guess we've settled the question over what to do with the furniture. I knew this was a dumb idea." Jack reaches into his pants pocket for his cell phone, dials, hands Connor a paper bag from the store, speaks into the phone. "Can I have the number for U-Haul road-side assistance?"

Connor pulls out a bottle of strawberry-flavored Gatorade.

"I'm allergic to strawberries," he says.

"I know; it's all they had." Jack swings the phone away from his mouth. "I checked the label, and there's nothing in it actually relating to strawberries. I think you'll be okay."

"You remembered I'm allergic to strawberries?"

"Sure." Jack nods. "Could this godforsaken place just answer their phone?"

"What's Jorie's middle name?"

"Aww, come on, Conn." Jack moves the phone away from his mouth again. "I don't even think I know *your* middle name."

"It was on the announcement Laine and I sent, and I said it in all those phone messages you never returned."

"You've *got* to be fucking kidding me," Jack says. "We're in the middle of ass-fuck nowhere, dying of salmonella. We have a van that got broken into because you couldn't work a goddamned padlock. I think I can skip the pop quiz."

Punching his brother isn't something Connor thinks about; it just happens. His right hand clenches into a fist. The fist arcs into the air and into Jack's left eye with an audible thud. Cupping his face, Jack hops around the parking lot, feet tangling with the golf clubs. Connor stares at his bloody swelling knuckles, tries to remember a time he hit anyone else and comes up blank. From the phone Jack dropped on the pavement, an operator announces they've reached the twenty-four-hour hotline, but it's not during the normal hours of operation.

"Jesus Fucking Christ," Jack screams, still holding his eye. "What's wrong with you? Is this because I'm selling the house? You want it? It's yours. If you and Laine and your kid want to move to Ohio, fine. Take the goddamned house. I don't want it anymore. I never wanted it."

"This isn't about the house."

"Then what? You're pissed off cuz I don't know the kid's middle name? I'm an asshole, I admit it. I'm a huge fucking asshole, but this isn't exactly a news flash."

Connor opens his mouth to say that Jorie isn't "the kid" or "some kid" but Jack's niece. To say that that should be reason for Jack to care, that Jack can't just slip out of his life because children make him uncomfortable. But then Connor changes his mind. Maybe it's simply that Jack is wearing sneakers and a sweatshirt instead of an Italian suit and wing tips, but Connor realizes he's taller than Jack now. Maybe it's that the side of Jack's head is turning the color of mushed berries, but the knot in Connor's throat is gone.

"I'm so sorry," Connor says. "Your eye looks awful; I'll get some ice."

Connor will go to the ice machine, wrap the rough cubes in a thin hotel hand towel, and Jack will shudder and swear when the cold touches his skin. Without discussing it, Connor will drive the rest of the way to Boston while Jack reads Illinois law, gingerly fingering his swollen eye from time to time. Laine will laugh when they show up, shake her blond head and say she can't even guess what happened. Jorie will be in a blanket in Laine's arms, and Jack will say appropriate, mindless things, then fly back to his own life. But before all of that, Connor turns from the van toward the vending area, and Jack calls after him.

"I'm doing the best I can," Jack says.

And Connor realizes Jack isn't just talking about Jorie anymore, but about everything. Realizes he's almost the age Jack was when their mother died, that the two of them have been on their own for nearly a decade. For almost ten years, Jack has been doing the best he could. But it's not enough anymore, or maybe it's not necessary anymore.

"I'm sorry," Jack says.

And Connor knows that he is supposed to turn around and acknowledge that he heard, to accept, because that is the right thing to do. But he doesn't want to look at his brother, because there's something more horrible about Jack falling apart than there is to Jack being selfish and awful. There's a traffic light leading out of the hotel parking lot, and he watches it change from red to green. His face crumbles, and he feels a hot tear run down his nose. It has been ten years, and Connor is a grown-up with a wife and a child of his own, but it's somehow still too much.

the only pregnant
girlfriend he ever
married

They're phrases Laine remembers from her childhood. Words murmured into her father's jackets by all those "aunts" who weren't sisters of either one of her parents, messages left on the answering machine of her father's car dealership. *I know it's not right, but it seemed right; I feel awful for your wife and daughter.* . . . Laine finds these exact words on a sheet of tear-stained typing paper folded and tucked in her husband's parka pocket when she looks for the car keys.

She'd been on her way to the gym, the first night she'd left Merrill Lynch before ten in nearly a month, but she marches through the tiny apartment to the bathroom, beats the closed door with a flat palm.

"I can't believe you did this to me." Her voice quakes with anger, the way her mother's voice used to.

"Lainey?" Connor asks from inside. "What's going on?"

"I found Beth Martin's note. Open the door." Laine reaches for the doorknob at the same time Connor reaches for the handle on the other side. Both knobs come off, clanging on the floor and locking him in.

"I hate this fucking apartment," she says. "This is absolutely ridiculous."

She tries twisting the inner workings of the lock with her fingertips. Through the pressed wood separating them, she hears him do the same.

"I guess you should call the super," Connor says. "Gimme a second, I think I'm going to be sick."

"At least you're in a good place for it. I might boot, too, and I'll have to do it on my shoes."

Actually Laine doesn't feel sick, but strangely calm, maybe because she's been expecting this, not this exactly but something like it, since she was a kid, because she never believed in happily ever after.

In the bedroom she finds the maintenance man's number. When there's no answer, she leaves an emergency page. The intercom buzzes. It's not the handyman but the day-care car pool dropping off their two-year-old. With Jorie balanced on her hip, Laine goes back to the bathroom door, where she can hear Connor tinkering with the lock inside.

It occurs to Laine that she's happy her husband is trapped in the bathroom, because if he could get out they'd have to have the same fight her parents always had, the fight she thought she'd never have to have because she'd chosen someone like Connor.

"I called the maintenance guy," she says to the door. "I'm going to go somewhere."

"Wait."

"Daddy?" Jorie reaches for his voice with dimpled fingers. "Come out."

"I'm working on it, cheesefry," Connor says. "Lainey, please just wait until we can talk."

"I don't want to talk. I don't want to know all the reasons why you did this."

"Whatever you want, but don't take off."

The room shakes as he throws his weight against the door in a poor attempt to knock it down. She tells him to stop before they lose their security deposit.

"I'll leave the front door unlocked so the super can get in," she says, glad she doesn't have to look at him, because he has that heartbreaking twelve-year-old-boy look that skinny guys in their twenties sometimes have. "I'm taking Jorie with me."

"Lainey, wait. At least tell me where you're going."

"Somewhere."

But behind the wheel of the Jetta, a business school graduation gift from her father, Laine isn't sure where to go. She suspects Steve Humbolt, the only real friend she has at work, might have a crush on her, so he's out of the question. More than anything she wants to go to her father, wants to inhale his scent of Lagerfeld and leather from the car dealership. She wants to cry on his shoulder and have him threaten to kill her husband or at least have his legs broken. But she can't go to her father, not for this. He'd made a second career of fucking around on her mother; anything he could say on the subject would be pretty hollow.

So she gets on 95 South and heads toward her mother's house in Providence, even though her mother forgot Jorie's last birthday and told Laine not to marry Connor when she got pregnant. In movies, women go to their mothers when their husbands screw around, and that sense of sisterhood seems right.

"Want to go see Grandma?" Laine looks in the rearview mirror at Jorie strapped in her car seat.

"Want Daddy."

On cosmic cue, Laine's purse starts ringing in the passenger seat. The caller ID on her phone shows the number for their Cambridge apartment.

"Lainey, don't do this to our family," Connor says in a rush, knowing there's a finite amount of time he has to say anything. "Please, let me explain."

"I take it you got out of the bathroom," she says, and turns off the phone.

Two months before Laine found Beth Martin's note crumpled in his coat pocket, Connor was floating in that place between awake and asleep, where he thought he was having conversations with people who weren't in the room.

"Baby," Laine shook his shoulder, definitely a real person, a real person home from work hours later than she'd promised. "Get up, you did that thing where you fell asleep with water again."

That thing—drifting off with a glass of water in his hand—had been happening a lot since their babysitter dropped out of MIT to follow Phish and Laine had started going to her office at noon till all hours of the night so Jorie only spent afternoons at day care. Connor always tried to wait up for Laine, but rarely made it.

"I'm sleeping," he said, though that was becoming less and less true, and the sheets *were* wet and his contacts had dried to his eyes. "Just lay on the dry parts."

"Come on, get up so I can change the bed before we get sick."

Connor moaned. Laine was a superevolved human who functioned on three hours of sleep, no food with faces, and decaf coffee; she didn't get sick, or tired, or unproductive. While she yanked off the bedding, he went to the bathroom. He couldn't find his glasses, and everything was fuzzy when he came back sans contacts. Tall, blond, and in her underwear, Laine looked good, even fuzzy. He touched the pointy bone of her shoulder.

"I almost forgot to tell you," she said. "Beth Martin called."

"Who?"

At the University of Colorado, Connor had almost married a Beth

Martin, but Laine had to mean some other Beth Martin, perhaps a Beth Martin graduating from college and looking for an AmeriCorps placement in Boston, maybe a Beth Martin who'd seen their ad in *The Crimson* for child care. He hadn't heard from University of Colorado Beth Martin in nearly four years and couldn't fathom a reason she'd contact him. Even so, his heart flopped against his chest at the thought of his Beth Martin.

"She's doing her internship at Mass General." Laine got into bed and the pulled blankets up to her chin. "She heard you were in the area and wanted to get together for coffee."

"My ex-girlfriend called here and talked to you?" Connor asked; Laine nodded. "How'd she even get the number?"

"We're in the book." Laine shrugged from under the covers. "She seemed nice. I told her you'd give her a call. I figured you'd want to see what she was up to."

Laine talking about Beth Martin had an unsettling nightmare quality of things being off. Not that he hadn't told Laine about Beth. In that part of a new relationship where you tell each other the reasons why you are the way you are, it was one of his sugar-packet stories—dead father, dead mother, living with his brother, and a brief engagement to his college sweetheart. What Laine didn't know were the details—that for years after breaking up with Beth Martin he'd start sweating at the mention of her name, that the thought of her made his fingers shake.

"I guess coffee would be okay." His hands weren't shaking per se, but his heart was pounding blood furiously enough to make him wonder if his eardrums might explode.

"Are you coming to bed? I thought you were tired," Laine said, and curled her body into his when he lay down beside her. "So I have a question. When you proposed to Beth, was she pregnant, too?"

"You know you're the only pregnant girlfriend I ever married." He patted Laine's hip, wondered if she could feel the blood in his ears. "Beth and I didn't even have sex."

"You never told me that." Laine propped herself on her elbow. "You never had sex with her? And you dated for two years?"

"Three and a half."

"You didn't have sex for almost four years?" Laine was incredulous. "Was she religious?"

"Not really. She just wanted to wait until she was married," Connor said. That wasn't the whole truth. Initially Beth *had* wanted to wait, but after they'd been together a year, she'd wanted to do it. By then Connor was convinced he would marry her, and it had seemed silly to compromise her beliefs. That didn't seem like something he should tell Laine—Laine who'd picked him up at a bar, Laine whom he'd gone to bed with when he still thought her name was Jane. "There are other things you can do."

"You got by on hand jobs and hummers for four years?"

"If you want to have these heart-to-hearts maybe you should try getting home before midnight." Connor sighed, mad at Laine for bringing the whole thing up in the first place. "Why is this so important anyway? I never hold it against you when I find your name scribbled in bathroom stalls."

Laine laughed, mock smacked his shoulder.

"So these bathroom messages," she said, "do they promise wicked good times?"

"A great lay, sound financial advice, that kind of thing."

"Wanna fuck?"

"That's romantic." He turned on his stomach. He'd wanted to fuck a lot three hours ago when Laine was supposed to have come home, before she mentioned Beth Martin. "We've got to be up in like four hours."

Laine crawled on his back, aligning her arms and legs with his, reaching for his big hands and feet with her big hands and feet.

"Come on, baby, we haven't all week." She licked the back of his neck, making his shoulders bunch.

"Whose fault is that?" he asked, but Laine's hands slid beneath the waistband of his boxers—it was a lost cause.

"Baby, a little longer," she said ten minutes later, as he held her long, lean torso, and she rocked back and forth on top of him. "I'm almost there."

But he just let himself go, not entirely on purpose, but not really an accident either. Halfheartedly, he apologized.

"That was a shitty thing to do," she said.

"I was sleeping, what do you want from me?"

"Sorry I bothered you." She rolled away from him, sounding like she might cry.

Then he *did* feel horrible. It wasn't Laine's fault they were on a weird crepuscular schedule, wasn't her fault Beth Martin had a copy of the white pages. Reaching over Laine's hips, he tried to open her thighs, but she swatted his hands away.

"Go to sleep if you're so tired."

"Let me make you happy, please."

"It's fine." Her voice was marginally softer. "Don't worry about it."

"I *am* really sorry." He kissed her dishwater blond head. "Can you get off work one night this week and come with me to meet Beth for coffee? I'd really like it if you came."

"I can try."

"I've never met anyone who needed a family more than Connor," Laine's mother says. "I never thought *he* would do this to you."

Even though she's saying the exact opposite, Laine is pretty sure her mother means *This always happens; you just thought you were special and it wouldn't happen to you.* The two of them are in the kitchen of the house where Laine grew up, and everything looks the same as it did then, only not as clean.

"That makes two of us," Laine says, missing her father's quiet understanding, wishing she'd gone there.

"And he just left the note in his pocket," Caroline says. Still thin and blond, an older Laine. "It's almost as though he wanted you to find it."

"I really don't want to talk about it," Laine says, and she doesn't. Because the note was so sad and chock-full of regret, Laine almost felt sorry for the woman fucking her husband, the short, dark-haired girl she'd talked to once on the phone and met briefly last week when she and Connor had bumped into her at the grocery store. She just can't shake the feeling that if it were a movie, she'd be rooting for Beth Martin and Connor to be together.

Laine opens the pantry and stares inside, just like when she was a kid. Even though she isn't hungry, just like when she was a kid.

"There's leftover spaghetti," Caroline says. It's Friday night, but her lesson plan book is open on the table—the same red vinyl kind she used decades ago, probably the same grammar lessons she used decades ago. Caroline became a teacher because all women of her generation became teachers; a mother because all women of her generation became mothers.

"With meat sauce?"

"I didn't know you were coming."

Taking out a box of oyster crackers, Laine funnels a few into her mouth and wishes she had gone to her father's condo in downtown Providence. But then she feels the same shot of guilt she felt as a kid each time her mother kicked her father out and her father asked Laine to go with him. Before she was old enough to understand why her mother was sending him away, to understand spare shirts her father kept in his office, the little square packets of condoms. Laine knew it wasn't right to leave her mother, even though she wanted to.

"Do you know what you're going to do?" Caroline takes a fistful of crackers from the box, shuffles them in her hand. "Leaving him could make things hard."

Laine fakes a yawn. "Do you want to watch Jor tomorrow, or should I take her back to the city with me? I'll only go into work for a few hours."

Her mother says of course she wants Jorie to stay with her, of course she wants to see her granddaughter, if it's really only a few hours, because she does have things to do, things Laine and her father never understood.

In Laine's old room, Jorie sleeps in one of the twin beds. The reading lamp casts a weird glow over Laine's awards and plaques from the debate and cross country teams, her honor cords and photos of friends she hasn't heard from in years. Her mother's school crap has taken over the desk and the surface of her dresser, but otherwise the room is the same as when Laine left for Harvard eight years earlier. A picture from her senior prom is even tucked in the corner of her dresser mirror. She'd gone to the dance with a twenty-four-year-old architect, and he'd been one of the younger men she dated in high school. Since Laine was thirteen, when she stopped eating to eat and started running to run, there'd always been men and they'd always been older, men like her father and Steve at work, serious men with serious plans. They were the ones who appreciated her graceful collarbones and the way her mind worked.

Five months her junior, Connor was the only younger person Laine ever dated, and it wasn't a great "how they met" story. She'd picked him up in a bar. Out for a friend's bachelorette party her first semester of business school, she'd been annoyed by the other girls—the bride-to-be was wearing a "Suck for a Buck" shirt, and everyone was doing body shots with BU frat boys. Connor was eating cheese fries and watching the Indians–Red Sox game at the bar. She asked if he went to school in the area, which was pretty much Boston slang for "wanna fuck?" The sex was good but forgettable; she was tall and skinny, and he was tall and skinny. But the next morning when her alarm clock went off, he pulled her back to bed, said, "Don't leave, lovely lady," and log rolled with her across the mattress onto the floor. He'd pretty much had her there. It turned out he was getting a master's in social policy from the Kennedy School, though she realized his getting in probably had a lot to do with the teaching he'd done with AmeriCorps and the fact that he was an orphan by fifteen. He seemed to be chilling out in graduate school because he couldn't think of anything else to do and his brother was footing the bill. When Laine got pregnant (how she could graduate at the top of her class and not remember to take a little white pill was one of the world's greater mysteries), she waited until she was sure she was keeping the baby before she told him. She knew he'd want it, having a child with her was better than any plan he had. At least that's what she'd thought.

Since Laine turned off her cell phone three hours earlier, Connor has left seven messages on the voice mail. *Lainey, please pick up. Will you at least tell me where you're going? I'm calling C.J. and Dan to see if you went there. Are you still going to work tomorrow? I'll get Jor if that helps you.* She stops listening when she hears a sob in his voice, because it makes her feel sorry for him, and she's furious at herself for feeling that way. The phone rings in her hand, and she clicks the talk button before it wakes Jorie.

"Can you at least let me say good night to Jor?"

"She's already asleep," Laine whispers and turns the phone off again.

Pulling down the blankets of the twin bed opposite Jorie, Laine changes her mind and crawls in the bed beside her daughter.

"Daddy?" Jorie murmurs, sleepy and perfect.

She looks almost exactly like Laine did as a child, fair, with wide-set gray eyes, more her daughter than Connor's, even if she does love her father more, even if she wants him more than she wants her mother.

• • •

A year before he would even meet Laine, at the top of a double black diamond slope in Vail, Connor got down on one knee and presented Beth Martin with a velvet box from his ski pants pocket.

"I love you more than I've ever loved anyone and can't think of any family without you," he said, squinting against the sun—he thought he should take his goggles off while proposing. "Beth, will you marry me?"

Saying yes, she hugged him through the layers of their down ski jackets and took off her glove so he could put the ring on her finger. They raced down the hill and when they got to bottom, he tackled her and they rolled around kissing and laughing, snow wet and cold on their cheeks and the slivers of flesh between their coats and gloves. It was Beth's twenty-second birthday, and he'd made reservations at the four star restaurant in the lodge. They were the youngest couple in the dining room, drawing attention to themselves by being giddy, giggly, and drunk from the cheapest wine on the menu.

"We'll have lots of kids, right?" Connor asked, dipping a two-dollar pomme frite in a pool of mustard and hot sauce he'd swirled together. "I want a whole gaggle of kids."

"No more than nine." Beth smiled. "Just enough for our own soft-ball team."

When he went to the bathroom that night, she wrote him a note on the lodge stationery. It said she was better expressing herself in writing and she wanted to make sure he knew she couldn't wait to start a life with him. She signed it "Cheesefry," and he actually kissed the paper.

Five weeks later, a month before *his* twenty-second birthday, a hyperventilating Beth Martin handed Connor back the ring and another note, this one on loose-leaf paper, blue ink smudged with tears, saying she was going to medical school alone.

"I'm so sorry. It's just that you're the only boyfriend I've ever had," she said over and over again, crumpled on the cheap carpeting of his apartment. "We're so young, and you don't even know what you want to do yet. I'd never forgive myself if I let you make my plans your plans."

He never told anyone, not Laine, not his brother, all of what happened after he finished reading Beth's note and she walked out. Guts mangled, he'd spent days on the toilet shitting out everything that had been a part of him for the previous three and a half years. One night he washed down a bottle of aspirin with a fifth of Gin and slept for twenty-nine hours. He didn't shower; didn't eat; swam laps at the U of C pool until he couldn't feel his limbs, then walked home in the March air in nothing but wet swim trunks. After twelve days, when he hadn't shown up to their child psych class, Beth timidly knocked on his door.

"I wanted to make sure you were okay," she said, pulling nervously at strands of her brown pageboy. "I was worried."

He wanted to slice open her belly and pull strands of intestines out by the fistful. Instead, he said he'd slept with her best friend, whom she always joked had a crush on him.

"Dana and I were kicking it on and off for pretty much the whole last year you and I were together," he said. "I was going to give her up when we got married, but she's a fabulous lay."

Without a word Beth left, shoulders slumped and defeated. He wanted to slouch her even more, to pound her into the ground. So he called Dana and made it as true as possible.

Connor didn't see Beth Martin again for four years, not until she walked into Café Paridiso for the coffee that Laine set up but couldn't attend because she had to work.

When Beth walked through the door shaking rain off the collar of a violet peacoat, he almost didn't recognize her. Not because she looked any different, but because she looked exactly the same, he'd just forgotten, remembering only her back, her hunched shoulders, and the hatred that made his fingers shake. Unlike Laine, who was aggressively attractive with the classic bones of a statue in the Art Institute, Beth was pretty in the most unassuming brown-eyed way. And like those dogs they'd studied in freshman psych, Connor remembered exactly how it felt to be in love with her. Remembered she used to rub her feet together before she fell asleep, that she wrapped herself in warm sheets when they came out of the dryer, the way her belly button had a slightly musty smell.

"Conn?" Beth asked. "Who would have thought we'd both end up in Boston?"

"Yeah, everyone in this city calls me 'Kahnah.' " He stood up, and she gave him a quick hug; she was easily a foot shorter than him. "So you're a doctor now or something?"

"Or something." She shrugged, rolled wide eyes, smiled at Jorie. "Is this your little girl?" Beth held out her fingers for Jorie to squeeze, and looked up at Connor. "She's so cute. I can't believe she's yours."

"*Hey.*"

"No, I mean, I knew you'd have a beautiful kid; I just can't believe you have a kid."

But Connor knew what she meant: she couldn't believe he had a kid that wasn't hers.

It's pouring rain, and Laine is already late to get Jorie from her mother's when she leaves her office on Market Street, still she goes completely out of her way back to her apartment. She tells herself she's going to get clean underwear and a change of clothes, but the only thing she takes is a shoebox of Connor's old photos they unearthed the year before while moving from their last crummy apartment to their current crummy apartment.

Pulling the car into the parking lot of a White Hen Pantry, Laine thumbs through the pictures. Most of the shots are Beth and Connor in L.L. Bean outerwear—apparently the two of them did nothing in college but ski and have snowball fights on the campus lawns. But there is one shot of Connor on a bed with the paisley coverlet in all hotels. Even though he's wearing jeans and a T-shirt and Laine knows he and Beth never had sex, the photo is decidedly postcoital. Half on his stomach, half on his side, something between surprise and a smile is on his lips, black eyes unfocused, like Beth whipped the camera out of a travel bag without warning. This is what Laine wanted to see—what it looks like for her husband to be in love with someone else.

Laine sets the box of photos on the wet asphalt in the parking lot, leaving it to confuse the next person stopping for cigarettes and soda. As she drives, fighting Big Dig construction and sheets of rain, she wonders for the first time in twenty-six years if her father loved any of those women. Wonders if that makes any difference.

"Ma, I'm really sorry," she says preemptively in the doorway, when she finally gets back and lets herself in.

"Jorie's with Connor." At the top of the stairs, her mother shakes her head. "He came by looking for you, but you didn't answer when we tried your cell. He waited around, but Jorie was hungry, so he took her to get something to eat."

"What?" White-hot anger burns Laine's lungs. "You just let him take her, just like that? God, for once I really thought that you would be on my side. Just this one fucking time."

And then she's running up the stairs to her childhood bedroom, grabbing her deodorant and makeup from the dresser, and shoving them back into her gym bag.

"There aren't sides here," her mother is saying. "You said you'd be home by noon, it was going on three. He's her father; she wanted to go with him. What did you want me to do?"

Laine realizes it's a perfectly legitimate question. If her childhood taught her anything, it's that children shouldn't be used as pawns in their parent's disasters. But she wants to be nine years old again to tell her father yes when her mother kicks him out and he asks Laine if she wants to go with him.

"Wait, where are you going?" Caroline's hand grazes Laine's shoulder as she runs past her down the stairs.

"I'm going where I should have gone in the first place," Laine says. "To Daddy's."

Connor hadn't realized Laine was someone he could love until the night he tripped over her on his way to pee. It was four in the morning, but she was on hands and knees scrubbing the splintered floors in her apartment.

"What are you doing," he asked, squatting next to her. "Don't you have a big test tomorrow?"

"Yeah," she said, cheeks red—the first time in the two months they'd been sleeping together that he'd seen her embarrassed about anything. "I just do this when I get nervous."

It might have been biological, OCD or something fixable with a pill, but it was the first crack she'd let him see, the first time he thought of her as a person and not some perfect droid.

It wasn't until half a year later, when Laine was six months pregnant, that he realized he *did* love her. It was the middle of winter, but the heat in their apartment couldn't be adjusted, so it was perpetually ninety-six degrees. They spent a lot of time languishing on each other on the futon. With her head in his lap, she looked like a dying queen ant, twig arms and legs protruding in all directions from her huge, round stomach.

"Baby, let's go out to dinner." Laine looked up from one of his heavy books on social policy—she'd started off editing his thesis but by that point was pretty much writing it. "I want you to eat a steak for me."

"If you want a steak, I'll take you to get a steak." Connor smiled down at her. "But I'm not gonna torture you by eating one in front of you."

"Please." She pushed plump lips into a pout. "I just want to be around meat."

He took her to Smith & Wollensky, where the waitress's annoyance became apparent when the two of them got iced tea instead of alcohol and Laine ordered a baked potato and creamed spinach. His filet au poivre came out tender and bloody. Since dating Laine, he'd only had steak once, when his brother came to visit, and he'd forgotten the sheer joy of meat. With the first taste, he actually sighed. Gray eyes lean and hungry, Laine watched him chew.

"Just take some." He held a piece on the end of his fork. "The cow's already dead, and he'd understand it's your hormones."

"Put it in your mouth," Laine said, breathing heavy, pink flush on pale cheeks. "Don't chew too much, then kiss me."

They were next to each other in a little romantic booth, and she slipped her tongue between his lips, licked juice and pepper off his teeth, sucked the meat. Sliding her hand under the table, she reached for his cock poking through his corduroy pants. The annoyed waitress walked by pretending not to notice.

"Men's room," Laine whispered, hand still on his crotch. "I'll meet you there in a minute."

They'd fucked in public bathrooms before, but her changing body made them clumsy. He could hardly lift her, and her swollen stomach created an odd distance between them. Stumbling, he knocked her head against the stall. Laine laughed; Connor cried. That was the moment.

"Baby, it's okay, I'm fine." Laine ran fingers through his hair, looked at him nervously. "It didn't even hurt."

He shook his head, put his palm on her belly, tried to think of a way to say what seemed unsayable.

"I'm just so grateful we're doing this." He knew she hated syrupy displays of emotion, but he needed to plow through it. "I feel, I don't know, blessed."

After he calmed down, Laine made a joke about how he was going to lose it in the delivery room (he didn't), but for a good fifteen minutes she just held his head while he sobbed in the restroom.

"Thank you," he said, again and again, into breasts she didn't normally have.

Turning off the ignition at Rosen Motors, Laine closes her eyes, waits for the rain to let up a little. When someone knocks on her window, she expects her father or one of the sales guys with an umbrella, but it's Connor, dripping wet, black hair molded into peaks on his forehead.

"What are you doing here?" she asks, but he twists up his palms indicating he can't hear her. Surprisingly, she isn't angry, but terrified. Terrified because Connor looks the same as always. There's the same faint scar on the left side of his forehead, the same right turn of his nose. Somehow she'd expected him to morph into something else since making it out of their bathroom, to have become someone entirely different. She rolls the window down a crack. "Where's Jorie?"

Connor lowers his head to the slit of space, and windblown water sprays Laine's face.

"She's inside with your dad," he says. "I've been looking for you for hours. Please talk to me."

Through the glass window of the showroom and the hard rain, Laine can see her father, Jorie in the crook of his arm. He's waiting to come rescue her if she needs to be rescued.

"I don't feel like talking," she says.

"Lainey, please open the door."

She shakes her head.

"I have the keys." He pulls a chain from his jeans' pocket, sticks it in the lock.

Like a cornered spider, she backs into the passenger seat. Just as Connor opens the door, she jumps out the other side and runs into the lot of new Volkswagens and Audis. On his stomach and elbows, Connor crawls into the car, over the seats and console, and out of the passenger-side door. Even though she doesn't want to, Laine laughs. But she starts running as he climbs out of the car. She runs; he chases. Around a Passat, though a row of Eurovans. She stops at the rear end of a Jetta, Connor at the front. He moves toward her, and she runs to a blue Beetle and rests her palms on the rounded hood.

"Wait, please," Connor yells, words garbled from the rain, but sincere as always.

She ducks behind a TT. He follows, and she starts running again. Crying and laughing from car to car. Within seconds her hair is wet and heavy around her face. Frigid air stabs her lungs as she splashes in puddles and muddy water seeps through her leather pumps and nylons. Coat and suit jacket in the car, Laine feels the thin fabric of her camisole mold around her nipples. And she runs like she hasn't run since high school track, since she ran away from her parents' crumbling marriage, ran out of her baby fat, ran out of Providence. Connor chases her down a row of convertibles. There's a mesh fence blocking her in, nowhere left for her to go. She turns, and he grabs her wrist.

"Lainey, talk to me please," he says between heaving gasps for air. "Just give me a chance to make it up to you. Don't do this to our family."

"You did this," she says, looking at the cars, her arm, everywhere but his eyes, because she's sure her mother has said that exact line before. "This, us—it was working for me, and I don't want to hear all the things that are wrong that made you do this. I don't want to know that you always loved her more."

"Of course not. Maybe we can go away next weekend, just the two of us—to Nassau or some other warm place."

She concentrates hard on the asphalt lot.

"Or maybe we could take Jorie to Disney World," he says. "It wouldn't be crowded this time of year, just get away with our family."

"Connor." He's still holding her wrist, but it's a gentle pressure she could shake off. "It's not like we can ride Space Mountain and you can unfuck that girl."

"I know, I just don't want this to be the end, and we need to start somewhere."

His voice catches, and she can't not look at him anymore. He rubs his wet eyes with raw hands.

"Your teeth are chattering," he says. "Let's go inside and talk."

She realizes her teeth *are* chattering and she's freezing. It can't be more than thirty-five degrees out, and the rain is chunked with ice. Connor is shaking, too, his breath coming out as white clouds.

"I don't—" She stops because she isn't sure where she wants the sentence to take them.

Leaning in, he starts to put his arms around her, then stops and holds her shoulders, a foot of rain and air and her parents' failed marriage between them.

"God, you're so beautiful," he says, blue lips trembling from the cold and because he loves her. Even if he could stick his cock in someone else, she's still the best plan he has.

His eyelids droop, and she knows he's going to kiss her.

She could stop him. If she leaves him she could find someone else, or she doesn't need to find anyone at all. She has two degrees from Harvard and cheekbones to cut glass. She doesn't have to stick around and become bitter for the reasons her mother stuck around, the reasons that have kept women stuck and bitter throughout history. And she knows this game too well. If she kisses him, he'll be sorry for a while, be crazy good to her for a while, but it will happen again and again. Everything she has done her entire life has been in preparation for this moment, to not kiss him back. But she's freezing and he's freezing. When his lips touch hers, she opens her mouth and lets him loop his arms around her. Wrapping her long arms around him, they hold each other until they stop trembling.

Beth Martin initially felt good in Connor's arms that first afternoon after the coffee shop. It was as if some astrological wrong had been righted—he'd finally had sex with Beth Martin. Almost immediately that karmic soundness was replaced with a terrific pain that seemed to stem from the base of his spine and radiate to his toes and scalp.

"I can't believe we did this." Beth rolled over to face him, her enormous eyes wet. "I talked to your wife on the phone last week, and you have that beautiful little girl. This isn't like us."

She was so sweet, so cute; it seemed impossible that he ever hated her or thought of her as anything other than warm and wonderful. He wanted to take her guilt away, so he kissed her forehead, her nose, her throat.

"It's just . . . I thought about you every day for four years," she said. "I don't know that I ever stopped loving you."

Something in his chest snapped then, and he made love to her again, almost because it hurt. They kept at it for six weeks, even though it made them both miserable. Beth developed a nervous blink; Connor couldn't sleep, jumped at all shadows and chewed the tops off his pens. Somehow it made him love Laine more—martyr Laine who compromised all her beliefs to work at a giant evil finance firm so he could work for Massachusetts Reads and they could still eat; beautiful Laine, on her knees scrubbing floors, forever fucked up from her parents' divorce.

He knew things had reached a critical low point when he called his brother in Chicago for advice. As an orphaned teenager, Connor had been disgusted by the revolving door of Jack's bedroom and the steady stream of girls sipping coffee in the kitchen in the mornings. But six weeks into his affair, nails gnawed to the quick, Connor found himself dialing his brother's office.

"Have you cheated on Mona since you got married?" Connor asked.

"What?"

"Have you been unfaithful?"

"Are you asking for me or for you?" Jack sighed. "Look, kid, if you're calling for me to condone fucking around on your wife, it's not like I can give you some green light. Do what you have to do. But you like your kid, you like Laine. You made choices."

That was what he told Beth, later that afternoon while they sat in his Nissan Sentra in a Twin Donut parking lot, words muted by buckets of rain.

"We made choices," he said, and watched her try to hold things together.

"Of course, you're right," she said, but she was talking to her Nikes.

A week went by, and Connor started thinking everything might not have to come avalanching down, that maybe Laine would never have to find out. Then Beth Martin came up to him in the grocery store, and Connor was pretty sure the stabbing pain in his chest was a heart attack. His father had been fifty-five when he'd had his first, but Connor was convinced he was going to die at twenty-five, on the linoleum floor of Star Market, while his wife examined prepackaged California rolls and his daughter sat in the shopping cart eating an organic oatmeal cookie.

"Conn? I thought that was you." Beth touched his arm. "And you must be Laine? We spoke on the phone that time."

It took a lot not to throw up or fall down, but somehow Connor negotiated an introduction between the two women. Laine apologized for missing coffee and talked to Beth about children's hospitals because Laine knew about everything, even hospitals. Connor leaned on the handle of the cart and shook his head no when Jorie offered part of her cookie.

"We should all get together and have dinner sometime, right, Conn?" His vision was actually blurring. Lower body loose as gravy, he couldn't even tell who was talking—Laine? Beth? Jorie? Probably not Jorie.

Mercifully the conversation ended. Telling Laine they needed olive oil, he cornered Beth in an aisle of imported Italian foods.

"You don't live anywhere near here." Connor grabbed Beth's arm. "You're not freaking Glenn Close. You can't stalk me."

"You know I'm not like that."

He did know, which made it so much harder.

"Then why are you doing this?" he asked. "Why are you here?"

Between rows of marinated artichoke hearts and balsamic vinegar, she handed him a folded piece of paper with his name on it, exactly like she used to do in college.

"I know it's stupid, but I wrote a note," she said. "Can you just read it? I didn't want to screw things up for you. I just, I wanted to see what our life could have looked like."

She blinked, and he knew she would cry. Promising to read her letter, he slipped it in his coat pocket and went back to his wife.

"I didn't think Beth would be like that," Laine said as he drove back to the apartment. "I thought she would be different. She's so bird-on-the-shoulder, you know. Like Cinderella or Snow White, the kind of girl that attracts cartoon woodland creatures. She just seemed so nice."

"She's not that nice," Connor mumbled, unsure he could actually have that conversation, with his heart still sprinting.

"From what you said the other night, I just thought she'd be this prissy little thing with a gold cross around her neck."

Laine folded long legs under her chin, resting her feet on the dashboard. She was five eleven but looked small and sad, and he felt the same way he did when he saw her scrubbing the floor. So he said the thing that could make everything the most right.

"Let's have another baby."

"Where'd that come from?" Laine laughed self-consciously. "We can hardly manage Jor."

"Aww, you know we're doing great," Connor said. "We aren't dead, so we're doing tremendous compared to my parents. Let's have another kid while we're still young. Come on, a friend for Jor." He leaned over the seat and let Jorie wrap her small hand around his index finger. "Hey, cheesefry, would you like a little brother or a little sister?"

"A sister," Jorie clapped her hands together. "Like Emily's sister."

"There you go, she wants a sister like Emily's sister." Connor's shoulders loosened. "But this time, can the kid look a little like me? I'm not asking for much, maybe dark hair, just so I know I have genes."

"I could try." Laine's gray eyes narrowed. "Are you serious about this?"

He *was* serious, maybe more serious than he'd ever been about anything in his entire life. If he could get her to agree to have another child, things would be okay, he knew it.

"Yeah. Why don't you forget to take your pills again?" He rubbed her head. "And we should get a house. We've got the money from when my brother sold my parents' place."

"We *should* get a house. I hate our apartment, and they're killing us in rent." Laine crawled under his arm. Resting her head against his side, she wrapped her arms around his ribs. "I thought you didn't want to stay in Boston?"

"I don't know, I've gotten used to being 'Kahnah,' " he said. "Let's get a big old house with that New England–y roof thing."

"Shaker?"

"That's it. A big old house with that roof and fireplaces."

"Do you know how to build fires?" Laine laughed.

"I can learn." He kissed her forehead. "And a dog, I've always wanted a dog."

"Not a yappy little dog, though. Let's get a big dog the kids can play with, a lab or a golden or something." Laine slipped her fingers under his belt and jeans and the waistband of his boxers, took him in her hand.

"Lainey," Connor whispered, nodded toward Jorie in the back.

"It's okay," Laine said in his ear. "She can't see anything."

all the words
to "thunder road"

It wasn't the best method of family planning. Three months after her thirty-sixth birthday, Mona unceremoniously stopped taking the pill. She didn't discuss it with her husband. Jack always waved away the topic when she brought up children, saying the time wasn't right, that they had their careers to think about, their lifestyle. But at his firm's company picnic last summer, Jack dove into the pool when a junior partner's son fell in. The boy in his arms, Jack emerged, water rolling off them in sheets. As Mona watched her husband try to calm the child, she'd had to look away, tears in her own eyes—a picture of what they could be.

Jack was forty-one, and they'd been together almost fourteen years. Mona knew he would never think the time was right. It was easier, she figured, to ask forgiveness than permission.

But she doesn't get to ask for either. Sitting on the white paper of an examining table, Mona doesn't realize she's pregnant. Next to her, Jack can't stop yawning and black stubble seasons his cheeks. He'd held back her red curls while she puked the last three nights, and still put in his fifteen-hour workdays. He'd insisted on taking her to the doctor, assuming she has food poisoning or stomach flu.

"Sometimes birth control is less effective because of an antibiotic," the physician says. "Is there a chance you might be pregnant?"

Right then Mona knows she is, even before she pees in a cup to prove it. Jack studies a diagram of the female body where blue and red lines depict arteries and muscles, but he flexes tapered fingers and shifts his square jaw; he realizes she's pregnant, too.

"It's a possibility," Mona says to the linoleum floor.

"You did this on purpose, didn't you?" Jack asks flatly when the doctor leaves so Mona can get dressed. He doesn't sound angry or even surprised, just disappointed. "Without talking to me."

Mona intends to lie, to say the pill is never a hundred percent effective, that even the doctor says so, that it probably *was* the antibiotic she took last month for strep throat, but instead she just nods, tears in the folds of skin between her eyes and nose.

"I wanted to talk to you," she says, but feels herself starting to whine and stops.

Jack hands her a stiff tissue from a box next to glass cylinders of cotton swabs and tongue depressors. Closing his eyes, he rubs his eyebrows like he does when the computer crashes or his brother calls with some new problem.

"I really wanted to talk about it," Mona says, wiping her lips. "But you never let me."

"Let's not do this here." He puts a gentle hand on her back, takes a deep breath. "Wait until we're home."

But they don't discuss it. He drives to their condo in the high-rise where Oprah Winfrey lives, stopping on the side of Lake Shore Drive so she can vomit while the October wind blows her long hair everywhere. Then he goes back to his office in a different high-rise farther down LSD.

"I thought I'd pick something up on my way home." He calls

around nine, like he always calls around nine. "Anything you feel like you could keep down?"

He brings back coconut soup and pad Thai, which they eat from the cartons while watching a syndicated *Seinfeld* episode in the living room.

"It's the one where George's fiancée dies from the envelope glue," Jack says, chopsticks midway to his mouth—the wormlike noodle strands making Mona question her decision to eat. "We've seen this one."

"We've seen them all," she says. "Want to see what else is on?"

He flips through the channels—more sitcom reruns, *Star Trek* with its language of strange galaxies, sports networks he knows she won't like, news channels with bad things they don't want to hear about. They end up watching Jerry and the gang, and then Letterman. Chin drooping to his chest, Jack dozes during the musical act but jerks awake when the phone rings.

"It's your brother," Mona says, checking the caller ID without picking up the receiver. "Do you want to talk to him?"

"I'll call him tomorrow," Jack says. "Let's just go to bed."

In the massive California king that allows them to sprawl and never touch, Mona stares at the smooth plaster of the ceiling and waits for Jack's snoring to start. After an hour she turns to face him, puts her hand on his shoulder.

"You want to talk?" she asks, but he pretends to sleep.

Because she's pregnant and not dying of salmonella poisoning, Mona tries to pick up a four-to-midnight shift from the other Metro editor who covered for her all week. But she's home sick by seven when Jack's brother calls.

"Everything okay, Mo?" Connor asks. "You sound down."

She wonders if Jack told him she's pregnant, decides he probably didn't, even though Connor is the only living member of Jack's family and the closest thing Jack has to a friend.

"I've got some sort of stomach thing," she says. "How are things with you?"

"Not so great, actually." His daughters, dog, and new age/investment banker wife all seem to be yelling in the background. "The big guy around?"

She tells him Jack is still at his office, asks if there's anything she can do.

"Naw, I'll just try him at work," Connor says, and Mona thinks he probably needs money or maybe he's having some sort of problem with Laine—Connor and his wife are always almost getting divorced. "If you want to help, come visit soon. It's been, like, forever."

An hour later Jack plows through the front door. Mona follows him to the den, where he flips up the laptop on his desk.

"My brother's sick," he says, flushed and hurried. "I told him I'd go to Boston this weekend and do money stuff. Do you want to come?"

"Of course, if you want me to." They watch the computer screen turn blue before Windows kicks in. "What kind of sick?" she asks, even though she knows it's a bad sick. Even before Jack says things like "advanced stages" and "spleen involvement," she knows to put her arm around Jack's waist.

"Let me see if I can get tickets for under a million bucks." He kisses her head, but brushes her hand away.

He plays around Priceline and Hotwire and finally calls United to cash in frequent-flyer miles. The newspaper wouldn't let her take home any work, so Mona thumbs through copies of *The New Yorker* and *Atlantic Monthly*, magazines she and Jack subscribe to and never read. Periodically she looks at Jack's back, studying the point his thick hair makes at the base of his neck. The loudest sound is the laugh track of sitcom reruns, easily overpowering the ink jet's hum as Jack prints page after page about external radiation and autologus marrow transplants.

"If Laine has him on some kind of crunchy organic shit, I'll kill her," Jack says. "This isn't the kind of thing you fuck around with."

"I'm sure they're not taking any chances," Mona says, though she's not certain he's talking to her. "We should go to bed."

"Go ahead, I'll be in in a minute," he says, then looks up, the panic flooding his face, making him younger than forty-something. "Conn said they're giving him all this crap that's making him sick. Do you think his hair fell out?"

But Connor has all his floppy black hair when he and his family meet Jack and Mona at Logan's baggage claim the next day. Mona expected he'd look worn and weather-beaten, like actors playing cancer patients in made-for-television movies, expected she might be unable to keep her face light and pretend nothing is wrong. But Connor looks pretty much the same as always, lanky and young. He could pass for twenty years Jack's junior instead of ten.

"Was the flight bad?" He hugs her. "You guys look like you've been used as soccer balls."

"It was storming at O'Hare. Things were kind of rough." Jack says, eyes red and puffy. When the alarm went off at seven, he was still staring at his computer's green glow, a dictionary-thick stack of printouts marked up beside him. He turns toward Mona. "And Mo's had a stomach thing for the past week."

"We've got some chamomile tea that's great for that." Embracing Mona, Laine's bones stick out in too many places. She's the one who looks sick, blond hair tied back in a limp ponytail, shed pounds making her classic features severe. "Say hello to your aunt and uncle." Laine prods her daughters—Jorie, seven, and Keelie not quite four. They stare blankly at their mother. "Go on."

Mona doubles at the waist and hugs her rigid nieces. It has been more than a year since she saw them last, she and Jack keep postponing visits. Mona can't remember how she normally greets them, but it seems important now. Leather carry-on bag still slung over his shoulder, Jack nods at the girls.

"You've got to get out here more often," Connor says. "My kids don't remember you."

"I know who they are." Jorie thrusts out her lower lip. Already tall and fair, she's a little Laine. "We're still going to carve pumpkins tonight, right?"

"Pumpkins," says Keelie—smoky and darker, with the same black eyes as Jack and Connor.

"If we don't get to them tonight, we can do them in the morning." Connor puts a hand on Jorie's blond head. "Your aunt and uncle are probably hungry and tired."

"It will be too late," Jorie whines, glares at Mona. "Tomorrow's Halloween."

That she could have missed it before seems ridiculous, because suddenly Mona notices signs of Halloween everywhere: goblin and vampire cutouts on the walls of the airline offices, "Monster Mash" on the Muzak, a few Delta employees are even sporting pointy black witch hats. Halloween had been insanely important to Mona and her sisters, growing up in Athens, Ohio, where their mother started sewing their costumes each August. When she was in college and her first years working, there were always parties where everyone used the day as an excuse to wear racy clothes—midriff-baring genie outfits, tight rubber cat suits. But October 31 is a day of no significance to her life with Jack in Oprah's building, where no children ever wander up to the eighteenth floor seeking candy. And Mona wonders when she began to forget.

In the parking garage, Laine clicks a key fob and lights blink on a blue minivan.

"When did you get this?" Jack looks at his brother. "You hate these things."

"We hate it." Connor shrugs, a daughter on each hand. "But it's the only thing that holds the girls and their friends. We still have the Jetta."

Getting everyone in the van is a complicated procedure, and choosing a place to eat is even more difficult. Though everyone insists Mona decide because she's the one feeling sick, Laine is a vegetarian, Jorie lactose intolerant, and Keelie is in a phase where she eats nothing white. The six of them end up at a round table in a Chinese place in Natick, where Jorie continues to whine about pumpkins and Laine orders a ludicrous amount of rice. Fried rice for Keelie and Jorie, who refuse to eat it. Keelie no longer eats brown or beige foods in addition to white ones, and Jorie recently learned fried is unhealthy. Despite Connor's insistence that he only wants soup, Laine orders white rice that sits on the table in front of him.

"Can you try it?" Laine looks at Connor, who has eaten maybe two spoonfuls of wonton broth. "It's something you could handle."

"I don't want any rice."

"It shouldn't be too hard—"

"I'm not hungry."

"Conn—"

They've gone from whispering to not whispering; Mona looks at the burgundy napkin in her lap. To her left, Jack chews sesame beef, oblivious or pretending to be oblivious.

"Laine, I don't want it," Connor says, quietly again. "Let it go."

"If Daddy doesn't have to eat the rice, do I *have* to eat it?" Jorie asks.

"Yes," Laine says.

"Yes." Keelie, apparently also in an echoing phase.

"Daddy," Jorie looks at Connor, "do I have to?"

"No one *has* to eat any rice," Connor says; Laine clicks her tongue and closes her eyes. "But do you like Aunt Mona's hair?"

Hearing her name, Mona looks up.

"Yes," Jorie says grudgingly. This aunt is the reason pumpkins aren't being carved. "The color's pretty."

"Well, look at all the rice your aunt ate." Connor winks at Mona. "How do you think her hair got so red and curly?"

"It's not from eating rice," Jorie says. "It's from her genes. Her parents probably have red hair."

"Everyone in my family does have red hair." Mona makes her voice cookie dough, and wonders if all seven-year-olds know about genetics. "But we all eat a lot of rice, too."

Before Mona can gauge Jorie's reaction, Keelie picks up a silver dish of rice and hurls it across the table, where it knocks a plate of barbecued spare ribs in Jack's lap. Laine and Connor are both on their feet—Connor lifting Keelie out of the booster seat, Laine wetting napkins from a water glass, handing them to Jack, who looks at Keelie as if he expects an explanation.

"No rice!" she screams.

Jack's pants spin in the dryer downstairs, and the *Seinfeld* where Elaine won't sleep with a guy who isn't spongeworthy is on the TV in the guest room. Jack and Mona have seen it at least twice, but he waits till the closing monologue before flipping off the power with the remote.

"Jack," she says when he clicks off the light on the nightstand. "We never did get around to—"

"I haven't slept in a week," he says. "Let's do this later?"

She wants to scream at him, but she also wishes he'd hold her and let her warm her hands on his stomach like he did in the early days when they slept tangled as phone cord, the days before the enormous bed in the condo. But she knows he's worn thin with worry about his brother and the work he's missing, and already she hears the rattle of "coming down with something" in his lungs.

"Sure," she says, and within minutes he's asleep.

It has been years since his snoring kept her awake, but tonight Jack's thick wheezing bothers her. Leaving him balled on his side, she wanders Connor and Laine's house: brick and stone laid more than a hundred years ago, innards clean and renovated. Connor is in the sunken family room, TV playing odd lights on his face, golden retriever at his feet. Mouse barks when she walks by, and Connor is up, shushing the dog, asking her if everything is all right.

"I just feel a little icky—" She stops mid-sentence and stares at her bare feet, blushes. Because Connor really *is* sick, even if he looks okay, even if they only talk about it in vague ways. "I can't believe how inconsiderate that was, I'm sorry."

"Don't be." He shakes his head. "And you're in the right place to feel sick, we've got all kinds of stomach stuff here. We have prescription stuff, over-the-counter stuff, this horrible herbal crap Laine keeps buying from some natural foods co-op. Name it, I'm sure we've got it."

She shakes her head—no, she's fine. He pats the cream leather sofa, and she sits next to him.

"Can I ask you something kind of personal?" Connor licks pale lips. She nods. "Are you pregnant?"

Mona says nothing, and blood rushes to Connor's thin cheeks. "I'm not asking because you look fat or anything," he says. "You look great, you always look great. It's just you and Jack are acting kind of weird, and I was wondering if that's maybe why you're sick."

When Mona's little sister got pregnant, she conference-called the entire family, burst into the conversation by screaming, "Patrick and I have news." Mona doesn't want to have to tell Jack's family this way, sheepish and uncertain, wants her baby to be special, too.

"We *have* been talking about it." Mona gives the story she wishes were the truth. "Nothing yet, though, except some wishful thinking."

"That's great."

"Did Laine get sick much with the girls?" Mona asks.

"In the eight years I've known Laine, the closest she ever came to sick was a cold sore. She may have actually worked while she was in labor. Pretty awful, huh?" Connor shakes his head. "But she knew all the words to 'Thunder Road,' so I married her anyway."

"That's funny." Mona smiles. "I never had you pegged for much of a Springsteen fan."

"Aww, Mo, I'm crushed." Connor brings a hand to his chest in mock agony. "All these years, and you don't know me at all. Ever since I was in junior high, I swore I'd marry the first girl who knew all the words to 'Thunder Road.' It happened to be Lainey. When we were in grad school, we'd drive for hours. And she'd lean across the stick of the Sentra and sing in my ear." Standing, he hands Mona the remote. "TV's all yours. I'm gonna go to bed before she realizes I'm awake and tries to make me take more ginseng."

"She loves you," Mona says, touched by the image of Laine, all five feet eleven inches of her, all two Harvard diplomas, singing a song about blue-collar Jersey kids who'd never heard of soy milk.

"Yeah, she's just like Jack, though. She's not good when she's not in control."

For fourteen years Mona has tried to figure Jack out, and his brother has done it with one sentence.

"Jack will make a great dad, though." Connor turns around halfway to the step out of the room. "After our mom died, I had these really horrible nightmares, where I'd wake up screaming. And Jack would come check on me, bring me a glass of water. For a couple weeks, they were like clockwork, and he started anticipating when I'd wake up. They tapered off, but even on nights I was fine, I'd wake up and there'd be water by my bed." Connor lowers his head, looks away. "I wish my kids knew him like that."

Maybe the story is true, or maybe Connor knows she's lying about not being pregnant and tells it to make her feel better, either way she's grateful.

He starts to leave again, but she calls after him, sings quietly. *"Screen door slams, Mary's dress waves. Like a vision she dances across the porch as the radio plays."*

"Don't tempt me, Mo." Connor smiles, which makes him look like his brother. "I'm a married man."

And she's a married woman, though she didn't marry Jack because he knew all the words to a certain song, she married Jack because she got a concussion. After living together for six years in Cleveland, they couldn't set a wedding date, and she realized it was because neither of them wanted to get married. So she took the job in Chicago; it was okay for a few months, she even dated a Channel 4 reporter she met on assignment. But while making coffee in the break room, she whacked her forehead on the cabinets. The paper was on deadline, so one of the copy editors just dropped her at UC's emergency room. Head in the giant white cylinder of the CAT scan, she started crying. The technician rolled her out, assuring her lots of people got claustrophobic during the test. But that wasn't it. It was being in a strange city, with no one waiting for her in the next room. She called Jack from a pay phone, and he got to the hospital in four hours flat. In the black Porsche he'd leased since she left, he was Batman. He stayed at her apartment that night, waking her every few hours like the attending ER doc had instructed. Each time he shook her back into consciousness, he told her how much he missed her. She told him how much she missed him, and by eight the next morning, they decided it was dumb for them to go on missing each other. So he sold his parents' house and got a job at a Chicago law firm. They moved to Oprah's building and were happier together than apart. But there were annoying hangnails of boredom itching to be chewed. Then that kid fell in the pool and Mona stopped taking birth control.

After a solid hour spent trying to ignore the chairs, feet, and paws scraping the hardwood floors and the voices and barks below, Mona touches Jack's shoulder.

"You awake?" she asks.

"Of course, there's a fucking carnival downstairs." He reaches for his watch on the nightstand. "Six thirty. When he was in high school, my brother slept until three or four in the afternoon on Saturday. I'd go to the office, come back, and wake him up to see if he wanted to get dinner."

"They've got two kids," Mona says deliberately, waits for Jack's reaction, any reaction. He says nothing, stretches his legs under the covers and rubs his feet together. She starts to sit up, but he holds her wrist.

"Let's sleep for an hour." He smiles, eyes arching into half-moons— it was the first thing she noticed about him when they met, when she couldn't believe someone with a smile like that would smile at her. "If we pull the blanket over our heads, we might drown out Family Circus."

They shift into familiar grooves of each other, her head in the dent between his collarbone and arm.

"What was it like when your mother died?" she asks, thinking about Connor's story.

"Why?"

"I don't know much about that part of your life at all."

"It was sixteen years ago," he says, lips on the crown of her head, close enough she can feel air come out of his nose. "I thought you wanted to sleep."

Below them something crashes.

"We should get up," she says.

"We should have stayed in a hotel. That's what we should have done. I hate staying here."

"He wanted to see you." There's a concrete edge in her voice. "Do you really think he needed you to do money stuff this minute? You haven't drawn a will since law school. It was an excuse to get you here."

"I know." Jack balls onto his side, eyes and nose bunching together as though he might cry. "But he's going to be fine."

"Of course he is." She inches back down, grazes his forehead with her fingertips. "We should be helping; he wants you to spend more time with the girls."

The phrase hangs between them.

"What do you think we could do with them, Mo?" Jack's black eyes are soft. "My brother's kids don't like us."

Everything in the kitchen is from the future—chrome and stainless steel, black lacquer, a flat-range oven, copper pots dangling from racks in the ceiling. Laine washes fat pumpkins in the sink, and Connor spreads pages of *The Globe* over the table. From a television built into the wall, the *Today Show* anchors give the mornings' top news stories dressed as Scarlett O'Hara and Rhett Butler.

"Feeling better, Mo?" Connor asks, and Jack looks at Mona—part guilt that he didn't ask, part terror she told his brother she's pregnant. "Can I get you some breakfast? We've still got pancake batter and Egg Beaters, and there's bagels and cereal and stuff."

Mona had a family like this, where everyone sat down to dinner at six thirty with Tom Brokaw and *NBC Nightly News*, where meals were served on plates with vegetables and rolls. She wonders if it's what she wants, and then wonders why she chose Jack, who never wanted anything like this.

"Bagels and cereal." Keelie puts her chubby hands in her mouth.

Hunched over a piece of orange construction paper, pencil in hand, Jorie doesn't acknowledge them at all. Connor scoops Keelie into his lap, guides her hands as they draw triangle eyes on the best side of a pumpkin.

"Coffee'd be great," Jack says.

"That pot should still be pretty fresh." Laine points to the machine at the end of the counter, tells Jack where to find mugs.

"Daddy." Jorie pokes her father in the shoulder. "He's using the cup I gave you."

In his hand, Jack has a ceramic mug proclaiming "World's Greatest Dad" in a font that's supposed to look like a child's crayon.

"Let's let Uncle Jack be the world's greatest dad for a while." Connor looks directly at Mona, and she's sure he knows she lied last night. He holds out his own mug to Jack. "Can you top me off?"

"Conn." Laine, toasting a bagel, using the rice voice. "If your stomach's bothering you, don't drink more coffee."

"Stop it, Laine." Connor nods at Jack, who stopped pouring. "You're being loony tunes."

"Like Bugs Bunny?" Jorie looks up, sets aside her paper, picks up a Sharpie and draws ornate, impossible-to-carve lips on her pumpkin.

"Exactly like Bugs."

"Bugs Bunny." Keelie, still in her father's lap, claps her hands.

"Ask Mommy, 'What's up, Doc?' " Connor says.

"What's up, Doc?" Keelie gurgles.

"That's just great, Conn." Laine presses pouty lips together, puts Mona's bagel on a plate. "Cream cheese, butter, or jelly?"

Sliding the sports section out from under a pumpkin, Jack sits next to his brother and disappears behind the quarterback's thoughts on Sunday's game and a photo of the Bruins loss. Mona takes a seat by Jorie and looks at her paper.

"Is this a poem you wrote?" Mona asks.

"It's a haiku." Jorie doesn't look at her, instead finishes eyelashes on her jack-o'-lantern. "This one is about Halloween."

"What's a haiku?"

"A Japanese poem with five syllables in the first line, seven syllables in the second, and five in the third," Jorie says as if Mona were an idiot. "They're very hard to write, but the one I did yesterday was the best in class and Mr. Marcus put it on the bulletin board. It was about Mouse."

Hearing his name, the dog under the table picks up his head, barks once. Laine takes a long knife from a chopping block and stabs into the circle around the stem of Jorie's pumpkin. Threads of pumpkin guts coat the blade, but the top won't budge when she tries to rock it off. She saws in again, jerking the knife back and fourth. The rotten, squishy smell hits Mona, and she sets down her bagel. Sweat dots pop onto Connor's forehead, and his shoulders bunch. He swallows slow and exaggerated, like he's a bad actor trying to indicate swallowing. Having thrown up for the past five days, Mona knows the signs and isn't surprised when Connor hands Keelie to Jack, who sets down the paper and holds his niece at arm's length.

"Take her for a minute," Connor says, and jogs to the bathroom.

Laine's gray eyes follow him, not the knife still lodged in the pumpkin. Even before it happens, Mona knows it will. The jack-o'-lantern top finally flips out, and the blade slices deep in the meat of Laine's palm.

"Fuck." Laine hops from foot to foot, grabs her injured hand with the other one, knocking the pumpkin off the table. It hits the hardwood with the dead thud of a corpse. "Fuck."

A blood ribbon unfurls down her arm, red drops rolling off her elbow onto the black and white newsprint. Eyes wide as gumdrops, Jorie opens her mouth like she's going to cry, but no sound comes out. When she finds her voice, it's primal, horrible and magnificent, truly one of the loudest sounds Mona has ever heard. Between a squat and a stand, Jack looks from Jorie to Laine to Keelie, still in his arms. Jorie sprints from the kitchen, screams floating behind her like a parachute. Nails clacking on the floor, Mouse chases her. In the bathroom, Connor is still puking.

Mona grabs a wad of paper towels from the dispenser. As she hands them to Laine, Mona sees the ragged edge of the cut. There's so much blood, plus something white and important looking. Her own shoulders bunch, her own exaggerated swallow.

"I'm sorry." Mona starts toward the bathroom, hand over her mouth.

"Wait, Conn's still in there." Jack grabs her arm below the elbow and reaches for the flip-top waste can. "Here."

His hand on the small of her back, Jack leads Mona to one of the futuristic chairs. Any question of whether or not she's going to throw up is answered by the funky smell of something in the can. Jack pats Mona's hair, and asks Laine about her hand.

"What's going on?" Back from the bathroom, Connor does look sick: dark hollows eat the spaces under his cheekbones and temples. He's bluish and pale, lips white.

"I cut my hand," Laine says matter-of-factly, as if blood weren't soaking through layers of quilted paper towel, weren't coating her arms and dripping on the floor. "Mona got sick, and the girls freaked out."

"Lemme see." Connor reaches for Laine's wrist, but she brings it to her heart.

"You'll get sick again."

"I'm fine; let me look at your hand."

"No." Laine's lower lip quivers.

"I've gotten more stitches than anyone. I just want to see how bad it is."

"It's really bad, all right?" Her voice trails off into a question, and her face crumbles. With the back of her sleeve, she wipes her eyes.

"Lainey." Connor pulls Laine against his chest, kisses her forehead. "It's okay."

"I'm sorry, baby." Her words are muffled by his crimson sweatshirt. "I meant to be so much better. I'm so sorry."

Connor makes soft sounds into Laine's hair. Mona takes Jack's hand, and he squeezes back so hard the diamond of her engagement ring cuts into her index finger. But when she tries to meet his gaze, he shakes his head, fixates on the floor. Except for puddles of pumpkin insides and blood, the honey-colored wood is immaculate and Mona wonders how

Laine can keep the floors so clean with two kids and a dog. Mona has Jack and a cleaning lady, but her floors never look like that.

"Can you wiggle your fingers?" Connor asks Laine. "That's good, you're gonna be groovy sweet like a peppermint stick. We'll just take you to the emergency room, get you sewn up. No big deal."

Things feel loose and melodramatic, like Mona wandered into one of the soaps she watched in college, everything fuzzy because it's shot on video instead of film. Somewhere in the big, old/new house, Jorie screams and Mouse barks.

"I'm sorry," Laine says again. "I'm so sorry."

"Don't be sorry, everything's going to be okay." Connor holds her, and she cries. Blood seeps through the balled paper towels onto her shirt and onto his. It's on their arms and on Connor's face, which she keeps reaching for. "I'll just get my shoes, and we'll go."

"You're sick," Jack says. "I can take her."

"I can do it," Connor says. "Will you watch the kids?"

Mona nods.

"Let me go tell them." Laine sniffles.

"We need to clean you up a little before you see the kids." Connor looks at Jack. "Can you go find them?"

"I'll take Laine to the hospital," Jack says.

"Jack, she's my wife, she's upset. I'm going to go with her. It won't kill you to spend an hour with my kids."

Jack opens his mouth, closes it, and looks at Mona who nods. "Okay."

Keelie is easy enough for Jack and Mona to find. In the den she's drawing on Mouse's side with one of the permanent markers, her own hands and arms already tattooed with black scribble. Mona picks her up, balancing Keelie's warm body on her hip. Trusting and docile, the girl loops her arms around Mona's neck and leans her head on Mona's shoulder. Having finally stopped screaming, Jorie proves more difficult to locate.

"This is what you want?" Jack asks. In Connor and Laine's bedroom he opens the closet, revealing rows of folded sweaters and hanging shirts but no Jorie.

On the nightstand there's a picture of Connor, Laine, and the girls that must have been taken last Halloween, everyone in costumes from *The Wizard of Oz*—baby Keelie in furry lion jammies; Jorie as Dorothy in a checkered dress and ruby slippers; Connor, face painted silver, in a boxy Tin Man's outfit; and Laine as Scarecrow. Beautiful children, beautiful parents. Mona hadn't realized just how idyllic they look, easy and perfect in a photo.

"That's not fair," Mona says.

"No, what *you* did wasn't fair," Jack says. "And not just to me. Have you thought about it at all? Are you going to quit your job? We moved to Chicago for your job."

"I'll figure something out," Mona says, but the truth is, she has only considered those things in the abstract, thinking of the pregnancy as the first obstacle, the step that would put all other steps into motion, the one allowing them to plan new and different things. "People do this every day—" Mona starts, but Keelie reaches up and puts her fingers over Mona's lips, laughs when Mona stops talking.

"Yeah, they do, and a lot of times they screw it up. My father's been dead twenty years, and Connor still hates—" Jack stops mid-sentence. A rustling in the bathroom.

Pale and placid, Jorie is in the shower stall, fully clothed. Opening the glass door, Jack takes her hand and leads her out.

"Your mom is going to be fine." Mona tries to sound light, but Jorie remains a haunted doll.

"Jesus," Jack says, under his breath, and Mona follows his eyes to the mirrored medicine cabinet open above the sink.

In neat little rows, there are a dozen amber vials with names like all those galaxies in *Star Trek*—prednisone, procarbazine, Procrit, Anzemet, and Neupogin. Jack shakes his head, and Mona wants to hold him, but Keelie is heavy in her arms, they haven't talked, and Laine is bleeding downstairs.

Looking for the Museum of Science, Jack, Mona, and the girls have driven by the same White Hen Pantry three times. Connor took Laine, hand swaddled in dish towels, to the hospital and left Mona and Jack with the kids, keys to the minivan, the museum membership card, and directions that didn't include Big Dig detours. Normally a human compass, Jack has somehow led them to a residential neighborhood, and Mona notices he's driving awfully near to the curb.

"Jack," Mona says. "You're kind of close on this side."

"It just seems close because this is twice the size of your car."

The White Hen Pantry appears again.

"Is Mommy going to die?" Jorie asks. It's the first thing she has said since Mona and Jack found her in the shower.

"No, sweetie." Mona looks over the seat. "Your mom just cut her hand."

"Is Daddy going to die?"

"He's going to be fine," Jack says.

"But he's sick?"

"He'll get better." Blue veins bulge in Jack's wrists because he's squeezing the steering wheel like he's trying to juice it. The side mirror next to Mona flirts with low-hanging sycamore branches.

"If Mommy and Daddy die, would Keelie and I live with you, like Daddy did after Grandma and Grandpa Reed died?"

"No one is going to die," Jack says; the car inches closer to the curb. "So we shouldn't worry about it."

"But if they *did* die, would we live with you?"

"Sure," Mona says.

"In Chicago?"

"Maybe." Mona wonders what the right answer is. "Or maybe we'd move here."

"No one is dying," Jack says again. "I don't think your parents would like this conversation."

"There's a lot of car on this side—"

"Mo, it's fi—"

On cue, the passenger-side mirror cracks against a black metal mailbox. Both objects spiral behind the van like flying saucers and land on the sidewalk. Jack pulls to the side of the street, rubs his eyebrows, as Jorie opens her lungs for more of the magnificent screaming.

And Mona understands the wounded impulse to make the loudest noise in your power, to break the silence that so often follows something bad. Why shouldn't Jorie scream? Her mother's blood is still smeared on the clean floor, and her father's blood turned against him in a way that even a seven-year-old who can write a haiku can't make sense of because no one can make sense of it. She's stuck in a car with an uncle she knows only as a grouchy onetime guardian of her father and he's just wrecked their car. As Jorie's screams crescendo, Mona actually feels a swelling of respect for her niece, because Jorie shouts out, doesn't wait for someone else to make the first sound.

"I'll go see if they're home." Jack shakes his head—*not good when he's not in control.*

While he knocks on the door, rings the bell, and waits, Mona says mindless things to soothe Jorie, but Keelie repeats the tail ends of Mona's phrases—an echo of her ridiculousness.

"We can fix the car. . . . It's not hurt too bad. . . . It will be okay."

"They're not here." Jack opens the driver's door, which starts the van beeping because the key is in the ignition. "I'll leave cash for the mailbox."

"You can't just leave money." They're yelling over Jorie and the car. "You need to write a note." Mona rummages through her purse for pen

and paper, but pulls out a bank envelope and a tampon. She digs back
in her bag.

Jack leans over the front seat. "Can you girls please be quiet?"
he asks, but Jorie screams louder, and Keelie joins her. "Please stop,
please."

"Here, Jorie." Mona swivels around in the seat, reaches for Jorie's
slender shoulder. "Help me write the note for the people who live here.
We can make it a haiku. How does that work again? Is it nine, five,
seven?"

"Five beats, seven beats, five beats." Jorie's voice is bruised and raw.
She sniffles. "My haiku about Mouse is on the class bulletin board."

"Okay." Mona writes on the envelope. "How's this:

> *"Sorry for your box,*
> *Uncle Jack didn't realize*
> *The van was so big."*

Together she and Jorie count the syllables on their fingers. Jorie nods.

"That's good," she says.

"You missed your calling, Mo," Jack says. "You should have been a
Japanese poet."

They drive in silence, passing the White Hen Pantry again. Jack
turns on the CD changer, and Bruce Springsteen's raspy voice fills the
vacuum of the van.

"Ohh Ohh Thunder Road, Ohhh Thunder Road."

Jack reaches to adjust the controls, and Mona grabs his fingers.

"Don't change it," she says, far more forceful than necessary.

He looks at her, and he looks forty-something. Still bushy as ever,
his hair has lost its blackness—not the jet paint of Keelie's and Connor's.
He's heavy, the lines in his face settled. In five years he'll have jowls.

"It's a really good song," she says.

"I was just going to start it from the beginning."

She'll take that. She'll take it because being bored wasn't a good reason to get pregnant, and they won't make good parents. She'll take it because Connor is sick, Laine is going nuts, and the Big Dig construction makes it impossible to get anywhere. So Mona will take "Thunder Road" as a sign that maybe it's not that bad.

"This is Mommy and Daddy's song," Jorie says from the backseat, and Keelie repeats her.

"Mommy and Daddy's song."

Mona is still humming it under her breath an hour later when they're shuffling through the museum exhibits among all the real families. There's the complete units where both parents are present and the kids have similar features. But there are also the families that have splintered and cracked. The dads with joint custody trying to cram whole weeks into a Saturday visit, the moms who don't have men to carry around the jackets and activity bags.

Mona thinks that she, Jack, and Keelie, propped on her hip, make a convincing enough family. Keelie could easily be Jack's daughter, but fair-haired Jorie throws them off. Standing apart from the rest of them, she still looks placid and haunted. She's the reason they get second glances from other museumgoers and the staff in costume for Halloween, the reason they're not fooling anyone.

Jack must see it, too, because he turns to Mona in front of a perpetual motion statue where plastic balls hurtle through gadgets designed to keep them going.

"I'll respect whatever decision you make," he says quietly. "I'd never ask you to do anything you didn't want to. But you know who I am."

Mona nods, Keelie's fingers in the spirals of her hair. She does know or she thinks she does. She also knows he isn't going to pack his monogrammed luggage and leave her in the obvious way, they've tried that before and it didn't work. But there are other ways to leave someone, and in some of them he's already gone—if he was ever there at all.

Connor and Laine, her hand and wrist in white bandages, are spooned into each other asleep on the couch, while the Soup Nazi *Seinfeld* episode plays on the TV. Mouse, at the foot of the couch, picks up his golden head when Jack and Mona and the girls get back. Mona hushes everyone, but Connor props himself on his elbow and massages unfocused eyes crusted with sleep. Both girls run to take his big hands.

"Let's let Mommy sleep for a while," he says. He still looks pale and blue and thin. "Then we can all go trick-or-treating, okay?"

"How is she?" Jack gestures to Laine.

"Ten stitches, no permanent damage." Connor shrugs. "They gave her Vicodin, and she's been out for hours." He nods at the girls. "These guys give you any trouble?"

"No," Mona and Jack say in unison, utterly unconvincing.

"Did you like spending time with your aunt and uncle?" Connor asks the girls.

"They broke the car," Jorie says.

"Broke car," Keelie says.

Mona feels a stab of betrayal. Even after "Thunder Road," after the haiku, her nieces still hate her.

"I knocked off your side mirror." Jack shakes his head, his hands deep in khaki pants pockets. "I'll take it in for you."

"Don't worry about it." Connor smiles, eyes crinkling into Jack eyes. "I hate that car."

Easing out from under Laine, Connor starts to get up, but winces because he's stiff from sleeping or because what makes him blue and pale hurts.

"Go back to sleep, kid." Jack looks as though he might cry.

"Naw, my girls need food and stuff," Connor says. "Mouse needs to go out."

"We can handle it," Jack says with absolutely no conviction. "We've got it under control."

Connor looks to Mona.

"We've got it under control." She borrows Keelie's technique, as if repeating it will make it true.

it's really called
nothing

At 36,000 feet, Jack's wife tells him she's keeping the baby. He knew she would from the moment in her doctor's office last week when he found out she'd secretly gone off birth control, the moment he realized he'd been wrong about her for fourteen years.

"Really, I'm at the last safe age to have a first child." As Mona talks, she stares out the oval window. All Jack sees is her curly red hair, always the first thing anyone notices about her. "More than anything, I want this, us, to work."

She is crying, but there's a metal edge in her voice. Because she constantly apologized for things not her fault, didn't get pedicures, and voted Democrat, Jack hadn't understood that edge was selfishness. But in the doctor's office, everything had snapped into focus so clearly, he couldn't fathom how he ever missed it.

"But if you don't want to be a part of it," she says. "I have to re-spect that."

Something between a chuckle and a snort comes out of Jack's nose. It's not the right response considering he may get divorced, not right considering they're on their way back to Chicago from Boston, where Jack's kid brother has a wife, two daughters, and freshly diagnosed stage III Hodgkin's disease.

"I'm sorry, Jack." Mona turns to him with mascara streaks on the apples of her cheeks, her nose red.

Laughing again, he takes her pale, cold hand, gives it a squeeze, and meets her confused amber eyes. Only five weeks pregnant, she looks like she always looks, but he barely recognizes her. It reminds him of a line in that Talking Heads song that was big when he was in law school—*And you may tell yourself, this is not my beautiful wife.*

"I'll understand either way," she says, but Jack suspects she's counting on him to stand by her, cemented with a glue of inertia, joint finances, and the fact that he walked around a world thick as Jell-O when they briefly broke up eight years ago.

The plane jerks, and everyone gasps and shuffles and grips the armrests as if they can keep course through sheer will. As the "Fasten Seat Belt" light dings, the pilot's smooth-jazz voice comes over the intercom, assuring "everything's fine, just a few bumps."

Jack has always thought the pilot would tell you things were peachy keen even as all four engines died and the tail fell away like bird poop—keep the passengers docile with pretzel sticks and soda as the plane goes down. And he's always envisioned a plane crash as an awful way to go, with those horrible last minutes of g-forces fighting against you, lungs exploding, nose squirting blood. But today a plane crash doesn't seem half bad. Better certainly than having your body turn against itself, than having doctors pump in poison so you puke and shiver and fight with your pretty wife about whether or not you can stomach steamed rice. In fact, Jack wonders if he'd mind if the plane belly flopped into a dramatic descent right now. Maybe not if it meant he wouldn't have to watch his brother's body break or deal with the giant mess of trial for his big firm's biggest client waiting for him in a high-rise office on Lake Michigan. Perhaps plummeting to the ground would be easier, too, than having to make decisions about his selfish wife's plan to screw up their selfish lives.

But the plane doesn't crash. The pilot takes them higher, and when he finds smooth air, everyone sighs in unison.

It makes Jack chuckle-snort again.

"Say something." Mona's brow scrunches, and she appears truly terrified. "Please."

"Well." He looks beyond her head to the window, where beads of rain ride the thick glass panel. "I guess I have nine months to decide anything, right?"

No decisions have been made eleven weeks later when Connor, his immune system Swiss cheese from chemo, is taken by ambulance to Massachusetts General with pneumonia and a fever of 103. His sister-in-law calls, and Jack, upset but not surprised, flies in to watch Connor sleep and sleep, thin sheets and thin gown blurring as though everything were a part of him. While Connor dozes, Jack and Laine speak a language of blood counts and lung function, frustrating the actual doctors by demanding to know about every bleep and drip from Connor's monitors and tubes, by bringing up clinical trials and experimental procedures they've read about online or heard about from nondoctor acquaintances.

"Can we *not* discuss the color of my snot anymore?" Connor asks when he rolls awake. Coughing a slimy cough, he tries to hide that it hurts. "I feel a billion times better. Where are the kids?"

"With my dad." Laine runs long fingers across Connor's smooth forehead. All his black hair is gone, as are his eyebrows; strangely, his lashes stuck it out—long and full. "He took them to the new *Jungle Book* movie."

"I wanted to see that with them."

"You'll have to watch it over and over again when it comes out on DVD." Laine's voice is gentle.

"Sure, in the summer."

Connor takes Laine's hand, and Jack turns away because it's teeth-gnashingly unfair that his brother is the one who got sick. Connor's the one who taught with AmeriCorps and works for the Massachusetts reading program, the one who occasionally remembers to recycle and doesn't wear sneakers made by Indonesian children. It's unfair because though he's a decade younger, Connor cares about his family more than Jack has ever cared about anything, and there's no guarantee that he gets another summer to watch sappy Disney cartoons. Jack would gladly hand over his stock portfolio and car keys to anyone who could make his brother better or even happy. And suddenly he realizes that even though Mona's pregnancy is something he has been trying not to deal with, it has the potential to raise Connor's spirits.

"Actually, I have some news." Jack licks his lips, and his heart hur-ries as it does whenever he lies. "Mo's pregnant."

"What?" Connor props himself on his elbows, jostling the IVs jammed in his purpling forearm. "This is huge. Why didn't you say something earlier?"

Shrugging, Jack tries to smile and not think of his wife, whom he has scarcely spoken to since their flight back to Chicago.

"Congratulations," Laine says.

"You're going to be the greatest dad." Connor is excited, his eyes bright and almost lucid for the first time since Jack arrived. "I tell every-one you're the only parent I ever had."

Heat floods Jack's cheeks and he nods, even though all he actually did for his brother after their mother died was sign a few checks, fill out a few forms. Connor left Cleveland less than three years later.

"We'll see," Jack says.

"Naw, you'll be awesome." Connor smiles, coughs, smiles again. "How pregnant?"

Wanting to keep his brother glowing and distracted, Jack makes up answers to Connor's questions—a combination of quick math, sitcom plots, and *Chicago* magazine articles. The baby is due in the summer, they think they'll turn their condo's second bedroom into a nursery, Mona wants to be heavily drugged during labor, "R" names are their favorites.

"Has she been sick much?" Connor asks.

"Constantly." This Jack does know because he has been helping Mona in the bathroom, while she throws up and they don't talk. "She hasn't spent a whole day at the paper in forever."

"That's rough." Connor wrestles sleep, eyelids closing and springing open like crazed garage doors. He looks at Laine. "You never got sick." Blinking, he shakes his head. "Can you tell them I don't need this much pain stuff, all it's doing is knocking me out."

Laine leaves to find a doctor she knows is already frustrated by her.

Connor looks at Jack. "I appreciate you helping out with Lainey and the kids, but you should be with Mo if she's not feeling well." He closes his eyes, and Jack thinks he's asleep. "All those hormones and stuff; it's really hard, makes girls crazy."

"I'll go home soon."

"At least call her." Connor waves Jack out with the back of his hand. "I'm sure she'd want to know you told us. It's a big deal."

"Sure," Jack says.

But in the hall he automatically starts toward the vending machines and searches his pockets for change. He absently slips coins in the coffee machine without thinking; it's probably his ninth cup of the day. Smoldering and bitter, it rouses the heartburn he has had on and off, mostly on, for weeks. He shouldn't ignore it, his father's ticker hadn't outlasted his fifties, but Jack can't decide if he cares enough to pay a doctor to tell him to change his diet and start working out. Like a plane crash, it's not a bad way to go, quick and easy, flicking off a light switch.

Then guilt socks him in the gut as he thinks of the question-mark curve of his brother's bald head. Jack reaches into his pocket for his phone. Mona left a message, but as he starts to call her back, one of Connor's doctors waves her hand in the universal "stop" motion.

"You can't use that in here." She's a short brunette in blue scrubs who only cares about Connor because it's her job. "There's a pay phone down the hall or you can go outside."

Having used all his change on coffee, Jack takes the elevator to the ground floor, whizzing past Maternity on the second, and follows exit signs to a parking lot. At half past five everything is shaded by the depressing sunset of a cold, gray place in winter, and he trembles in the January air as he looks at all the cars with old snow caked on their roofs, crusted salt on the tires.

A second message on his phone is from the beautiful first-year associate working with him on the department-store case that may go to trial. In her message, Kathy says she's drafting a memo about similar cases found on the legal databases, a nervous excitement in her voice. Since starting the project, Jack has been trying to gauge if Kathy has a crush on him or if she's simply grateful he put her in charge of more than her first-year status warrants. He starts to dial Mona, but calls his office instead, punches in the digits of Kathy's extension.

"Hey, partner," she says. "Everything okay?"

Though he's never brought his personal life to the office, there's something knowing in Kathy's voice that makes him want to tell her everything.

"I'm in Boston," he says instead. "Family emergency."

"Can I do anything to help?"

Because she went to Penn for undergrad and law and he went to Penn for undergrad and law, he'd been assigned her partner-liaison when she was a summer associate two years ago. When she'd graduated and joined the firm in the fall, a plethora of partners had asked for her help, primarily because she has great tits, creamy pink skin, and legs that look sexy in conservative suits. Jack, on the other hand, likes her because everything she does is unnecessarily excellent, the way his work was when he was just starting out. Giving her the fax number at

Laine and Connor's house, he tells her to finish the memo if she finds time, knowing she will.

"I'll have it to you by the end of the day," she says, and Jack pictures her behind the faux-cherry desk in her office, her blond hair brushed back, boxy black glasses on her nose like a prop—*I'm not a hot twenty-five-year-old, but a serious attorney.* For the first time in a long time, he feels himself smiling.

"No rush, Kath," he says.

He forgets he was supposed to call Mona until he's back in Connor's room, where his brother sleeps again. Laine lies next to him, curled on her side, eyes closed. Both of them have gotten so thin since Connor got sick, as if they're evaporating into clouds of Connor's wet breath.

A wall-mounted TV is tuned to CNN, where a pretty newscaster shivers in a light blue jacket and matching earmuffs. The volume muted, a logo at the bottom of the screen shouts, "Twenty Dead in Vail Chair-Lift Accident." The screen switches to defeated people in parkas and hats looking over yellow tape at smashed lift chairs and twisted cable. One woman raises the back of her hand to wipe her eyes. So easy, then it's done.

His phone rings in his pocket, and Jack reaches to turn it off, but not before Laine and Connor squirm awake and the brunette in scrubs materializes in the doorway.

"You can't use that in—"

"I know." As he pushes the power button, he sees the call is from Mona. "I forgot to turn it off."

"There's a pay phone down the hall."

"It's not important."

"What time is it?" Connor asks, and they all look at the institutional metal wall clock. "Lainey, you need to pick up the girls."

"They're with Dad." Disoriented, Laine hops off the bed like a teenager caught snogging her boyfriend, not a Harvard MBA. "I want to stay."

"You need to let him rest," says Scrubs.

"I've rested enough for fifteen years." Connor coughs up more sludge. "But you should get the girls out of your father's hair. Are you okay to drive?"

Everyone looks at Jack expectantly, as if he can fix things, because Jack always fixes things. He does the best he can—driving Laine home for a few hours with a promise to bring her back later.

"They'll call us if anything changes, right?" Laine chews a hangnail, fidgets in the passenger seat, as they pass huge stone houses in Boston's wealthy suburbs.

"Of course, and we'll call the hospital anyway." Trying to calm her, Jack asks about her childhood. "Conn says you used to live here when you were a kid?"

"Yeah, for a few years before my parents split up. It's a really good family neighborhood." Laine points out the window to a house with turrets. "See that one?"

Jack nods.

"There's a story that the woman who lived there during the twenties had an ongoing affair with the man next door. Supposedly they built a tunnel connecting the houses. When we were kids we were always coming up with stupid plans to sneak in and see it."

"Really." Jack looks at the two houses, maybe half an acre apart, thinks about how much easier and cheaper it would have been to just walk. "Didn't their spouses get suspicious during the digging?"

"They knew," Laine says. "It was that old-money deal where protecting your reputation was the most important thing. I guess they were okay with it."

"Yeah." Jack isn't sure what he's saying or why. "Maybe you take what you can get, and sometimes the best you're going to do is a tunnel under your house."

. . .

Mona's puking again sometime before dawn, her palms pressed against the porcelain toilet. Jack holds her hair away, feels the spasms of her back muscles, and tries, for the nine billionth time, to decide if he can forgive her. His hand is on her bare arm, but his fingers seem to pass through her. It's been a week since he left his brother, fever broken, lungs still gooey, and Jack has yet to tell Mona that he told Connor she was pregnant. He tells her nothing anymore. When she asks about work or his brother, he offers useless packets of information. He doesn't tell her about the trial date in early July or about Laine's father asking him how to set up trust funds for Connor's daughters.

Helping Mona sit on the edge of the Jacuzzi, Jack rinses his hands and fills her a glass of water.

"You don't have to get up with me," she says. "You must be exhausted."

"It's fine." Jack wonders if she really means he doesn't have to help her or if she only says it because she knows he will continue drawing her hair from her face night after night. "I was working anyway. Do you need anything? Saltines or something?"

"No, thank you." She takes a tentative sip of water and chews her lower lip. "I think I told you about it before, but I have the appointment for the sonogram tomorrow, and they should be able to tell the sex. I made it late, so you could come, if you want."

"There's a huge mess at work," he says, feeling the familiar pain in his chest. "I'll come if I can. Just make sure you give me the address and everything before I leave."

She nods, and he helps her back to their giant bed, where he gets in beside her but doesn't hold her. Instead he picks up the xeroxed documents he brought home from his office, shuffles through for anything he may have missed the first time. In the sixteen years he has practiced law, Jack has seen the inside of a courtroom all of three times. Those times were exciting, but this case, a giant Midwestern department store chain that breached hundreds of purchasing contracts, he knows he'll lose.

Reaching over Mona for the roll of Tums on her nightstand, he notices the light freckles peppered across her nose and the delicate creases of her eyelids, decides he will go with her to the appointment, if he can.

But he can't go to the doctor with Mona, because Kathy, three other young associates, and a handful of paralegals are trapped in a dark-wood conference room, sinking under thousands and thousands of forms, carbon copies, and slips of paper the department store accumulated over three decades. For the past two nights Kathy hasn't left, trying to organize it all in a way Jack can use. But the other associates are careless, counting the days until they leave Kirkland to go in-house somewhere cushy and unimportant. The paralegals are worse, all of them twenty-two or twenty-three, working at the firm only so their own law school applications look better. They hurry through so they can meet friends at the bars on Rush and Division. It's the kind of work Jack hasn't done in years, but all the documents for the trial have to be filed by Monday night, so he takes off his suit jacket, rolls up his sleeves, and sifts with the others, even though they're going to lose and it's all as useless as panning for gold in the bathtub.

Around eight the gouging pain in his chest resurges and Jack realizes he hasn't eaten anything since a glazed Krispy Kreme at a morning meeting.

"Let's order in," he says.

One of the associates suggests that they try the sushi place that opened on the corner, and the horrible associates and paralegals come alive as they pencil mark the menu checklist with an obscene amount of food because they know that the client is paying for their dinner as well as their time.

The order arrives, and they spin in leather office chairs, talking about places they've been where the sushi is really good and about those places that are "overrated." Jack and Kathy take absent bites and continue reading, marking, piling. His sinuses explode when he puts too much wasabi on a piece of toro. Eyes dripping, throat melting, he coughs, gropes for bottled water.

"Don't drink that." Kathy reaches for his arm. "It will only make it hotter. Have some ginger."

Maybe she does have a crush on him or maybe she simply likes that he's most likely going to be named assigning partner of corporate when the current partner retires, but when her fingers graze his wrist, he feels a current of something all the way to his ears and toes. He looks at her, and she smiles as though they share a secret. It *will* happen. Maybe in a week or a month, maybe a day, but it will. He's not sure if he wants it or not, knows only that he can't stop it. His life is no longer up to him. He's at the mercy of others—his wife, doctors in Boston, this lovely young woman.

"Thank you," he says, ginger grinding between his molars. "You were right."

One of the paralegals says the yellowtail smells funny, but everyone eats everything anyway. An hour later they all feel sick. The associates and paralegals complain so much that Jack finally suggests they go home, even though there's no time for going home. An hour after that he feels awful enough to join them. Kathy remains cross-legged on the floor, pen tucked behind her ear.

"All this crap will still be here in the morning," he says, packing a laptop and the most useful stack of the useless papers. "You should go; we're all sick."

"I must not have had much yellowtail." She smiles the secret smile again and pats his ankle. "I'll go home when I get tired."

In the cavernous concrete garage under the office building, Jack reaches into his pants pocket for his phone to call Mona. If their life worked the way their life used to work, he would meet her at the condo and they'd watch *Seinfeld* reruns until he fell asleep on her shoulder. At eleven she would nudge him awake and make toast and the one can of soup they'd had in their pantry for years. But things don't operate that way anymore.

Seeing she left a message, he remembers the sonogram.

"Hey, um, you didn't make it today." Mona's recorded voice is wet with tears. "But I thought I'd let you know, it's a boy. My sister came, so I wasn't alone or anything. Um, oh well, I guess I'll see you at home."

At the end of the message her words are rushed, as if she's fighting back a sob. A lead foot squashes his chest; he's never been able to listen to her cry. And the part of him that's used to fixing things wants to sweep her into his arms and fix this. But he can't because he doesn't know how to fix this, isn't sure it's fixable at all, and misleading her seems worse. He can't, because he hasn't slept well in months, is sick from bad sushi, and needs to work more on a case he can't win. So he puts his phone back in his pocket and takes the elevator back up. He stops at the men's room, where he runs a paper towel under the faucet and wipes it across his forehead. His reflection shows skin the color and texture of a grade school gymnasium and giant purple bruises under his eyes. With his clean jawline and broad shoulders, he used to command a certain attention, but there are only faint traces of that now.

"You're back." Kathy stands when he appears in the conference room.

Stacks of documents are in each of the chairs, leaving nowhere to sit. He rests his ass against the edge of the table and gestures to the mess with open palms.

"We're going to lose," he says. "I want you to know that before you pull another all nighter."

"There's nowhere I have to be." She shrugs and smiles and looks at him with blue eyes like the ones described in novels from a time before when he used to read novels.

Folding his arms, he bows his head, rubs his eyebrows.

"Jack?"

"My brother's sick," he says.

"I know. The first- and second-years talk a lot." Putting her hand on his shoulder, she's close enough that he feels her breath on his neck. "I can't imagine how hard that must be."

"And my wife is pregnant."

"I know that, too."

When he lifts his head, she's still looking at him. Everything is suddenly quiet and tense. More vague memories of a life prior to Mona make him realize that Kathy will kiss him. She doesn't. She touches his cheek, his lower lip, his chin, then sinks to her knees. In quick, easy movements, she has his belt and pants undone, has him hard in her palm. His fingers gravitate to her blond head.

It's been years since Mona has gone down on him. It always made her so uncomfortable, Jack found it hard to enjoy. Kathy, however, seems to like what she's doing.

"I'm married," Jack says, but not until he's at the point where he knows he can't not come, where his voice catches in his throat, comes out a moan. "And I'm sort of your boss."

Of course she swallows, and Jack wonders briefly if she exists at all or if he isn't delirious. If he's so sleep deprived that he's hallucinating this girl who does great research and sucks cock like it's a second vocation.

"This doesn't have to mean anything," she says. "I like you, and you needed that more than any guy I've ever met."

Unsure what he's supposed to do, Jack zips his pants, kneels next to her, and hesitantly kisses her forehead. He wants to believe her, that it doesn't have to mean anything, but the guilt he feels isn't over Mona, it's over Kathy, who's young and pretty and should be blowing someone young and pretty.

"May I return the favor?" he asks.

"Someday, if you want. You should go home and sleep now."

"You're the one who should go home," he says.

"In a little while."

But he knows she won't. She'll stay in this conference room all night and the night after that. He thinks of warning her that in a decade and change she may be contemplating the end of the world in various ways. He says nothing, however, because he isn't sure he'd change anything in his own life knowing what he knows now.

"Leave soon," he says again. He doesn't follow his own advice, instead goes up a floor to his office.

Unlike the other partners, Jack doesn't have his desk facing Lake Michigan. Heights make him nervous, so his desk faces the Robert Longo painting on the wall. But tonight he stands with his nose against the full-length window, his breath leaving circles on the cold glass. He wonders about people who jump to their deaths, what it feels like in those minutes before you hit the ground, if some primal instinct kicks in and you fight against it, if that's why your arms kick and flail. He thinks about those people in the ski lift, about plane crashes. Then he remembers his brother, sick and swinging blindly against the thing that's trying to kill him. Recalling Connor's ridiculous happiness over Mona's pregnancy, he picks up the phone.

"Hey, Laine and I were reading to the girls, and *we* fell asleep." Connor sounds groggy, like he has every time Jack has talked to him since he started treatment. "Things you can look forward to. You calling to check up on me?"

"A little bit." Jack closes his eyes against the burn in his chest. "And I wanted to tell you that we found out the baby is a boy."

"Really? Jack, that's great," Connor says. "You'll do much better with a boy. I wasn't going to say anything, but I thought a little girl would confuse you."

"What's that supposed to mean?" Jack fakes a laugh.

"You're just gonna get to do so much cool stuff. Seriously, I'm jealous. I totally want a boy next time."

"What next time?" Laine is on the line, groggy herself, and then sound explodes in the Boston suburbs. Connor's dog, his daughters, everyone is making noise. "Jack, it's one in the morning here."

"I forgot about the time difference."

"Jack's just excited cuz he and Mo are having a boy," Connor says. "I want a boy next kid."

"I'll see what I can do," Laine says. "Congratulations, Jack, but it's a school night."

"We're going to have to take all of the kids to Cleveland one day," Connor says. "Go to an Indians game, show everyone where we grew up."

"Conn," Laine again. "Come on, it's late."

"Sure, kid, we'll all go," Jack says, wondering if Connor has more summers for visits to Cleveland and Indians games.

"Sure, kid," he says to no one as he's waiting for the elevator to the parking garage an hour later.

As it descends, there's a snapping of something mechanical, and he imagines the unhinged car racing down the shaft to unforgiving concrete, everything over in under twenty seconds. But the doors part, and he gets in his sleek, black car. LSD is nearly empty so late at night, but Jack drives uncharacteristically slow, watching the waves crash against the sand, everything sinister in the darkness.

Their building, with its cold doormen and cold marble and mirror hallways, never lost the feel of a hotel—*And you may ask yourself, what is this beautiful house?* Then he's speeding up in another elevator that doesn't crash, to his front door with the heavy silver knocker. Keys in hand, he stares at his distorted reflection in the metal for nearly ten minutes before finally going in. In the master suite, face smeared with tears and faded makeup, Mona sleeps on top of the bedspread. Jack slides her shoes from her flattened feet and tucks her under the covers.

She squirms and murmurs his name, eyes still closed.

"I'm here," he says, positioning a pillow under her head.

"You didn't come to the appointment today." Thick with sleep, the sentence is really one long word. "Picture's in the kitchen." Then she's out again, in some deep pregnant-woman slumber.

It wasn't as though Jack grew up thinking he would never have children, they always seemed something certain but distant, like root canals and taxes. His own father hadn't been a parent until he was thirty-nine, and Jack had only been twenty-seven when he met Mona. Back then he'd thought she was cute and simple, that they'd date a few weeks, maybe a month. It took him years to realize he cared for her, had taken her leaving Cleveland for him to realize he wanted to be with her. He'd probably promised her children to win her back. He'd promised her everything else—the move to Chicago, the lavish wedding at the Drake Hotel. But after a few months, everything defaulted back to normal, and things like kids seemed distant again.

Held to the refrigerator with a Cubs magnet is a black-and-white printout from the sonogram. Looking at swirls of their blended genes, Jack isn't sure what he's supposed to feel.

Everything is pulled tighter and tighter, like fabric stretched too thin, but somehow things don't tear. As the days blur into weeks, weeks into months, Jack carries Tums in his pockets and keeps bottled antacid liquids in his desk drawer and glove compartment. And things continue to stretch.

Mona stops throwing up and everything about her rounds. Her curls tighten to Victorian ringlets, her breasts and stomach inflated beach balls, her cheeks soft and full. Surprisingly Jack thinks she looks good. It doesn't change the astral quality of her touch, doesn't make him forgive her, doesn't stop him from screwing Kathy on his office floor, but he *does* recognize the empirical beauty of his pregnant wife.

Even though he's going to lose the department store case, he works late because he has always worked late, calls Mona from his office because that's routine, too.

"I'm going to pick something up for dinner and stop home for a while," he says. "Is there anything you want? Something you feel like?"

"No, just get the usual wherever you go," Mona says. "Anything's fine."

Having watched enough movies, he knows pregnant women have cravings and he finds odd things in the kitchen—glass jars of pimento olives and maraschino cherries, twigs of beef jerky and licorice ropes—but since the missed sonogram appointment, she has asked him for nothing.

In a big, old house in Boston's suburbs, Connor also stops throwing up. Having finished a course of chemo treatments, the doctors have started him on radiation, which makes his skin itch. At night he calls Jack's office.

"Tell me anything to keep me from scratching," Connor says. "Tell me about Mo and the baby. Are you still thinking 'R'?"

Tucking the phone between his ear and shoulder, Jack glances at the stacks of documents on his desk. The department store chain is owned by Donald Ryan, and that seems fitting.

"We like 'Ryan' this week," Jack says.

"Ryan Reed? Sounds like a character on *Days of Our Lives*. I guess it could work if he grows up to be a Wall Street guy."

"Yeah, it's a name that doesn't mess around."

"Did you finish the nursery?"

"Not yet. Mo bought everything from some catalog, and it came in four thousand pieces. Her sister is coming over to help us put it together."

Parts of the story are true. The other day Jack noticed boxes in the extra bedroom and heard Mona tell her sister she'd ordered furniture. But she didn't ask Jack to help.

"How is Melanie?" Connor asks. "I haven't seen her since your wedding."

Chugging another unmeasured dose of Mylanta, Jack weaves together more half-truths, until he hears sleep creep into his brother's voice across the line.

As night morphs into morning and the janitor's vacuum buzzes down the hall, Jack strokes Kathy's dewy buttocks when they finish fucking.

The trial starts in a month, and the two of them dress and drive to Cook County Courthouse to drop off a motion they don't trust to the messenger service.

"I always wanted to live in one of these houses," Kathy says as they pass the huge brick houses in the suburbs. Jack realizes he has no idea where she's from—he'd assumed somewhere in the East. In fact, he realizes he knows very little about her at all other than that she never asks more from him than what he gives. Remembering Laine's story about the love affair in Boston, he decides to test her.

"See those." Jack points at two of the larger houses. "The wife of the one there had a long affair with the man of the other house. For convenience they dug tunnels linking them underground."

"Really?"

"Yeah," Jack says carefully. "It was the kind of arrangement where the spouses knew."

"Didn't they hit water from the lake?" Kathy asks. "A lot of these places don't have basements for that reason."

"It's just something I heard."

They stop to shower at Kathy's apartment, where everything is orderly and sterile like the rooms in furniture stores with cardboard display appliances. He wonders about the artifacts of her life—photos, papers, open envelopes of mail she hasn't dealt with, sections of the *Tribune* she is saving to read—but all that is hidden. Her CDs are alphabetized on freestanding metal racks, and he thumbs through them for any hint of who she really is. He notices she has one by the Talking Heads.

"Is that song on here?" He flips over the case and looks at the play list on the back. "That one about the days going by and the water flowing?"

"I don't really know." She comes out of the bathroom with a towel fashioned into a turban around her head, her body bare and damp. "I think it originally belonged to someone else."

She doesn't specify if that someone is an ex-lover, a current lover, an old roommate, or some sibling she hadn't mentioned. He doesn't ask.

Putting the CD in the changer, they skip forward until they find it. *"Letting the days go by, let the water hold me down. Letting the days go by, water flowing underground."* And things stretch farther and tighter than Jack ever thought they could.

It's a call Jack almost forgot he was expecting, but it comes on a Saturday evening, while he's in the kitchen reheating leftover sesame beef, the smell of Kathy still under his fingernails.

"It's in the fluid around his lungs and heart." The voice on the other end is his sister-in-law's, toneless and beaten. "They're going to give him six cycles of MOPP and targeted radiation. They want to get started by the end of the week."

Seventeen years ago Jack had halfheartedly been studying for a Literature and the Law exam that didn't really matter because he'd already accepted a job with the biggest firm in D.C., when Connor called to tell him their mother had dropped dead of an aneurysm. It had been such a large idea that Jack hadn't been able to react. Finally he simply asked Connor where he was, because that information seemed something for which there was a logical course of action—find orphaned fifteen-year-old brother.

He asks the same thing of Laine now, even though he saw the number on the caller ID and knows she's at home.

"I'm in the kitchen; he's outside with the girls," Laine says. "He wanted to wait until after Mona had the baby to tell you, but I thought you should know."

"Fuck." Jack hurls the food into the garbage. "What do you need me to do?"

"What can you do?" Laine asks. "We were supposed to go to Orlando next weekend—this stupid Women in Finance conference, where Merrill Lynch parades me around cuz I don't look like a troll. I have to give a speech, but we figured we'd take the girls to Disney. He says we should go without him or he can go with us and wait a week to start treatment. But I want to hit this thing with a fucking truck now."

"Should I come there?" Jack asks. "I could stay with him, and you could go with the kids."

"I don't know; Mona's really pregnant."

"She's not due for another month," Jack says, absently surprised he knows.

"Maybe."

When he gets off the phone, nothing has been solved. He's dazed, more so even than when Connor initially told him he was sick. Then there had been so much research, doctors, treatment centers, disease history. At this point Jack could write a dissertation on Hodgkin's disease, knows its spreading follows a pattern, each stage lopping off chunks of the survival rate. Like all things in Jack's life, however, it's not up to him.

On the cream couch, Mona, open *Harper's* in her lap, drifts between awake and asleep.

"What's wrong?" she asks, instantly alert. "Who was on the phone?"

"Laine." He shakes his head, looks at the ground. "He's sick again."

Mona's up, fast as her rounded body allows. Jack should offer his arm, but everything in him is heavy and planted on the Oriental rug.

"Jack, I'm so sorry," Mona says, and he believes her. There's an honesty in her cool arms around his neck, her head against his shoulder. "It's not fair. I'm so sorry."

And then he's kissing her like he hasn't kissed her in a year. Faces pressed close, he feels her tears on his cheeks, salt water bitter on his tongue. He can't even remember the last time they made love, but he lays her on the sofa and rips at her gauzy maternity shirt as if his life depended on it. In some ways it might. Every taste and touch about her is different and the same, like they're underwater. She's still crying, though it's probably not about his brother anymore. When they finish, he kneels on the floor, rests his head on her alien breasts, and she strokes his brow with swollen fingers.

"I think I have to go to Boston," he says, checking to see if that glimmer of selfishness is in her eyes, hopes it's not, because if it's gone, maybe things between them can be fixed.

"Do whatever they need."

"So I should probably try to get some work done."

In his hair, her fingers stop moving, and he feels her holding her breath.

"Mo?"

"Melanie's college roommate heads IT at Kirkland," she finally says. "I know about Blond Ponytail, Jack."

He doesn't say he's sorry, because he isn't sure he is. Inching up so they're at eye level, he touches her enormous belly, wanting their unborn child to kick or shift, to give some sign. It does nothing.

"You need to make some decisions." Mona's voice is gentle, but she says it with more authority than anything she has ever said in all the years he has known her. "Your nine months are almost up."

And he knows his red-haired wife means she isn't going to be okay with tunnels.

Strangely, for the first time in months, Connor looks good. He has gained weight, softening the angles in his face, and his hair has started to grow back, the shorter length neater than the foppish mess he had before. He fastens his daughters into the seats of the limo Laine's company sent, while Laine speaks to Jack on the front porch.

"This whole thing is ridiculous," she says, nervous and jumpy, hair haphazardly tied back. "I shouldn't go. You know what cocksuckers those doctors are. They tell us everything's manageable, they've got drugs to make everything a-okay, then Conn's ralphing for hours."

"Lainey, it's three days." Connor comes up behind her, musses her hair. "Jack and I can watch the Indians game and pick up girls; it's much easier to pick up girls when you're not around."

Her lips turn up in something not quite a smile. "I don't want to leave you."

"Please. If I get really sick, the girls shouldn't see."

She nods, leans in, whispers something in his ear, and Jack looks away, because Connor is so certain of his wife and children. Reaching for the antacid tablets that leave white powder in his pockets, Jack realizes if he could switch bodies with his brother, he would without question.

"Why do they make this so difficult?" Connor asks on the drive to the hospital two hours later. He's trying to cram new batteries into a portable CD player, but they're upside down. "It's not like I want to put the space shuttle into orbit."

One hand easy on the steering wheel, Jack reaches across the gear console, turns the batteries around and slides them in.

"You nervous?" He hands Connor the Walkman.

"COPP wasn't so much fun." Connor sighs, shoves the radio into the backpack with a Harvard sweatshirt and crayon drawings his daughters made; if he *could* switch bodies with his brother, Jack wonders what he would bring. "I can't imagine I'm going to dig MOPP any more. Let's talk about something else. I told you not to come, at least tell me you and Mo have everything ready?"

"We're getting there." Jack assesses things he knows about Mona's pregnancy. "She had this painter do the walls in different colors—one blue, one red—it sounds stupid but it looks great."

"Yeah, it will be nice for Ryan, too, all that color stimulation." Connor relaxes in the leather seat, asking questions about kicking and weight.

Jack makes up answers and it gets them into the parking lot and up the elevator to the comfy chairs in Oncology. While Connor is poked and measured by the nurses, Jack gets coffee from the machine in the hall—the familiar burned taste, the familiar burn in his chest. Kathy gave him cross-exam questions he could read, but instead he looks at the sign by the elevator listing Maternity on the second floor.

"Excuse me," says a doctor he and Laine haven't exasperated yet. "Can you hit down?"

Jack does, and the doors pop apart. The doctor steps in and cocks his head at Jack.

"Are you coming?" he asks, hand holding the elevator open.

"No," Jack says, backing away. "Just looking."

Connor meets him in the hall. "I'm all full of nuke juice," he says cheerfully.

He looks okay, but on the drive back to Natick, the antinausea meds kick in, and he rolls in and out of sleep. Waking up, he pulls on his sweatshirt and fiddles with the vent until Jack shuts off the air conditioner even though it's eighty-five degrees outside. Connor's head droops again, and his breathing changes. Jack yawns himself and thinks about what would happen if he fell asleep at the wheel, if Connor's Jetta drifted off the side of the road into the median. Is there a way for his brother to escape unscathed? Some way to wreck only the driver's side?

"We're here already?" Connor asks when they safely pull into the driveway ten minutes later.

They turn on the game on the flat-screen TV in the den. Connor starts trembling, and Jack brings him an afghan from the hall closet.

"How much time are you taking off after Ryan is born?" Connor balls into the blanket, Mouse at his feet. "If you can swing it, you should try to go part-time for a while."

"Maybe," Jack says, though the department store trial should be in full throttle right around the time Mona has the baby. "At least at first."

The Indians give up three runs in the second inning; Connor is out before the bottom of the third. Lowering the volume, Jack tries reading over Kathy's questions, but they're perfect.

Then he isn't reading. His neck is cramped from falling asleep at an odd angle, the papers are on his head, and somewhere in the house Mouse is barking and Connor is calling him. Both feet asleep, Jack hobbles to the powder room. Still wrapped in the afghan, Connor is on the toilet trying to shit, puke into a waste can, and shoo the dog from vomit on the floor. It might be the most horrible thing Jack has ever seen—more horrible than news footage of the ski-lift disaster or plane crashes or car wrecks or elevator accidents.

"Can you put him outside?" Connor wipes his mouth with the back of his hand, points to the dog. "He tries to eat it when people throw up."

Taking Mouse by the collar, Jack leads the dog through the sliding door to the yard, with its enormous trees and sturdy wooden jungle gym. Though he'd absently been aware of the warming temperatures and the changing of his suit fabrics from wool to linen/silk blends, Jack realizes for the first time that everything is green. They *have* made it through winter; his nine months really are up.

Back on the bathroom's floor, Connor is balled, groveling to an imaginary king, the afghan a cape over his shoulders, jogging pants and boxers at his ankles. Trying to avoid the vomit, Jack squats beside him.

"Come on, kid." He puts a hand on Connor's blanketed back. "Floor's not where you want to sleep. Let me get you upstairs."

Sitting up, Connor leans against the side of the toilet but doesn't make any move to leave the bathroom.

"You want to know the funny thing?" he asks, voice splintered and cracked as kindling.

And Jack nods even though he doesn't want to know, because it's not going to be funny, it's going to be terrible. What can *really* be funny when you're crumpled on the floor, stomach heaving, teeth chattering, eyes watery and red. What's funny when you're thirty-two years old, and MOPP has been leaked into your veins to weed-whack hair that just grew in.

"Sure, what's the funny thing?"

"Pretty much my whole life I figured our parents screwed us genetically," Connor says. "I thought I'd live to be fifty, fifty-five tops. So I try to do everything the way *they* didn't—have my kids young enough so I can make it through their graduations, maybe see them squeeze out a pup or two of their own, you know?"

"Conn, stop—"

"I have no memories of Dad, Jack, and I was ten when he died. Keelie won't even be six until November."

"Don't do this," Jack says. "You're going to be okay."

"Look at me. Do you *honestly* believe that?" Connor means the question rhetorically, sarcastically, but Jack answers with more sincerity than he has ever had about anything.

"Yeah, I do." For months Jack has expected Connor to die, but suddenly he doesn't think so. Other than obligatory weddings and bar mitzvahs, Jack can count on one hand the times he has been to religious places. He doesn't believe in God or fire waiting for him below (though fucking around on a pregnant wife would probably be a good way to get there). He doesn't believe he can win the department store case, or that he'll be able to fix the unfixable things with Mona; always, he believes, the plane will crash. But for some reason—karma, the cycle of the tides, something—Jack knows his brother isn't going to call it quits before thirty-three. "I really do believe that."

. . .

Of course the baby is born when Jack is somewhere over Indiana. It's only fitting of his unsettled life—half in Boston, half in Chicago; half with Mona, half with Kathy—that his son comes into the world while Jack is in the air, an unnatural place where he has never been comfortable, where his guts bunch with uncertainty. Years later he will still regret having missed Ryan's birth, even when living with Mona seems some distant dream and he knows her only as the woman who takes care of his son on the days he doesn't.

But before he becomes a father, Jack helps Connor to the master bedroom, spot-cleans the bathroom, and lets the dog in. Upstairs, he strips to boxers and an undershirt and gets in bed beside his brother. Neither one of them mentions that there are three other beds and a pullout couch where Jack could sleep; neither mentions it's two in the afternoon.

"I'm tired," Jack offers as the only explanation.

Almost his entire adult life, Jack has been tired. Since starting at Jones Day in Cleveland, he felt a need to be first in the office and to stay after the cleaning crew finished at night. It was about proving he was more than the old managing partner's son. Through the flu, back strains, bad breakups, and most weekends, Jack worked. He grew to like the grudging respect, awed head-shakes from associates who billed half his hours, and the flurry of summers wanting to work with him because he was the guy to know. Sleep was recreational, something you did on vacations. But his poisoned brother needs sleep, his pregnant wife needs sleep, and it's the best idea Jack can come up with now, too.

So they sleep.

The first time the phone punctures the vacuum of the bedroom, Jack knows it's Laine and the girls in Florida. Even if Connor weren't asking questions about the Dumbo ride and the Enchanted Castle, he would know. It's the way Connor relaxes when he speaks to them. They must put Laine on because Connor shifts, gets quieter, asks about the conference.

"I'm fine," he says. "My stomach was screwed up earlier, now I'm just zonked out." Connor hands Jack the phone. "Tell my wife I'm groovy sweet, she doesn't believe me."

"Honestly, Jack, do you need us to come home?" Laine asks across the line. "We can be on the first flight out of here."

"Naw, he's going to be okay," Jack says. "Thank you, though, for loving my brother."

After hanging up, Jack lets the dog out again. It's early evening, but everything is dimmed by a gathering storm. At a lunch counter on the corner in the suburb's throwback square, he orders two grilled cheese sandwiches and steaming strained chicken broth. Optimistically he adds french fries, because his brother has loved them since he was a kid. The red-haired man behind the counter waves Jack's money away.

"You're Connor's brother, yeah?" He says "Connor" with a strange hard "K," ending it with a long "A." "You just take this home and make sure he gets better."

"He will," Jack says.

"Good. Try to stay dry; it's going to be wicked out there."

The first crack of thunder makes Jack jump on his way to the car, and by the time he pulls into the driveway, fat drops dot the pavement. He brings everything upstairs, where they eat in bed, feeding fries to the dog.

"You're gonna make the best dad." Connor licks salt from his fingers, looks exactly how he did as a child of six and seven, when their mother left ten-dollar bills magneted to the refrigerator and notes saying Jack should pick up something for dinner. "Really, you'll be amazing."

"We'll see," he says.

Jack doesn't read through the rest of Kathy's questions, knowing they're good, certainly better than any he could write at the moment, probably better than any he could write at any moment. He calls and tells her she can do the cross exam for those witnesses.

"Really?" she asks. "I don't have any courtroom experience other than moot court."

"You'll be great, Kath," he says. "You know you're great."

"We're still going to lose though?"

"Yes, but we can lose with finesse."

"I kind of miss having you around, partner," she says, and he knows she will say it again soon, that she's getting tired of the tunnel.

After he hangs up, Jack gets back into bed with his brother. Outside the storm is in full force, branches banging the windows, wind rattling the house, but Jack falls asleep instantly.

Eleven hours later, at six the next morning, the phone rings again. Disoriented, Jack thinks something must be wrong with Connor in Boston, but he realizes his brother is beside him.

"It's Melanie." Connor hands Jack the receiver. "Mo's in labor. You've got to go home."

Then Jack is awake, talking to Mona's sister, who speaks to him in a different medical language, one he didn't bother to learn—one of centimeters dilated and minutes between contractions. His wife is on the phone, voice hurried.

"Can you come back, Jack?" she asks. "I'd really like for you to come home."

What she's saying is that she can forgive him. And there's a chunk of him that wants her to forgive him, but he's not sure. He looks at his brother.

"You have to go," Connor says. "I'm fine."

Jack nods, tells Mona he'll try to get the first plane out, and Melanie gets back on the line with instructions. When he hears the click of the receiver, Jack means to reach over his brother, put the phone back in its cradle, find his clothes, and make arrangements to get to Chicago. But he doesn't do that. There's a horrible pain in his chest. Bunching over, he claws through his undershirt to massage it.

"I can't," Jack says to his knees. "I can't go home to her. I don't love her and I don't want this baby."

"You're freaking out." Connor sits up. "Everybody freaks out. But I've heard the way you talk about Ryan, you're going to be great."

"The kid's not called Ryan." Jack can hardly breathe, and he notices the hand not in his shirt is shaking. He balls it in a fist to make it stop. "Everything I told you—about the furniture, about Mo and the baby's room—I made it up. We never even called it Ryan, it's really called nothing."

"Jack, it's going to be okay."

"I'm serious. I haven't talked to Mo in months; I haven't made it to a single one of her doctor's appointments, and I'm sleeping with a twenty-five-year-old in my office. Do you still think I'm going to be winning awards for father of the year?"

Connor reaches for Jack's clenched fist and puts his own hand on top of it. They don't have the kind of relationship where they touch often, and his brother's warm flesh on his makes Jack look at him.

"Listen to me, I don't know what's between you and Mo and this girl," he says. "But none of that has anything to do with you being a good father."

"Do you *honestly* believe that?"

"I do," Connor says. "I really do believe that."

When Jack rewrites his history in a way that's congruent with his love for his brother and his love for his son, he will make this moment into the epiphany. Say he realized he'd always been a parent to his brother and that was one of the great joys of his life. Say while looking at Connor he imagined Ryan, not as a baby, oozy and needy, but as a young man of seventeen, smart and slender, looking at college brochures but deciding on Penn. Say the pain in his heart subsided, and he knew things *would* be okay. But that's not the way things happen. What happens is this:

Jack gets out of bed, finds his clothes, and haphazardly packs his suitcase. Fighting against the storm, he drives his brother's car in the general direction of the airport, wind throwing sheets of rain against the windshield, tires skidding on pooled water. Eventually he goes in, exchanges his ticket, and even grips the armrests in an attempt to keep the plane from crashing when the air traffic controller finally gives permission for the pilot to take off in the storm. But for hours Jack rides the circular drive of passenger pickup, wiper blades smacking at the water, praying for just a little more time.

defending the
alamo

Months before the dog starts dying, Laine feels the already-wide distance between her and her husband getting wider, but neither of them mentions it. When they notice Mouse is having trouble climbing upstairs, Laine takes the dog to the vet by herself. The vet thinks it's a simple infection, tells a joke about a Zen Buddhist and a hot dog vendor, and gives her pills she has to trick the dog into taking by covering them in peanut butter. The medication doesn't help, so Connor takes the dog back to the vet, who says he thinks Mouse has arthritis. But the new tablets don't fix the golden retriever either. Then Laine notices Mouse isn't eating, not even the scraps Jorie and Keelie pass him under the table, and Mouse isn't peeing when she walks him through their neighborhood of big old houses. They go back to the vet together. This time he doesn't tell Laine and Connor clean jokes or ask about their daughters. He draws his lips into a thin white line, pokes and prods Mouse, and then sends them to the animal hospital downtown for exhaustive tests.

"Just make my dog better." Connor throws their MasterCard on the reception desk when a veterinary assistant starts giving them a list of potential tests and prices. "I don't care how much it costs."

Connor looks to Laine, as if he remembered she makes ninety percent of their income, that he has only worked sporadically for various not-for-profits since he got sick. But she nods, she'd go into debt to make Mouse better, too.

Serious people in white coats shave patches of the dog's paw, run plastic tubing through the pink skin under his fur, and attach catheters to every orifice. All the while Laine and Connor stroke the dog's soft head, call him a "good boy," a "brave boy." The only time the dog cries is when Laine leaves to pick up their daughters from her father's house in Cumberland. By the time she and the girls get back, the vet has determined Mouse's kidneys are failing; there's nothing they can do. Putting a gentle hand on Laine's forearm, the vet says they should probably just put the dog to sleep. Mouse is in pain and it's only going to get worse.

The bones in Connor's jaw shift, and Laine can tell he might cry, feels the sting of tears in her own sinuses.

"But look how happy he is." Connor points to Mouse on the examining table, tail wagging as Jorie and Keelie pet him in the careful way Laine said they could. "Do we have to do it so soon?"

Laine hasn't eaten an animal in twenty years, since she was sixteen, because she can't tolerate cruelty to living things, but the dog does look happy, slapping his pink tongue against Keelie's nine-year-old hands, nuzzling Jorie's face.

"Can we have a few days to say good-bye?" Laine asks the vet.

So they take Mouse and a stash of pain suppositories back to Natick, where they set old blankets and pillows on the first floor by the door so Mouse can rest. For two days Laine and Connor take turns shoving the syringes of medication up the dog's ass—truly one of the most disgusting things Laine has ever done. Keelie reads the dog pages from a chapter book she's massacring, and Connor stands outside with him in the gray wet air, praying that the dog will pee, which in his mind would signal an impossible recovery. At night Connor sleeps next to the dog on the floor in the living room, and Laine misses their warmth in the bed.

Jorie gets on the Internet and finds a veterinary clinic in New York that does kidney transplants on dogs for an obscene amount of money. Connor calls, and the clinic says Mouse isn't a good match because the disease is so far along, but if they want to bring him out to the city, they'll take a look.

"We've got to try, Lainey." Connor's black eyes are wide and hopeful, and he looks decades younger than thirty-six. "We owe it to Mouse."

"Conn—" she starts, but remembers how when Connor was sick and always freezing, Mouse followed him from room to room, sitting on his feet. "I'll call tomorrow and see how it works."

But later that night the dog starts crying, even after they insert the painkillers. When he tries to stand, he stumbles and falls onto his hind legs, nails clanking on the hardwood floor. Keelie starts crying, and Jorie runs upstairs so Laine won't see her crying. She's only twelve, but Jorie is already at the stage where she hates her mother and everything she does, hates that they look almost exactly alike, pale and blond and willowy.

Laine looks at Mouse, then at Connor.

"Baby." She shakes her head, realizes this is the first time she's called him "baby" in a long time. "This isn't fair to Mouse, it's time to put him down."

Probably because he knows she's right, Connor doesn't say anything, just stares at his sneakers. So Laine takes the cordless from its holster on the kitchen wall and calls the vet at home, makes an appointment for the next afternoon, then leaves voice mail messages for her team at work, canceling tomorrow's meetings. When she gets off the phone she goes upstairs, where Keelie, her sweet daughter, is already getting ready for bed.

"Can I go down and say good night to Mouse?" she asks.

Laine nods, bends down to kiss the crown of Keelie's head, with its thick blue-black hair—Connor's hair. She wonders if she should say something about Mouse now or explain it to the girls later, forgiveness versus permission.

The handle to Jorie's door won't turn, and Laine knocks lightly. "You know the rule about locked doors," Laine says.

"Go away." Jorie's voice is scratchy and worn with tears. "You're going to put Mouse to sleep."

"I won't come in, just unlock the door." She hears Jorie's light feet on the carpet and the mechanical twisting of the lock. "Don't forget to brush your teeth and lay out your clothes before going to bed. Did you get any work done on your Alamo project?"

"Daddy said he'd help me tomorrow," Jorie screams. "Just leave me alone."

Downstairs on the pile of blankets, Connor lies next to the dog, strokes its golden head, and looks into its brown eyes in a way he hasn't looked into Laine's eyes in months, maybe years.

She bends at the knees to touch his shoulder. "Conn, the vet can get us in tomorrow at one, so I thought I'd go to work early and come back."

"Fine," he says without looking up at her.

"Are you going to sleep down here again? It can't be good for your back."

"There's nothing wrong with my back, and for all this dog did for me, I think I owe it to him to spend one more night with him."

"Sure. Do you want an air mattress or one of the sleeping bags?" Even in her own ears she sounds pathetic and meek. "I could bring some stuff down and sleep with you?"

"That's okay." He's still not looking at her, but his voice is softer. "You've got to go to work in the morning, why don't you try to get some sleep."

She does go upstairs, strips down to her underwear, but doesn't get into bed. Instead she goes back down, tiptoeing past Connor and Mouse, both snoring lightly. In the kitchen there are dishes in the washer that Connor forgot to run, so she takes them out, scrubs and dries them by hand. Noticing crusted food on the shelf liner in the cabinet, she takes everything down, wipes the cabinets with nonpoisonous cleaner, and rewashes all the dishes just to be on the safe side. She's already awake, so she sweeps and mops the kitchen floor, and cleans the big bay window in the breakfast nook.

When Connor first got sick—and that was how they always referred to it, not as cancer or Hodgkin's disease, just "sick"—their house had been clean like this. During those early weeks, when she tried to convince him to eat macrobiotically, to drink prepackaged shots of ginkgo biloba from the natural foods store. But then they'd settled into it and simply stopped using the lower rooms of the house.

Their bed, an enormous California king with a rounded metal sleigh frame, had become a strange island. She worked from home, propped on pillows, laptop on her crossed legs. Next to her, Connor slept or glanced at books their friends gave him, mostly he slept; if the antinausea drugs couldn't stop his guts from swirling, they could certainly knock him out. For lunch they had whatever he wanted, whatever he could keep down: sugary prepackaged snack cakes, drive-thru french fries, canned pasta with an astronomical fat content. They ate at one, so they could watch *Days of Our Lives*, becoming intensely invested in the lives of Bo and Hope, John Black and Marlena, characters who could die and be buried but come back to Salem a few months later. On nights when they didn't send the kids to Laine's father's house (Connor was adamant the girls not see him when things were very bad), they'd let the girls get into bed with them. The Japanese place on the corner had a miso soup Connor liked, and they brought the cartons of noodles and vegetables into the bed and fed pieces to Mouse. They read aloud from books about other fantastical islands—*The Island of the Blue Dolphins, The Isle of Doctor Moreau, Treasure Island*. They kept the heat cranked to eighty, and it was quiet—muted by the blanket of snow, extra afghans, and the hushed voices people use when someone is very sick. *If something happens, move to Chicago, so the kids can know my brother. If something happens, put the life insurance into trust for the girls. If something happens, cremation, no graveyard stuff, for years I've felt guilty for not going to my parents' sites, none of that for the girls.* But the something didn't happen. They found that they hadn't made any arrangements for that possibility.

On the drive home from the vet's office after putting the dog down, Connor refuses to look at Laine. Instead he stares out the passenger-side window, lower lip thrust out the way Jorie does sometimes.

"I loved the dog, too," Laine says. "But we had to do it."

"I know," he says.

She suggests they go somewhere for lunch, maybe even a place where they can sit down.

"Whatever," Connor says, but across from her in a booth at John Harvard's Pub, he says he isn't hungry and orders only coffee.

The waitress sets Laine's glass of iced tea and Connor's mug on the table, and they both reach for the container of sweetener packets, fingers knocking together over the white porcelain.

"Go ahead." She smiles, but he shakes his head.

"Mouse's dead," he says. "I don't think I can drink coffee ever again."

And she wants to shake him, to say it was purely selfish they had kept the dog alive as long as they had, to say it isn't fair for Connor to take it out on her and it's pointless to deny himself something he loves because their dog had bum kidneys. But Laine doesn't say any of this, because when Connor got sick she promised herself, and a God she hadn't thought much about before, that if her husband got better she would never yell at him again, never admit she was smarter than him.

"Do you really think Mouse would want you to not drink coffee anymore?" she asks, amazed at her own ridiculousness—between the two of them, they have three Harvard diplomas. "I think he would want you to be happy and go on without him."

"I don't care," Connor says, then stares aggressively at the black-and-white photo of Jack and Bobby Kennedy on the wall above her head.

She pushes spinach lasagna around her plate, plunks down her debit card, and refuses a box when the waitress asks. On the drive home it starts raining, but neither one of them comments on it. In fact, they don't say anything until she pulls the Jetta into the garage and he gets out and revs the Harley he got three years ago. Wheeling it from the garage, he cracks the pipes, loud enough that the busybody soccer mom in the house across the street appears at her window to scowl.

Laine always hated motorcycles, knew all the statistics about crashes, but she understood that it was a way for Connor to take control of the things in his life that tried to kill him. So she hadn't told him not to get it, had even ridden behind him, arms locked around his leather jacket, pretending it was fun. But that was before the long spells of silence between them got longer.

"You promised you'd help Jor with her report," Laine yells over the roar of the bike. "When are you coming back?"

"I'll be home before the girls get here," he says with no further explanation.

Then he's off, in a flurry of twisted images reflected in the Fat Boy's chrome. Splotches of rain dot his shirt, and his dark hair flaps in the wind, the helmet she *did* insist on still hanging on its nail in the garage.

They'd promised to never again be careless.

Perhaps the worst moment of Laine's life, the one that still crams white-hot coals into her stomach when she recalls it, was when Connor passed out at the bat mitzvah party of her regional director's daughter. Neither Laine nor Connor had wanted to go to the dinner; earlier that morning they'd suffered through a service in a language they didn't understand. Plus, Connor had been complaining he felt "flu-y." But Laine had been up for vice president and her director's input would be crucial, so she had Connor zip her into a crimson cocktail dress and she pinned the waist of his tuxedo, which had somehow become two sizes too large. Once at the Colonnade ballroom, they found themselves having a surprisingly good time. There was dancing, and Connor and Laine loved dancing, and because they were young and pretty, people loved to watch them dance. After an hour Connor put a heavy hand on her bare shoulder.

"You're wearing me out, girlie," he said. "I've gotta sit the next one out."

She started back to the table with him, but her director offered to take her for a whirl, and then the VP of marketing wanted a dance. When her friend Steve Humboldt stepped in too close, Connor appeared at Laine's side and cut in as if they'd all fallen into a Fitzgerald story.

"Lainey, when you dance I want to make it rain"—one of those nonsensical things he said instead of *I love you.*

But his steps were off, and sweat beads rolled down his throat to stain his white collar. He stumbled in her arms, and she took several steps backward, suddenly supporting his weight.

"Baby?"

"I feel weird." He shook his head, straightened up, took a labored breath. "Really dizzy."

"Let's sit down." In some horrible slow-motion universe, she tried to lead him back to their table. "I'll get you some juice or maybe a soda—"

Then Connor was on the floor, and hundreds of arms were reaching toward her as if she were a rock star. The director's wife, a gynecologist, and someone's plastic surgeon husband swooped to Connor, who blinked and tried to sit up. Steve Humboldt's hands were on Laine's shoulders, as he told one of the kids to call an ambulance. Connor shook his head and waved away the attention. But then he looked at her, and it was the closest Laine ever felt to another person before or again. When she took his hand, the joining was welded platinum.

With both his parents buried by the time he was fifteen, Connor had always been convinced he didn't have much time to knock around the earth, which made the fact that they hadn't recognized he was sick all the more awful. For months they'd been fighting over it without knowing that was what they were fighting over. *"I know you're tired, Conn, but I'm tired, too." "Lainey, could you stop cranking up the freaking heat, every morning I wake up drenched." "If you ate better, maybe you wouldn't feel like shit all the time." "You're not my mother."*

Four days later, hands linked across the armrests of the oncologist's black leather office chairs, they got the results of Connor's tests and learned that the likelihood of a cure would have been better than ninety-eight percent had they caught it a year earlier. Instead the oncologist offered them half of that. But they weren't surprised; they'd realized that the night of the party, that's when they made all their promises to each other. It was sometime between the floor of the Colonnade and now when they broke them.

Of course it falls on Laine to tell the girls the dog is dead, because Connor isn't back when the yellow bus deposits them in front of the house. Keelie simply starts crying when she hears, but Jorie looks at Laine with accusatory gray eyes.

"So you finally convinced Daddy to put Mouse to sleep?" she asks. "You promised you were going to call the place about the transplant.

You didn't even try." Her skin is blotchy, face suddenly soft and squishy, and then Jorie is running up the stairs, slamming the door so hard everything in the house rattles.

"Jor—" Laine calls after her and then just stops.

Keelie is still crying, strings of snot leaking from her nose, wide eyes wet and sad. Laine tries to gather her daughter into her arms, but Keelie shudders, stiff in her embrace.

"Did you really kill Mouse?" she asks.

It isn't fair that Laine has to do this by herself, which is what she screams at Connor when he comes through the door twenty minutes later.

"I can't believe you fucking did that to me," she yells. "You hung me out to dry. I've got Jorie screaming that we killed the dog and now Keelie thinks I'm a murderer. Where were you anyway?"

"Lainey, calm down." When Connor gets exasperated, Laine sees exactly how he must have looked as a child and knows she wouldn't have liked him then. "I just went to get the stuff for Jorie's project," he says. "And I had to go to like three places, because she wants real mulch and they didn't have that at Frank's. Then I was right by Ben & Jerry's so I stopped to get some ice cream, cuz I thought we all might need it."

It all seems quasi reasonable. He does have plastic bags from two different craft stores, and sticky pints of Chubby Hubby and Cherry Garcia.

"It was just awful to do by myself." She feels her voice catch.

"I'm sorry," he sighs. "I thought I'd be back in time; I'll talk to them. Let's just order a pizza, then I'll work with Jorie on the Alamo thing."

Even though he does talk to them, Jorie won't come down for dinner. Laine starts upstairs to get her, but Connor puts a hand on her wrist.

"Let it go," he says. "When she gets hungry she'll come down and eat the leftovers."

There are lots of leftovers. Though Keelie puts away two huge pieces, her round face rouged with marinara, Laine and Connor just pick at the toppings on their slices. As she's putting the wide, flat box in the fridge, she asks Connor if he wants coffee, but he shakes his head, says he's still not drinking it. She bites her tongue so hard she tastes blood.

He does the dishes, and she goes to the study to check all of the e-mail and voice mail messages she hadn't checked all day. On her way to the kitchen to get juice, she pauses outside the door, hearing Connor and Jorie inside.

"I don't understand why it matters," says Jorie, always so serious. "I don't know anything about world politics, and this is just one dumb battle. The Texans lost anyway."

"Yeah, well, they tried really hard to save it," Connor says. "Sometimes trying counts enough, cheesefry."

"Whatever," Jorie says. "They probably shouldn't have even been there in the first place."

Through the gap between the door hinges, Laine watches. They're at the table with all the things Connor bought earlier in the day—Popsicle sticks, clear glue, green gobs of mulch and tempera paint. The "A" volume of *Encyclopedia Britannica* is open to a picture they're using as a model. Laine smiles when she sees the plate of pizza crust next to Jorie.

"How are things going in here?" Laine walks in, tries to look casual. "The Alamo rising again?"

"Hey," Connor says. "Thanks, by the way, for taking off today, I know it's your busy season."

"Sure." Laine nods.

"You don't have to be nice to her for me," Jorie says, staring at the Alamo on the table so she won't have to look at her parents. "I know she killed Mouse."

"Come on," Connor says, unusually parental. "She didn't kill Mouse. He was sick, and we were being selfish keeping him alive. It's okay to be sad, but you can't take it out on your ma, okay?"

Jorie says nothing, looks at the sticks and paint. Laine tries to meet Connor's eyes to thank him, but he's fiddling with the clogged orange Elmer's nozzle, so she pours a glass of carrot juice and goes back to the study, lets Connor put the girls to bed. From the living room, faint sounds of *Late Night* filter through the walls. When she hears Connor click off the TV, she goes upstairs, where he's climbing into bed. Sliding out of her clothes, she gets in beside him, touching his bony shoulder.

"Thank you for sticking up for me with Jor," she says.

"I told you I felt bad about leaving."

She lowers her hand from his arm to his nipple, feels the bump harden under her fingers, but he brushes away her touch.

"Lainey, I can't. . . . Mouse." He kisses her cheek, rolls away from her onto his stomach.

On one hand Laine could count the number of times they made love when Connor was on the very hard drugs. But one night, even after hours spent shitting and shivering on the toilet, he woke up with his cock hard against her thigh.

"I know what to do with this," she said, trying to sound sexy as she ran long fingers down his gaunt body, and took him in her hands, lowered her head. She'd wanted only to go down on him, unsure if he was even supposed to have sex—all those amber vials with so many restrictions: no operating heavy machinery, no driving or drinking, no taking on a full stomach, no taking on an empty stomach.

"No, Lainey, please." He pulled up her head to his, kissed her. "Let's not waste it."

On top of her, he felt brittle. Fat splotches of sweat falling from his forehead onto hers. Laine had never faked an orgasm before with anyone, but she knew Connor wouldn't stop until she came, his face contorted as he thought about whatever it was he thought about to distract himself. She'd loved him so much then, more than she loved her children, more than she loved herself. So she rolled her eyes back, bit her lower lip, and called his name until he believed it.

Three weeks after they put down the dog, when they still haven't had sex, Laine comes home from work, late and tired, and steps in a pile of dog crap in the living room. Her first thought is that Mouse must be sick, because he never has accidents. Then she remembers Mouse is dead, and Connor still isn't drinking coffee. But there's barking, and through the screen door Connor and the girls are playing with a dog that truly seems to warrant the label "mangy mutt."

"It's Mouse Two," Jorie says when Laine slides open the door to the backyard. "Because Mouse is dead we don't use junior."

"I see," Laine says. "Conn, can you come talk to me in the kitchen for a minute."

Of course Connor has a story about finding the dog stuck in the broken fence in the woods behind their house, about how it seemed like fate.

"We talked about getting a new dog, and we said we were going to wait until the summer," Laine says. "Then I'd have some time off and the girls would be home, and it wouldn't be such a bitch to train it."

"But I found this dog now," Connor pleads, actually whining. "And it's a good dog."

"I'm sure it is," Laine says. "But it's really awful timing."

"You're such a hypocrite," he says. "You walk around all holier than thou because you won't eat a cheeseburger, but when there's actually an animal that needs help, you totally bail. It's all theory with you."

"Conn—"

She's starting to feel guilty, starting to reconsider, when she notices Connor has one of their kitchen towels tied around his left hand, a giant crimson blotch in the middle.

"What happened to your hand?" she asks, even though she knows exactly what happened, and Connor doesn't say anything, which just confirms it. Anger swells in her chest. "The dog bit you, didn't it?"

"It was just a little nip when I was helping it out of the fence. She was really scared. You saw her, she's a good dog."

And Laine is running through the living room and out to the backyard, screaming for the girls to get away from the dog. Keelie obediently goes inside and up the stairs, but Jorie stays behind, looks at the dog, then at her mother, shrugs, annoyed as always.

"Now," Laine yells with enough force that Jorie kicks the earth in front of her and shuffles through the sliding door.

With the girls gone, the dog rubs against Laine's wool pants. Laine backs away, leaves it outside and shuts the screen door. Sitting on haunches, it watches Laine and Connor through the glass.

"The dog bites you, and you bring it into our house and let it play with our children," Laine says. "You probably have fucking rabies."

"I don't have rabies."

"How do you know?"

"I know."

"God, what is wrong with you? It's one thing for you to try to kill yourself on the fucking motorcycle. But your kids?"

"Aww, Laine, you know I'd never do anything to hurt the girls; you're just screaming at me to scream at me."

Then she can't take it anymore, feels blood pounding through her system, in the back of her head.

"Just get out," she says, trying to breathe. "I can't deal with you right now, so just go somewhere for a while."

"Where do you want me to go?" Red fills the spaces under his cheekbones.

"For starters, why don't you go to the hospital and have them check out your hand."

"What about the dog—"

"Just go."

The garage door rumbles up and the Fat Boy's pipes crack.

Muffled by the screen, the dog barks. An unfortunate cross between a collie and dalmatian, she has messy spots under a layer of dingy, rough fur. She does look sweet though, with her mouth slightly open, kind of like a smile. It's a look Mouse used to get. Connor had set out a dish of water and some type of food by the door, but both dishes are empty. Sliding open the glass door, Laine bends down to pick up the bowls, and the dog licks her hands, pink tongue rough and not really wet. Mouse II starts to follow her inside, but Laine points a stern finger, tells her to stay, which the dog does. In the basement, there's a twenty-five-pound bag of Mouse's dog food; somehow it had felt wrong to throw it away. Laine hauls it back up the stairs, fills Mouse's old bowl, and sets it on the concrete step for Mouse II, slides the door shut again. She sits in one of the wooden chairs watching the dog eat.

Jorie's model Alamo is on the kitchen table, fat red A+ on the corner of the cardboard base, the report she wrote is beside it. Laine picks up the loose-leaf paper and skims her daughter's eloquent prose. *Whether or not the story of the battle with Santa Ana is true, the Alamo has become an important part of our national history. It has come to symbolize the courage it takes to fight against overwhelming odds.* At the end the teacher has simply written, "Excellent," like all Jorie's teachers are forever writing "excellent," just as Laine's own teachers used to. Realizing it's after ten, Laine goes upstairs. Keelie is in her bed with the sheets pulled up to her round chin.

"You're such a good girl, going to bed without being told." Laine strokes Keelie's forehead, kisses each of her eyelids with their dark lashes.

"Daddy called Jorie's phone and told us to go to bed," Keelie says.

"Oh." Even when Connor is absent, their children still love him more, obey him first.

Jorie's bedroom door is shut, but it pops open when Laine turns the handle.

"Jor, I just wanted to say that I'm proud of your history report," Laine says quietly.

Arms crossed in the pose of an Egyptian mummy, Jorie lies perfectly still, pretending to be asleep, ski-slope nose pointed due north. Laine lets her pretend, goes to the den, and stares at a chart she has opened on a laptop without processing the information.

The dog outside barks, and Laine screams, startled. Then she screams again for no real reason.

The garage door opens and closes and Laine hears Connor's feet on the stairs. She sets down her book and waits. "How's your hand?" she asks flatly when he comes into the bedroom.

"It needed stitches." Something between a laugh and a sigh comes out of his nose. "But I waited too long for them to stitch it, so it will probably get infected."

"Did they at least clean it?"

"Yeah, and they gave me antibiotics."

She nods; he nods. He's at the foot of the bed, so close, and she feels that thing that she's always felt, but she also feels removed from him, has no idea what it is he will say next.

"I came back to get some stuff." He looks at the ground. "I talked to my brother; Mona's got Ryan with her for spring break and Kathy's in London for business, so I thought I'd go see him. I haven't been out there in ages."

"What about the girls—"

"Everything's cool, I called Tiffany, and she can stay with them after school until you get back. She can sleep over if you need her to."

"How long are you going for?" Laine asks, stomach loose and hollow.

"A week, ten days." He shrugs, looks beyond her out the window to the pool, which will stay covered for months. "Jack must be really lonely, he even suggested I bring the girls out for the weekend. They haven't been to Chicago in a long time, it might be fun for them."

"Maybe," she says.

"You're right though," Connor says. "I think maybe we need to not be together for a few days. See how things look from the other side, you know?"

Laine hears herself agreeing, hears herself saying she feels the same way.

"My flight's pretty early in the morning, but I'll take the dog back to the shelter before I go." He smiles, and Laine looks up. "You knew I was lying about the fence."

"Yeah, you're a terrible liar," Laine says. "I can do it on my way to work. I fed her and everything, so she's fine in the yard for now."

Connor says he can do it, but Laine insists until he agrees. So he packs a duffel bag with jeans and shirts, underwear and socks, tells her he'll get a room at a hotel by the airport, that he'll call the girls when he gets to Chicago. Then he's gone, carried off by the sounds of harnessed metal.

The next day Laine takes the morning off and drives Mouse II to the vet's office, where the vet tells an incomprehensible joke, and Laine chuckles politely. She spends more than four hundred dollars on shots and flea medication, only to be told that Mouse II has an enlarged heart and will probably only live for a year or two.

"Your family was pretty upset when Mouse died," the vet says, suddenly serious. "You might want to consider that before you bring another dying animal into your home."

Laine nods and tells the vet she'll think about it. But on the drive home, the dog lays its front paws and head on Laine's lap, and she knows that keeping her won't be the problem. That part won't be hard at all; it's easy to love something when you know it's only for a finite amount of time.

It's after noon by the time she gets in, so she calls her office and tells them she'll work from home, to call her there if they need anything. The dog sits on the floor by her desk, and she rubs its ugly head while she waits for the screen to turn blue and Windows to kick in.

At some point Laine realizes she's crying, because the dog is on its feet barking at her. She's never talked down to children or animals before, but she speaks to the dog in a voice that sounds smushed, the kind people reserve for small, submissive things.

"I think you're the reason I'm going to get divorced. Do you know that?" She bunches the extra skin on the top of Mouse II's head. "You're the reason I'm getting divorced, yes you are. Yes you are."

Hearing the front door open and close, Laine wipes her eyes with the back of her sleeve, tries to inhale the gunk leaking from her nose. The girls look at her hesitantly when they see her on the living room floor with Mouse II. The dog barks a friendly bark, wags her tail.

"It's okay." Laine cringes at her own voice, which sounds full of tears and snot and worries. "I took Mouse Two to the vet, and she's healthy. You can play with her if you want."

Keelie gingerly sets down her pink backpack, walks toward Laine and the dog as if the carpet were made of lily pads.

"Go ahead," Laine says, and Keelie reaches a hesitant hand to the dog, who licks it, barks and wags. Keelie likewise giggles and wags. "It's all right, Jor—"

"This is so like you!" Jorie screams. The dog barks, and Keelie freezes. "You're all nice to the dog now that you made Daddy go away. You're always mean to Daddy—"

"Did Daddy tell you that?"

"I'm not stupid." Jorie throws her backpack on the floor, runs up the stairs, slams (and no doubt locks) the door. The dog barks again, and Keelie looks at Laine with a quivering lower lip—in a minute she'll be crying. Laine takes a deep breath and tries to smile at her younger daughter.

"So how was school, swee—" she gets out before Keelie starts to howl.

That night Mouse II sleeps in Laine's bed, head on Connor's pillow, warm dog breath on her neck. The dog follows her around the next morning as she makes sure the girls are up and getting ready for school. In the kitchen while Laine makes oatmeal, Keelie plays with Mouse II, but Jorie can't seem to decide what a pro-Connor position on the dog would be. She scowls and doesn't speak directly to Laine, going so far as to ask Keelie to ask Laine for orange juice.

At her office in the high-rise on Market Street, Laine finds herself online, looking for experimental procedures to cure the dog. Steve Humboldt knocks on her office door when she's on the phone with a veterinary school in Ohio.

"Everything okay?" he asks when she gives him the go-ahead to come in.

"Sure, sure." Laine wonders why she's lying to Steve, whom she's had lunches and coffee breaks with for more than a decade. By all accounts he's her best friend. When Connor was sick, Steve was the one who fought hardest to keep her position for her.

"I was just worried. When I stopped by yesterday, Rita said you were working at home. I just wanted to make sure that everything was all right."

"Yeah, it's fine." Laine nods. "We got this new dog, and Conn was out of town. I didn't want to leave it alone right away."

Steve sits in the chair across from her massive oak desk. Attractive in the way that all average-looking men with good jobs can be—expensive haircut, well-made suits that broaden rounded shoulders—he looks nothing like Connor, with his pretty, genderless features.

"That's great, another golden?" Steve seems a little disappointed that there isn't something more wrong, something that he can help her with.

"No, it's some mixed breed we got at the pound. You know my kids, they wanted to 'rescue' a dog."

She knows she could tell Steve, he'd listen and give advice. Even though he's wanted to kiss her for ten years, he wouldn't do that, unless she made it clear that she wanted him to. And she thinks that maybe someday she *will* want Steve Humboldt to kiss her. Someday when the white flag has been hung and she and Connor decide that the battle is lost. But now is not the time. So the conversation with Steve ends, and she asks him to shut her door on his way out.

By midweek Jorie slips and speaks to Laine directly, says that her book report on *To Kill a Mockingbird* was selected by the class to be on display in the school's main office.

"That's m'girl," Laine says.

"Daddy called," Jorie says. "You're supposed to call him at Uncle Jack's."

Five years ago, while Connor lapsed in and out of consciousness with chemo-related pneumonia, Laine had fainted because she hadn't eaten or slept in days. Jack had scooped her off the hospital's linoleum floor, cradled her in his arms, force feeding her peanut M&M's and Gummy Bears from the vending machine.

"Hi, Laine," Jack says now, stiff and formal, as if none of that had ever happened. "I think Conn ran out to Starbucks; I'll have him call you back in a minute."

"Wait, Jack." Laine licks her lips. "Can I ask you something?"

There's a pause, which tells Laine that Connor has confided in his brother, or at least something close to confiding, and she can't tell if that makes her happy or sad.

"Sure," Jack says.

"Has he been drinking coffee?"

"Wha— Oh, here he is, hold on."

A shuffling, words exchanged, Connor is on the line.

"Yeah, I booked a ticket back for Friday. Is it cool if I come back to the house?"

"Of course."

"I get in around one, but you don't have to pick me up. I left the bike there."

"Okay." She considers telling him about keeping Mouse II, about the girls, about not kissing Steve Humboldt. "So I'll see you sometime on Friday then?"

She waits for him by the terminal exit, tries to look beyond where security will let her pass. Fifteen minutes after the monitor announces his flight arrived, there's still no sign of Connor and she wonders if he wasn't on the plane or if he somehow found some other exit. A strange panic flutters in her chest. Maybe he changed his mind about coming back? Maybe he decided to hop a plane to Rome instead? But then there he is, tall and limby, in a leather coat she got him years ago.

When he sees her he stops, grins, shakes his head.

"Hey, pretty lady," he says.

"I kept your fucking dog."

"I know, Jorie told me. I knew you would anyway."

"Yeah, it's a good dog. It doesn't have rabies."

They get his duffel from the baggage carousel, and she asks about his brother, about Chicago. She wants to ask what he said to Jack, how he explained his strange familyless appearance, but she doesn't.

"Can I hitch a ride with you to long-term parking?" Connor asks. "Probably quicker than waiting for the shuttle."

"Actually"—Laine feels herself blushing, and she never gets embarrassed about anything—"you said you had the bike here, so I took the T. I figured *I* could hitch a ride with *you*."

He says nothing about how she hates the Harley, about how she hasn't ridden it with him since he first got it. Instead he smiles again, nods. During the tram ride to the lot, it starts to drizzle. By the time he gets the motorcycle, it's raining hard.

"You sure you don't want to take a cab back?" he asks, starting the bike. "I know you don't like to ride without a helmet, especially in bad weather."

She thinks of Connor on the floor next to their dying dog, how if she hadn't said anything, he would have kept that dog alive forever, taking it outside day after day as if suddenly it would start making urine again. And Jorie and Connor at the kitchen table a month ago, resurrecting the Alamo from Popsicle sticks and construction paper. His daughter passing on the lesson she already knew at twelve, one he hadn't learned at thirty-six—you don't get points for fighting a hopeless fight, you just get dead.

Laine's hair is already wet and cold around her face, and she knows her windbreaker will hardly keep her warm once they get on the road. But maybe Connor was right about the Alamo, too. Sometimes you get recognized for trying, a footnote in a history book and the sleep that comes with knowing you did all you could.

"I don't mind the rain," Laine says. "I'll ride with you."

He nods and she climbs on behind him, wrapping her long arms around his waist. Fat raindrops pelt her face, so she closes her eyes and rests her head on his neck. At first his skin is hot, but it loses warmth as they continue.

And she remembers five years ago, when Connor was sick, his oncologist warned he shouldn't take hot showers, that with the anemia he could pass out. Point blank, Connor had refused—*"I'll get out if I feel dizzy."* But Laine had been terrified of finding him slumped against the glass walls, so she had sat on the edge of the Jacuzzi, arms looped around her knees, watching him through the beveled glass.

"Lainey, if you're going to sit there, you might as well come in," he said, voice warbled from the spray.

Silently she took off her jogging pants, T-shirt, bra, and panties, pulled open the vacuum of the doors, and stepped onto the rubber floor mat. They rarely showered together because Connor always ran the water too hot, but that time it felt purifying—like they were made of metal and could be melted down, reshaped and changed into other things. She took the loofah sponge he'd been using, squirted on more body wash, and began to clean him. Before running the webbed material against any part of his body, she kissed it. A blessing more than sex—touching lips to a prayer book that touched the Torah during that horrible bat mitzvah. When she finished, he held her, smashed against him. Because of sickness and drugs and worry, their bodies were both stripped down to the bare necessities. Their bones sought their counterparts, his hips reaching for hers, ribs pressed against ribs. They stood under the spray until her fingers shriveled and aged, until it was unbearable, until there was no more heat in the water.

the way
he said "putz"

Unfortunately for Mona, Jack's girlfriend isn't a bimbo. Kathy *is* blond, *does* have great tits (probably real), and *is* seventeen years younger than Jack. But the truth is Kathy just made partner at a prestigious firm, has an Ivy-covered education, and probably made more her first year out of law school than any newspaper has ever considered paying Mona.

Still "Blond Ponytail" is what Mona's sister insists on calling Kathy.

"Jack still making an ass of himself with Blond Ponytail?" Melanie asks when she and Mona have one of their Bloody Mary brunches on a Sunday morning.

"They seem happy." Mona threads a red curl behind her ear, and lets Melanie be bitchy for her. The girls weren't close as children, but found themselves single and in Chicago as they slipped into their forties. "Its been so long, I wish them no evil."

Melanie blows air through her lips, says: "You're a better woman than I am."

"Eh," Mona says, takes another spicy sip. "She can have him."

But when she gets home from brunch, Mona showers, dries her hair, and reapplies makeup, even though she has no plans for the evening. Waiting for Jack to bring back their son, she puts on new jeans (she may not have Kathy's cleavage, but she's still got a great ass), and the kind of sexy casual top that only works on soap opera people.

The doorman buzzes the intercom.

"Jack Reed and Ryan are here," he says from eighteen stories down. It's the same doorman as when Jack lived in the building, and Mona wonders if they have the same mindless conversations about sports and the weather they had six years ago.

"Send them up," she says. Almost as a reflex she fluffs her hair in the mirrored foyer, shoves her lips forward in a pout. She has the door open when the elevator delivers her ex-husband, in pressed pants and a dress shirt, even on the weekend.

Without acknowledging Mona at all, her six-year-old son dashes by her. "SpongeBob is on." His words float behind him, followed by the elastic voices of cartoon characters.

Jack lingers in the door frame, looking uncomfortable and a little sick, sweat beading his brow, flush across his cheeks.

"Can I talk to you for a sec?" he asks.

"Sure," Mona says, heart rattling with uncertainty. "Do you want coffee?"

Jack nods, and she leads him to the kitchen. The espresso machine—sleek and black with a single button that grinds the beans and brews individual cups—had been something from their bridal registry. But Mona makes the coffee, as if Jack wouldn't know how.

"Thanks." He sits at the kitchen table, sips. His bushy eyebrows crimp with worry and he presses his lips into a tight white line. This is the kind of moment she relished when they were together, one of the rare times when he lets her help him.

"What's up?" She sits in the chair next to his.

"Mo—" He looks at her, his mouth not quite open and not quite closed, like he doesn't remember how to use it. Realizing what he's going to say, she stops him so she won't have to hear it.

"You're marrying Kathy, aren't you?" she asks, feeling sobs and screams ripening in her belly. Bowing her head, she rubs the bridge of her nose.

"I'm sorry," Jack says.

He hadn't ever apologized for sleeping with Kathy in the first place, hadn't apologized when he moved out or when he asked for a divorce.

"I'm sorry," he says again.

And something surprising happens: Mona doesn't break down. Her sinuses dry up, and she takes Jack's hand from the table, feels its familiar weight. Leaning into him she touches her lips to his forehead where his graying black hair parts.

"It's okay," she says, realizing it's true as she says it. "And, frankly, it's about time."

When he looks at her again, there's something in his eyes that can only be described as gratitude. It's a private moment she will share with no one. When she tells her sister, she will let Melanie say things about blondes and home-wreckers, nod, and order another Bloody Mary. But now she holds Jack, feels his torso tremble.

"I'm happy for you," she says, and he thanks her again and again.

Kathy Kreinhart decided she had a thing for Jack Reed when he called Paul Billings a putz. She'd been a summer associate and Jack had been assigned her partner/liaison because he'd gone to Penn for undergrad and law school and she was on the same track, set to start her final year in the fall. Jack had given her a few assignments, and she'd thought he was kind of cute in a square-jawed, overpriced-haircut kind of way. But when he invited her into his office and told her she'd done a stellar job on a brief she'd helped write, he shook her hand with command and smiled at her firm grip.

"If you're sure you want to do litigation, you don't have to go to corporate for the second half of the summer." He waved her into a seat across his massive desk, from his important-looking chair on the other side. "I can find some interesting projects for you here."

He looked genuine, as if he *were* truly thrilled by her five-hundred-word brief, and she felt comfortable enough to tell him that Paul Billings, a junior partner, had asked her to do all kinds of ridiculous crap—proofread his memos, get Krispy Kremes from the bodega in the lobby, pick up his dry cleaning.

"That's not your job." Jack shook his head. "If he asks you do anything else, just tell him you're doing stuff for me. That guy is such a fucking putz."

It was the way he said "putz," the way he rolled his eyes (nice eyes, that dark brown kind where the pupil bleeds into the iris). The other summers had been complaining about Billings for weeks, but when Jack definitively gave him the thumbs-down, Paul Billings became their private joke. She smiled, knowing how she looked when she smiled. At twenty-four, enough people had told her she was pretty that she figured they couldn't all be lying.

"I really learned a lot from that last project," Kathy said, which wasn't true. "I think I would like to stay in litigation." Which was true.

Jack nodded, told her about an upcoming case, asked if she wanted to discuss it over lunch. Just as Kathy was thinking about what it would be like to be out in the world with Jack Reed, she noticed the picture of the redheaded woman in a platinum frame on his desk.

That had been almost eight years ago. At the time, the redhead had been Jack's wife. Kathy didn't sleep with Jack until a year and a half later, when she'd joined the firm and Jack brought her in on the Ryan department store trial, when the redhead was pregnant with a child Jack hadn't wanted, and Jack's brother was almost dying. There'd been a challenging absence in Jack's kiss, in his eyes, but she'd attributed it to the guilt and gruel of his life. She pretended it would abate with time.

They lost the case, Jack's brother got better, the redhead had the baby, and she and Jack broke up, got back together, and broke up again. After Jack's divorce was final, he asked Kathy to move into the new condo he bought a mile and half down Lake Shore from the one he used to share with the redhead. For the past four years, Kathy and Jack have been driving to the office together most mornings, eating Asian take-out together most nights. On Sundays Jack has his son, and some weeks Kathy goes with them to Wrigley Field or the Lincoln Park Zoo. Some weeks she eats lunch at her parents in Rodger's Park instead.

"He's never going to marry you," her father says, sipping an Old Style and fiddling around with a model airplane at the same dark wood table that had been in the kitchen since she was a kid. Only six years older than Jack, Kathy's father, bald and shriveled, could pass for Jack's father.

Kathy's mother says nothing and busies herself making tuna sandwiches and coffee, despite Kathy's offer to take them out to brunch.

"I don't care about getting married," Kathy says and means it.

"You're thirty-one years old," her father says. "You should think about those things."

"I don't," Kathy says, resisting the urge to point out that marriage hadn't made her father nice, had made her mother frumpy and complacent with frosted hair and sagging breasts. "I'm happy," she says.

And she is. Until two weeks later when Jack gets up in the middle of surf and turf at Gibson's. He bends down, and Kathy takes another bite of lobster, assuming he dropped his napkin on the way to the men's room. On one knee in front of her, Jack takes her hand.

"Kath," he says. "I was wondering if you might like to get married."

If Jack hadn't spent a chunk of the previous year finding a Massachusetts' divorce lawyer for his brother, she might believe him. If he ever so much as kissed her in public, she'd think he's sincere. She doesn't think he is, instead assumes the whole thing is an uncharacteristically mean joke, and she wonders if she mentioned her father's comment.

"Aren't you supposed to have a ring when you do that?" she asks flatly.

Jack smiles; he looks good when he smiles, like men on TV who sell Viagra.

"Yeah, I've got one of those." He reaches into the pocket of his suit jacket and pulls out a velvet box with a ring—a very, very big ring. More accurately, a normal-sized platinum band with a very, very big square diamond in the center.

Something surprising happens then: Kathy starts crying, sobbing actually. There are audible gasps from restaurant patrons, who stop slicing sirloin and sipping red wine to watch. The creases in Jack's brow deepen, and he puts his hand on the thigh of her suede skirt, asks if she's okay. Kathy nods and sniffles, reaches for the cloth napkin in her lap to wipe her nose.

"Is that a no?" Jack asks.

"No, I mean it's not a no . . . I mean . . . I just didn't realize how much I wanted to marry you until you asked." As she says it, she realizes it's true.

"If I'd known you'd fall apart, I would have done this at home. I thought it might be romantic here."

Taking her hand, he slides the ring on her finger, and the people clap. Jack waves and grins, while Kathy feels heat on her cheeks and dabs at her eyes. The waiter clears away their plates of steak, seafood, and creamed spinach, returns with a molten chocolate cake. A lit candle glows over the hills of ice cream.

"Make a wish for a long and happy life together," the waiter says.

Kathy and Jack exchange looks about who's supposed to blow it out, and the small flame dances between them, the light reflected in Jack's eyes. And she thinks that she catches something in his gaze that she hasn't seen before, something open.

That look is still there later that night when he lays her naked on the bed, licks her body starting at the big toe of her left foot and continuing to her blond widow's peak. It's there the next morning when he pulls her under the sheets after she comes back from the bathroom.

"Ohmygod, I'm going to be Mrs. Reed. Just like Donna." Kathy laughs, and Jack rolls on top of her, squashes air from her lungs, making her cough. He's a tall man who's put on ten pounds in the years she's known him, not really fat, just filled out, and she likes his heaviness on her.

"You're going to take my name?" He brushes his straight nose against her straight nose. "How very fifties of you."

"Katherine Reed sounds like an attorney you'd trust." Her voice is strained from his dead weight. "I've always thought Kathy Kreinhart was kind of ducky."

"Okay, Mrs. Reed." Jack rolls off of her, swats her butt. "I'm hungry. Make some eggs."

But he makes the scrambled eggs and fresh ground coffee, brings it to her on a tray. They eat in bed and tumble around until he goes to pick up his son from the redheaded woman. While Jack takes Ryan to the Shedd Aquarium, Kathy drives out to the southern suburbs to show her mother the engagement ring.

"I never thought he would ask you." Cupping her daughter's hand in her own, Kathy's mother cries and talks about places where they could have the reception. "This is a miracle."

"Come on, Mom, it's not as though he figured out who shot Kennedy," Kathy says, but feels herself caught up in something, too, wonders if maybe she does want a wedding with a lacy white cake and a cover band after all.

As usual, her father is cantankerous and unhelpful. "Well if you want kids, you'll have to do it right away," he says without really looking up from the model airplane he's putting together on the kitchen table. "Jack's almost fifty."

"It doesn't matter how old Jack is." Kathy's mother perks up in a rare moment of defiance. "Kath's got twelve good years for kids."

Kathy starts to say that she doesn't want kids, but doesn't. Instead she smiles at her mother and helps chop tomatoes.

When they finish looking at fish, Jack and Ryan meet Kathy for deep-dish pizza at Carmine's. Across from her in a red vinyl booth, Ryan nods at her the way he always nods at her, completely unfazed at the prospect she'll be his stepmother. The boy's complacency might be due to the handheld video game system Jack bought him—Ryan's own engagement present. Thumbs working the buttons, he plays until the pie comes out, greasy and gooey, then burns the roof of his mouth on the volcanic layer of cheese between the sauce and crust. He cries, and for a minute Kathy hates his soft round face and red hair. Then the sensation passes, and she gives him ice from her water glass to soothe his tongue. He climbs over to her side of the booth and rests his head on her side. She looks at Jack, but the openness is gone. As he tries to catch the attention of the waiter to get more crushed red peppers, Kathy catches a flicker of the challenging blankness.

"So when is Jack marrying Blond Ponytail?" Melanie asks a month later. She and Mona aren't having Bloody Mary brunch, but coffee in Mona's kitchen on a Thursday night because Melanie has a literary conference in San Francisco over the next week. "Will you go to the wedding?"

"I don't know," Mona says. She still feels good about her exchange with Jack. "If I'm invited, I guess I'll go."

"I'm sure he'll be an ass to her, too."

Melanie is going to California with a married University of Chicago colleague she's been sleeping with for more than a year. Mona makes no reference to the irony, though, understands her sister is trying to be nice.

"I don't really care."

"Ryan taking it okay?" Melanie asks.

"What's there to take? Kathy's lived there for years," Mona says, but bad-mother guilt socks her in the stomach—not once has she asked Ryan's opinion on the subject. She glances at him in the den, watching an inane cartoon where the main character appears to be a block of cheddar cheese. "He's never complained about her."

"Yeah, I guess Blond Ponytail's been around his whole life." Melanie fluffs her own red hair; she's always been a shade less pretty than Mona.

They talk about the married professor and debate if his wife knows about Melanie. They talk about the doctor who writes a medical question-and-answer column in Mona's paper, who Mona's slept with a few times. They talk about their younger sister and her four brats, about their father's retirement party next spring.

Melanie gives Mona the keys to her apartment so Mona can feed the cat and water the plants while she's gone. "I'm just not sure this Jack remarrying thing has really hit you," Melanie says as Mona walks her through the mirrored hall to the elevator. "Don't hesitate to call me if you freak out."

Kissing her sister's milky cheek, Mona says she'll be fine, and Melanie tells Mona not to keep the cat waiting too long. "You can cuddle up with Fido," she says. "He's better than a guy anyway."

But Mona doesn't spend much time playing with Melanie's Siamese cat on Sunday night because she has to rewrite a horrible story by the horrible intern at work and doesn't get to her sister's until after dark. She's already late to get Ryan from Jack's, so she runs in, throws water on the plants and food in Fido's bowl, leaving the litter box for her next visit.

Melanie's condo is in a neighborhood *Chicago Magazine* has been describing as "up-and-coming" for ten years. As far as Mona can tell, it still hasn't hit. The streets are empty and the graffiti fresh on the sides of uninviting businesses—check-cashing services and auto-parts stores—all of which are locked with rusted chain-link doors. Somewhere in the distance a car alarm warbles. She fumbles for the Mercedes keys, *actually* thinking it's not a safe place to be at night, when she feels a hand on her throat, another around her middle, pinning her arms against her sides.

"I want your purse and your car keys." The voice is male, though not particularly masculine, very young. For a full two seconds, Mona fantasizes about crashing her elbow into his ribs, wrestling him to the ground—the kind of heroism she sometimes fantasizes about when she jogs.

"Now, lady!" The man attached to the voice squeezes her tighter, and she thinks she feels metal on her throat, maybe a knife, maybe a gun, it's hard to discern through her wool scarf and the cold of Chicago in February. If nothing else her attacker *is* bigger than she is.

"I can't reach them," she says, her own voice squeaky and high. "You're holding my arms."

"Smart-ass bitch," he says, but behind her, she feels him trying to negotiate the transaction.

He takes the car keys from her fingers, yanks the leather strap of her handbag, and shoves her to the dirty, hard snow on the curb. Catching herself, she twists her wrist, the pain sharp enough that tears pop into her eyes. A spray of street salt and asphalt hits her face as her assailant drives off in her car.

It can't be more than fifteen degrees out, but for a minute she sits on the cold concrete, studying the rip in her leather glove and the thin tributaries of blood running down her palm. Her cell phone was in her purse; she can't even call anyone. She thinks she may have seen a pay phone a few blocks away, but when she shoves her good hand into the pocket of her long black coat looking for change, she finds Melanie's apartment keys.

Back in Melanie's kitchen, she calls the police and they tell her two officers are on the way. She briefly contemplates the litter box, but decides against it. Her wrist hurts, so she wraps ice in a towel, but there's really no good way to hold it on her arm, so she takes four Advil from the bottle on top of the microwave instead. She calls Jack, who insists on coming over.

A big, burly boy cop and a big, burly girl cop arrive and sit awkwardly in the kitchen at the pearl vinyl bar stools and vintage 1940s table. Mona offers them coffee, but realizes she doesn't know if her sister even has any coffee.

"Don't worry about it, honey." Boy Cop puts a fat hand on her shoulder. Studying the gun on his hip, Mona decides there's almost no way that was what her attacker was carrying.

Girl Cop takes notes as Mona tells the story. Did Mona get a good look at the man, no. Did she see how tall he was, no. Was he Caucasion? Asian? African American? Mona's not sure. "You haven't really given us much to go on," Girl Cop says, and Mona rubs her wrist.

Boy Cop asks if she'd like to go to the hospital, calls her "honey" again.

"No," Mona says. "It's not that bad."

Jack arrives, tall and authoritative in a cashmere trench coat, and Boy Cop lets him in the front door.

"Are you her husband?" Boy Cop asks, and Jack simply nods. He asks them *Law & Order* questions, even though his job working for giant corporations has nothing to do with the criminal justice system.

"It sounds like the guy was pretty amateur," Girl Cop says. "We'll put out a call to body shops to be on the lookout. We'll let you know when it turns up."

"Keep ice on your wrist," Boy Cop says. "Go to the hospital if it gets any worse."

Jack walks them out, returns, and pulls out the bar stool next to Mona's.

"You hurt your wrist?" he asks.

"It's okay," she says, but it does hurt, is turning red. "Where's Ryan?"

"He'd already fallen asleep before you called," Jack says. "I'm going out of town tomorrow; you can just use my car while I'm gone."

"I can rent a car."

"Yeah, but for tonight and tom—" Jack stops. "You're holding your hand, are you sure you don't want me to run you to the emergency room?"

"It's fine."

"Jesus, Mo." Jack shakes his head, leans forward, elbows on the table. "It's Hyde Park. What were you thinking?"

"I guess I wasn't thinking," she says to the table and to her bruised arm. "I'm sorry."

"Well, I'm just glad you're okay." There's something in his voice that rallies all the hurt and loss she didn't feel in her own kitchen when he told her he was marrying Blond Ponytail.

She looks at him. Really looks at him.

For the past six years she's dressed up on Sunday afternoons, but that was different, that was about her wanting him to want her, about her pride. This might be larger, might be about their life and what it means to have your existence tightly braided to someone else's.

He looks at her.

His cell phone rings in the pocket of his coat draped across one of the stools, but he doesn't answer, just keeps looking.

She kisses him.

He kisses back, his lips more familiar than the sound of her name.

As Mona's fingers work the buttons of his oxford, he fiddles with the zipper on her skirt. He pulls her sweater over her head, unhooks her bra with one hand, the other in her curls. And then they're on the ugly linoleum of Melanie's kitchen floor, rolling around, bumping into the table and chair legs.

The last time they'd made love had been six years ago, when they'd already decided they were separating, but he hadn't closed on his condo yet. She'd been asleep on the bed with Ryan, and Jack was looking at them when she flittered awake. "What a lovely picture," he'd said, sitting down next to her to touch his son's small arm, then Mona's larger arm. Their bodies had taken over then. By that point they'd been so committed to uncommitting that they never talked about it.

And Mona wonders if they will talk about this time. When they finish, he holds her against him, and she notices subtle differences in his body. He's heavier, grayer. There's a scar on his lower abdomen from a hernia operation she'd only heard about.

It could be seconds or years that they lay there, nothing said. She's uncertain of what she wants to have happen, knows only that they can't stay on the floor forever, because her wrist hurts and the cat is licking her naked thigh, because she saw a line of ants scamper past, because he's engaged to Kathy, who's watching their son. She props herself on her elbows, her skin sticking to the floor.

"I'm sure this kind of thing happens all the time," Mona says, reaching for her panties and bra.

"Probably." Jack sits up.

She hopes he'll kiss her head once more, but he doesn't, doesn't touch her again. She looks away, notices the clock on the microwave says it's after one thirty, makes a comment about how late it is.

"You can drop me off and get Ryan," Jack says, as if he isn't pulling on his boxers, hopping into his pants. "I'll be gone through Friday; you can just keep the car until then."

"Sure," she says.

Jack hadn't told Kathy he'd call her when he'd gone to help Mona with the police, but three hours go by without any word from him and she tries his cell phone. Her heart pinches with worry as the voice mail picks up. She checks on Ryan, innocent and round, as he sleeps in his race car–shaped bed. As she runs her fingers along his hairline, she wishes it weren't red. Putting on a pair of Jack's old boxers and a T-shirt, Kathy goes to the bathroom brushes and flosses. She washes her face and applies unneeded wrinkle cream; this spring she'll be thirty-two, but she still gets carded in bars and worried looks from clients the first time they meet her.

She gets into bed, but doesn't sleep. At two the front door opens and closes, and she peeks into the living room. Ryan is asleep in Jack's arms, and Mona's bunched over her son—a family.

"Do you think he'll be okay?" Mona whispers. "Should we try to put his coat on?"

"You're going from one garage to another," Jack whispers back. "I'm sure he'll be fine. If your wrist hurts, don't try to carry him, make him walk."

As Kathy watches, she remembers the first time she met Mona all those years ago when she was a summer associate and she and Jack were not yet lovers. She'd gone to Jack's office to show him a case she'd found on Westlaw—partly because it pertained to their client, partly because her attraction to Jack had avalanched in the weeks since he'd called Billings a putz. His door had been ajar, and she could see him packing a leather case full of papers, talking quietly with someone hidden behind the office doors. When he saw Kathy, he waved her in. And there, ripped from the photo, had been the redheaded woman. Not as pretty as the picture really—maybe a few pounds heavier, even paler—but frighteningly real in a breezy sleeveless dress.

"Mo, this is that brilliant law student I've been raving about." Jack had pointed appropriately. "Kathy, my wife, Mona."

It was the way he had said "wife," pride in ownership, that made Kathy double over. Leaning on his desk, she'd felt sweat rolling from her hairline, down her back, to the waist of her nylons.

"Kath?" Jack had put a hand on her arm. "Are you feeling okay?"

She shook her head, mumbled she was sorry.

"You poor thing," the redheaded woman said. "You should go home."

"Yeah, we can give you a ride—"

She'd said she'd be fine, but Jack and Mona insisted on escorting her out of the building. As he hailed her a cab, Jack slipped a twenty into her palm, as if he were a better father than Kathy's own.

And there they are now, Jack and the redhead in the hall with the child that they'd made. Only now everything is different. Kathy has only to walk out and claim Jack, and it will be Mona who has to mutter something about how late it is, about how she should be going. But Kathy says nothing and gets back into bed.

A few minutes later she hears Jack trying not to make much noise as he undresses and slides between the sheets next to her. Kathy touches his collarbone, and he flips over to face her.

"Did I wake you?" He kisses her forehead.

"I was already awake. Is everything all right?"

"She's fine, a little banged up. I let her have my car. I can take a service to O'Hare."

"I can take you," Kathy says.

He tells her it's too early in the morning, but she offers until he accepts.

Curling into familiar sleeping positions, Jack on his stomach, arm across her back, they sigh and relax. Kathy flirts in and out of sleep. Though Jack keeps his breathing regulated, she notices he never starts snoring.

Three hours later the alarm goes off; Jack hits snooze until they have to get up.

On the ride to the airport Jack drives her Saab, and neither of them mentions the previous night. They toss a yawn back and forth and fill the awkward space with talk about Jack's client.

As he follows the signs to passenger drop off, she confirms the time his return flight gets in. Putting the car in park, he gets his roller suitcase from the trunk. She meets him at the rear of the car, where he gives her the keys and a closed-mouth kiss good-bye.

"Are we going to have kids?" The question is so odd; Kathy can't believe she asked it. Doesn't even know what the right answer is.

"What?"

"I just figured if we're going to get married it's something we should talk about."

"Well, you're right about that, but your timing sucks." He flips up his wrist and looks at his watch. "I have a plane to catch in thirteen minutes. You decide you want kids now?"

"Not now, but maybe in five or ten years . . . I've been . . . it's just something I've been thinking about."

"Jesus, Kath, let's talk about this when I get back." He shakes his head, puts a hand on her shoulder, and rubs the back of her neck. "Or call me tonight. We can talk then, okay?"

She nods and they exchange "I love you"s. The automatic doors to the terminal part when he walks on the floor mat; he doesn't turn around to look back, but she watches him until he's through security, until the car behind her honks.

All morning Mona flounders around the newsroom in a haze of pain, her hand swelling to elephantine proportions. She lets an incomprehensible paragraph by the horrible intern stand, because it hurts too much to retype it. It's more than her wrist though; there's an odd lump of something lodged in her throat. She expects Jack to call her at work, but doesn't answer the phone when it finally rings. The voice mail isn't from Jack but the horrible intern lost en route to a fire that's probably extinguished. Her hand hurts too much to call him back. By four she goes to the hospital, where they put her hand in a splint. Then she flounders in a haze of painkillers, somehow driving Jack's car home without totaling it. She's at the kitchen table looking at *Atlantic Monthly* without really reading it when the phone rings. Thinking it's Jack, she lets the answering machine get it, but picks up when she hears Melanie's voice.

"It's like his wife is here with us," Melanie says, two time zones away. "Like she's watching the freaking seals at Fisherman's Wharf, walking with us across Golden Gate Bridge."

"Sure," Mona says, distracted and high.

"Mo? Are you even listening?"

Telling her sister about the robbery and the car, Mona leaves out the sleeping with Jack part. Melanie apologizes for being insensitive and asks appropriate questions.

"This is my fault, I should have warned you not to go there too late," she says, and Mona likes that everything—car theft, her gimpy hand, sleeping with her ex-husband—can be blamed on Melanie.

When the phone rings a few minutes later, Mona answers, assuming it's her sister again.

"Hey," Jack says. "Any word on the car yet?"

She tells him that they didn't call, and he asks about her wrist. She says it's fine.

"I'm buried under about a hundred feet of snow in Minneapolis," he says, and Mona wonders if this is his way of saying that Kathy isn't around, that they can talk.

"Yeah," she says. "I think it's a snow belt."

A silence and four hundred miles between them.

"Is Ryan still awake?" he asks.

"No, he went to bed early; he was pretty worn out from last night." Her way of saying it's okay to talk?

"Well, I'm here until Friday," he says. "I guess we'll have to rent something when I get back."

"Yeah, I talked with the insurance rep today. It's a little tricky because it's still in your name." Their entire division of property is sketchy—they'd never gotten around to switching titles and deeds. When they'd decided the separation would be permanent, Jack had told her she could have whatever she wanted. It had been the saddest moment of her life because she realized he had no desire to hurt her, he simply wanted to leave.

"We'll figure it out. Call me if you hear anything."

"Yeah."

The big hand on the wall clock makes a half turn before either of them speaks again. There's a ringing in the background Mona recognizes as Jack's cell phone, but he doesn't answer it.

"Do you hate her?" he asks. "Kathy, I mean?"

"No." Mona realizes it's true as she's saying it.

"I was just wondering . . ." He lets the sentence die. And the big hand makes its way from the twelve and back.

"Are you still there?" she asks.

"I guess I should go," he finally says. "It's late here, and I got like no sleep last night." The part of the conversation where he used to say "I love you." And then he hangs up. Mona watches the big hand make seventeen more revolutions.

Probably the most difficult time in Kathy's life was the time after she and Jack became lovers before he ended things with the redhead. She'd worked with him every day, felt the white-hot tumor of attraction flare in her gut every time she passed his office or a coworker mentioned his name. Somehow she'd managed to keep it together when she actually had to interact with him, but afterward, she'd find her heart in her ears, racing as if she'd finished a marathon. She feels that way again, when Jack finally answers his phone in a hotel in Minnesota.

"I've been trying to reach you." She realizes she sounds rushed and panicked, stops to take a breath.

"Yeah, my phone's not working so great here." He sighs, and she can almost see him settling into the bed, closing his eyes, steeling himself for a conversation he doesn't want.

"About this morning, I'm sorry," she says, even though she isn't and he once told her one of the things that bothered him about the redhead was that she apologized for everything.

"It was weird, I had to catch a plane. Don't worry about it."

She asks about the transaction he's working on, and he gives an uninspired account.

"It would be nice if you were here," he says. "There's all this snow, we could just stay in bed and order room service."

"That would be fun." Things seem normal or normalish. "So I was thinking about when we first met, about our first real conversation. Do you remember?"

"About Billings? Sure."

"What did you think of me when we first met?"

"Great rack, nice legs."

"I'm serious."

"So am I. You terrified me when we first met." Jack's voice is soft, and she wonders if this is all in her head—this worry over Mona and Ryan and their own potential children might just be that thing that people do to screw things up when they're going well, to sustain drama. "You were this beautiful kid. The joke among the partners was that I'd be sued for sexual harassment by the end of the summer."

"Really?"

"Yeah, but then you were so grown-up, so capable."

Kathy nods into the phone. "Tell me about when you first met Mona."

A pause. A siren sounding somewhere.

"Why?"

"I've done the math," Kathy says. "She must have been younger than I was when you met me."

"I was younger then, too."

"I know. Just tell me."

"I've told you," Jack says. "I was at the courthouse with my brother for a traffic ticket. Mona was a lackey for the *Plain Dealer*, getting records or something, and she bumped into me at the water fountain."

"What did you think when you first met her?"

"I thought she looked cute. And she was really flustered, which was endearing."

"Did you think she was smart?"

"I didn't think she was stupid."

"That's not what I asked."

"I don't know; I guess not." Jack sighs. "What do you want me to say, Kath, that meeting you was like meeting her or that it was completely different? I'll say either. I'll say it was just like meeting my high school sweetheart, if that's what you want."

"I'm not sure." The fear bobs in her belly again.

"I'm not necessarily opposed to more kids," Jack says from nowhere. "But if you haven't noticed, no one in my family lives very long. Having babies in ten years wouldn't be very fair to you or to them."

"Yeah, better if we'd met ten years earlier," she says, but thinks, better if she'd met him first.

After he hangs up, she wills him to call back, then distracts herself with some non-real reality show. Finally she turns on her computer and Web searches Mona. It's the kind of thing she used to do all the time before she and Jack were lovers. There's a cluster of articles Mona did on area museum funding. Kathy reads the whole series as night bleeds into morning.

The phone rings as she's putting on her coat to go to work.

"This is the Chicago police department," the canned voice says into the answering machine. She jogs back to the kitchen, takes the cordless from its cradle. "May I speak with Mr. or Mrs. Reed?"

"Speaking." It seems easier than explaining the truth.

"We found your Mercedes." The disembodied voice gives directions to the police station, and Kathy starts to call Jack but hangs up.

After she and Jack became lovers, after he gave her keys to the condo and let her move her clothes into his drawers, Kathy had only gone with him once to pick Ryan up from Mona's. The redhead had met them in the doorway and Jack had reintroduced the two women.

"We met a long time ago." Kathy had extended her hand. "When I was a summer."

"Of course," Mona said lightly. Neither one of them mentioned that she'd slept with Jack or any of that. And what Kathy was looking for, that symbiotic connection she'd seen in Jack's office, wasn't there. In a way that was sadder; if she'd told her father he would have said, *See, he was happy with her once, too.* After that, Kathy hadn't had any desire to see the redhead again.

Until now. Mona's phone number is on a chart magneted to the refrigerator along with the numbers of Ryan's doctors and the poison control center. Kathy dials, and Mona answers on the second ring.

"They found your car," Kathy says.

"Who is this?"

"Kathy Kreinhart, Jack's girlfriend. The police called, they found the car. They want someone to come get it."

"Oh, thanks, I guess I'll go before work."

"Would it be easier if you picked me up and we went together?" Kathy says with more force than needed. "That way you wouldn't have to worry about returning Jack's car." No sound but the hum of central heat. "I was just thinking it might make the most sense. My schedule's pretty flexible, maybe once Ryan's at school?"

"Sure." Mona sounds like an actress in a high school play who doesn't know how to deliver the line.

An hour later Mona pulls Jack's car into the circular drive, and the doorman opens the passenger side for Kathy, gives a confused look when it's not Jack behind the wheel. After an exchange of mindless greetings, Kathy tells Mona where the station is located.

"Did your hand get hurt in the robbery?" Kathy points to the splint on Mona's arm. On Mona's right hand is a large diamond, obviously her engagement ring reset in a platinum band with an emerald. And Kathy wonders if Mona is only wearing it on her right hand because her left is in a splint.

"Yeah," Mona says. "Nothing's broken; they said it was just a bad strain."

"Do you want me to drive?" Kathy asks, realizing she's never driven Jack's car before, wonders if Mona used to drive it when she was married to Jack. By the way she cautiously slows into the turns and sits straight and stiff as Sheetrock, Kathy guesses Jack always drove her, too.

She wants to ask, but doesn't. She wants to ask if Jack made her feel alone sometimes. If occasionally Jack's eyes had held all the warmth of a Popsicle for her, too. When Jack had gone out for coffee, had the redhead ever wondered if he might just never come back?

"I wonder if they'll catch the guy," Kathy says instead.

"I doubt it," Mona says. "He'll probably get away with it."

The first time Mona met Kathy, she hadn't really thought about her. In fact, she didn't even recall their meeting in Jack's office until a year and a half later when news of Jack's affair filtered down to Melanie from a friend who worked in the firm's IT deparment. Then the memory of the blond girl in Jack's office had smacked Mona in the face, and she didn't realize how she ever could have missed it. She'd been eight months pregnant at the time, not the best moment to stand in front of the mirror and compare yourself to a pretty woman twelve years your junior.

Next to her in the car, Kathy is still pretty, with dewy skin and eyes blue and faceted as cut sapphires. But apparently that wasn't enough to keep Jack from being Jack. Guilt percolates in Mona's guts, and she wonders if she only slept with Jack as some sort of karmic payback—squaring things up with Blond Ponytail. She hopes it's something more noble, something about fate and things "meant to be."

"I think that must be it." Kathy points to a low-rise building with a police crest on its side.

Mona hasn't been at a police station since her early days picking up arrest reports as a general assignment reporter, but the place feels old hat, not too far a cry from the worn and weathered precincts she's seen on TV.

Boy Cop, arm draped around the watercooler in the corner, talks to another blue-uniformed officer. "How's your wrist?" he asks when they come in, and Mona holds up the cloth cast. "I told you, you should have gone to the hospital."

"You were right," she says, half-expecting him to ask where her husband is. He doesn't, instead hands Mona stacks of paperwork to fill out.

Kathy thumbs through the Most Wanted flyers dangling from a ring on the wall, and Mona notices her engagement ring. Not identical to the one she and Jack picked out in St. Thomas more than sixteen years ago, it *is* similar, the same princess cut and a platinum band. Maybe it's just classic, but Mona can't help looking at it and thinking how unoriginal.

"If you need to go to work, I think I can handle this from here," Mona says to Kathy. "You don't have to stick around."

"No, I should stay, just to make sure that the car works and everything." Kathy smiles. "Maybe we should drop it by a mechanic? I don't want to leave you with something broken down and useless."

It occurs to Mona then that the ball of something dark and sticky in her gut isn't guilt but sympathy. With her injured hand, she reaches for Kathy's shoulder.

Hours later, as Mona skims another horrible story by the horrible intern, she'll still be thinking about the exchange. But now Kathy turns her head, looks at Mona, eyes wide and searching for something. Her pinked lips open and close, and she waits for whatever wisdom Mona can offer.

"By the way," Mona says, "congratulations."

more fluid than
you think

It seems impossible to Jack that his brother could be forty. But Connor's kid, the younger one with the dark hair, Jack thinks, calls him at the office on a Tuesday morning and invites him to a surprise party.

"I would love for you and Aunt Kathy to come," the girl says, calling Kathy her aunt even though she technically is still only Jack's fiancée. "And I don't have to tell you how much it would mean to my father."

Phone balanced between his ear and his chin, Jack opens the calendar on his computer screen and looks at all the meetings scheduled in the days immediately before and after the Saturday afternoon in two months.

"Do I have to tell you right now?" he asks. "Let me get back to you after I check with Kath."

But Jack doesn't ask Kathy about it when he goes down a floor to her office to eat Thai takeout in the cartons or when they're in bed that night. He doesn't bring it up in the morning over coffee and the *Tribune*. Not the next morning or the one after that. It's not simply his hectic schedule making it a problem, nor is it just the idea of his kid brother getting old—he and Kathy celebrated Jack's own fiftieth birthday at Eli's last month. There *is* something unsettling about the idea of him and Kathy going to his brother's, but he can't quite define it. So the party doesn't come up again until he drops his son off at Mona's on Sunday.

In the foyer, seven-year-old Ryan acknowledges his mother with a nod, mentions Kathy took him to the new *Superman* movie, and scampers to his room to resume his love affair with a handheld game system. Jack follows Mona to the kitchen, where he sits at the table that used to be his.

"You look really nice today," he says as she makes coffee.

She thanks him and asks about his week. It has become their ritual. Thirteen months ago, when he'd slept with her for the first time since the divorce, Jack figured it was going to be a one-time kind of thing. It had evolved into a Sunday-afternoon-when-he-dropped-Ryan-off kind of thing. They'd start with coffee and a prospect and end in the bedroom, the study, or the floor of the bathroom, depending on where Ryan was in the house. But today when he reaches for her hand, she draws it back against her breast.

"Not now, Jack," she says, and he notices one of the reasons she looks so good is that she's wearing a low-cut shirt and high-heeled sandals. "It's not such a great time for that right now."

He doesn't need to ask, but he does anyway. "Do you have a date or something?"

"Yes, actually." When she blushes, she looks like she did when he met her more than twenty years ago, and something, maybe jealousy, maybe relief, pinches at his chest. It's uncharted territory, and he's not sure of the correct response.

"Well, there you go. It's more fluid than you think," he says, inexplicably adding a wink. Mona looks at him and cocks her head. "If you'd have told me, I could have kept Ryan a little longer, so you could have some privacy."

"No, no, it was kind of a last-minute plan." She waves for emphasis. "It's some guy from work . . . we dated a while ago, we figured we'd try again. It's no big formal event. I got a sitter."

"Sure," he says. Realizing he's drumming his fingers on the glass table, he stops. "I understand."

"Yeah, one of those type of deals."

"Hey," Jack begins unsure of what he's going to say until he says it. "Do you want to go to Connor's fortieth birthday party with me?"

"Yes," she says without blinking or asking when it is, or where she'll be staying, or if Kathy will be there. "I would love to."

When Connor picks Jorie up from the mall so she can practice driving, he doesn't tell her he spent the afternoon in Mass General's oncology ward or that his hip aches from where technicians extracted a marrow sample. He doesn't mention he's woozy because they took enough blood to feed a family of vampires. He certainly says nothing about how he didn't believe his oncologist when she'd told him again, everything looked great, no sign of any relapse.

This leaves very little to talk about as they weave in and out of Boston's lesser-trafficked streets. Her skills are nervous and wobbly, which isn't making him feel better physically or better about her chances of passing the driver's test when she tries again next week. Still, he tries to be encouraging, until, mercifully, she jerks the Beetle to a stop in a visitor-parking space in front of the condominium tower where her mother and stepfather live.

"Maybe brake a little sooner next time," Connor says. Twenty-some years ago his brother had screamed and yelled and turned tomato red trying to explain the finer points of the manual transmission; Connor had felt sick then, too. "You're getting much better, though."

"That's a gross overstatement," Jorie says. "I still suck."

"Well, you're sucking less and less."

Popping the trunk, she gets her backpack and meets him at the driver's side. Hands on her bony shoulders, he kisses her forehead, tells her he'll pick her and her sister up the next afternoon, suggests she try to get along with her mother.

"You should come in for a minute, Mom wants to talk to you about a few things." Oddly nervous, Jorie balances on one combat-booted foot, flipping a piece of coal hair between her thumb and forefinger.

Two days ago she'd been a blonde—a tall, beautiful blonde, with the translucent skin and gray eyes of her mother. Yesterday morning Connor found her at the kitchen table eating scrambled eggs and drinking coffee, her waist-length hair looking like an oil spill. A week shy of forty, Connor's own hair is still as dark as ever, but it's nothing compared to what his daughter did. She looks like something in a children's coloring book, where none of her shades are true to life. The black hair makes her eyes almost purple, her face unbleached cotton.

"I don't feel so hot, cheesefry," he says. "Tell your mom I'll call her tonight."

Jorie's eyes narrow, the same way her mother's narrow, into a concern that's oppressive.

"What's wrong?" she asks. "When's your next appointment?"

"Next month." He feels his eye twitch; he's never been able to lie convincingly to people he cares about. "I'm really just tired, that's all. Tell your mom I'll call her later."

"But Keelie's probably home, and you know she'll throw a complete fit if you were here and didn't say hi."

Connor sighs. There are many reasons he doesn't want to go into his ex-wife's condo. If he had to pick the top three, he'd start with Jorie's hair. Then there's Laine's new husband, though Steve is likable enough, his "Gosh, I'm lucky you let this girl go" attitude makes Connor uncomfortable. The real reason, however, is that he feels ill, and it shows—his belt is in the last notch and his pants still drip from his hips, his skin is the color of boiled chicken. Even if his doctors can't find anything wrong with him, Laine won't miss it. Laine never misses anything.

"I can barely keep my eyes open—" he starts.

"You have to go in because Keelie planned this stupid surprise party," Jorie says, words jumbled and rushed. "And Uncle Jack flew in from Chicago and Grandpa Rosen and all the stupid friends you guys used to have. They're crammed upstairs, waiting to jump up and throw confetti and crap."

"Oh." He smiles and flicks the key fob, locking the car. "I guess I have to go in then, don't I?"

"I tried to tell Keelie you wouldn't want anything and it would be weird to have it in the dweeb's house, but you know she can be a total cunt."

"Jor—"

"I know, I know," she sighs. "We're family, blood, water. Yada, yada, yada."

Connor considers lecturing Jorie, but then he notices that she's wearing a dress, moss-colored and gauzy, but a dress nonetheless, for his party. Something about that is so sweet, it makes his chest ache. So he rolls his eyes and wraps his hand around her index finger. The doorman nods them through to the elevator, and they shoot up a dizzying thirty floors. He blinks and leans against the railing.

Jorie eyes him nervously. "Are you sure you're okay?"

"I'm fine now," he says. "Once your mom sees your hair, I can't promise anything."

The doors part, depositing them at the penthouse, where all the people from his former life yell "Surprise," and do actually throw blue and gold confetti, the shiny foil dots splintering light in all directions.

The first person he sees is his ex-wife; Laine is always the first person anyone sees when she's in the room. "Happy birthday." She leans in to kiss his cheek, smells the way she's always smelled, simply clean.

He's known her seventeen years, her own fortieth birthday slipping by five months earlier, and he's still struck by her.

Steve Humboldt, standing next to Laine with his dopey aww-shucks expression, gives Connor a banker's handshake. Connor straightens up and tries to make his grip as firm.

Connor's older brother is there with his ex-wife, not his fiancée, and the way Jack's arm snakes around Mona's waist seems to indicate the title "ex-wife" may be subject to change. Connor wonders why Jack has told him nothing about it. In fact, can't recall his last conversation with his brother at all.

There's Laine's father, who still calls Connor "son," even after all the things Connor did to hurt his daughter. And the rest of the room is filled with the friends he and Laine used to have. People they'd go skiing with, other couples from graduate school who stayed in the area after Harvard, people with whom you discuss politics and weather and other things of no consequence. Near the end of his marriage, he'd had an affair with one of their neighbors, and that woman is there now, next to her husband, smiling and throwing metallic dots, as if nothing ever happened.

"Do you like it, Daddy?" his thirteen-year-old daughter asks. She has Connor's dark hair and eyes and C-cup boobs neither he nor Laine can account for.

"It's wonderful," he says, even though the catered appetizers—feta and spinach puff pastries, skewers of chicken, scalloped potatoes, chocolate fondue—aren't things he likes. A bunch of her friends roam the plush rooms, pretty girls in pretty dresses, young men in suits they wear to dances, and he sees that his birthday was her excuse to throw a party, because she's not Jewish so she didn't get a bat mitzvah at the Four Seasons. But Connor doesn't mind. He wants Keelie to be happy, and if this party—paid for by his ex-wife, who has oodles of money, or by his brother, who has even more money—makes her happy, then he's happy.

But he feels alone.

At the doctor's office earlier that day, when everyone kept insisting everything looked okay, he'd started to feel woozy. His oncologist had offered him Compazine, a drug he'd never been able to take. On a desk in front of her she'd had his medical records, records she'd authored for nine years saying just that. He'd looked at her blankly and felt profoundly isolated.

He feels the same way now, in this room of people who think they love him.

It's Jorie's goal to slink past the party and back to her bedroom. On Monday she was voted Girl You Most Want to Fuck in an unofficial poll by the boys of Natick High School. She actually did have sex with her boyfriend after school on Wednesday, and then skipped school on Thursday and Friday because she hadn't wanted to see Brandon afterward. These aren't things she feels like discussing.

For a minute, every one *is* too busy kissing her father and wishing him a happy birthday to notice Jorie or her hair. But then she smells Brandon, overpriced aftershave and Prell shampoo.

"Where have you been, babe? I've been trying your phone for days." He reaches for her arm. "Your hair looks awesome, like Cleopatra or something."

The comment has a domino effect. Jorie's mother, sister, grandfather, and all the friends turn to stare.

"Ohmygod," Keelie gasps, covering succulent lips with manicured nails. "What did you do?"

"It's different." Her mother's face reflects a true horror, but she tries to smile. She reaches a hand out to caresses Jorie's forehead, but Jorie brushes her away. "Is it permanent?"

"Yeah, it is," Jorie lies. "I was just really sick of being a blonde."

Her mother blinks and walks away, and Jorie turns to Brandon. "What are you doing here?" she asks.

Brandon had been assigned her chemistry lab partner in September. He'd broken a lot of test tubes and started a small fire with the Bunsen burner. "You make me nervous," he'd said. Because he was two years older, on the soccer team and student council, Jorie had thought he was making fun. When she realized he was serious, it hadn't made her like him; it made her feel sorry for him, which was why she'd finally gone out with him. But when they'd had sex Wednesday, his face had twisted like the melting clocks in a Dali painting and he'd told her he loved her. She'd hated him then, hated his toothpaste-commercial smile and the way that he told her about the Girl You Want to Fuck poll with a mix of offense and pride.

"Keelie invited me." Brandon nods at her sister, who perks up, momentarily forgetting Jorie's hair.

"I made you that drink you wanted." Keelie smiles and hands Brandon a blue plastic cup. When she starts high school next year, she won't be voted Girl You Most Want to Fuck, she'll be voted Girl You Want to Be Stranded on an Island With. "And, Jor, you have to say hi to Uncle Jack and Aunt Mona."

"I thought he was marrying Kathy," Jorie says sharply.

"I don't know the details, but they came a really long way."

Jorie is about to tell Keelie to fuck off, but her sister waves over the aunt in question.

"Aunt Mona," Keelie says with the affected diction she reserves for important adults. "We haven't had much time to talk, but Jorie and I just wanted to make sure you knew how glad we were that you could come, right, Jor?"

Jorie nods and takes a sip of Brandon's drink, feels the burn of rum in her throat. She doesn't have strong feelings about her aunt one way or the other, associates Mona with the blur of grown-ups from her father's illness, forever whisking her and Keelie off to G-rated movies, Disney On Ice shows, and children's museums.

"I just can't believe Connor is forty," Mona says, and Jorie can see the line where her ivory makeup stops on her ivory skin, a pretty but aging woman. "When I met him he was just this skinny kid who didn't like me."

"What was he like, Aunt Mona?" Keelie, so sincere Jorie almost believes her.

"Well, he was a terrible driver, always getting into accidents." Mona shakes her head, and Jorie stifles a snort, assuming her mother said something about Jorie failing her driver's test. "He was funny and sooo cute, and he was always losing things."

"He still is," Keelie says.

"And there was this one time, right when I first started dating Jack, when I opened the bedroom door and Connor literally fell in," Mona says, as if she isn't speaking to them but to some distant, different time. "He was sitting outside Jack's door, wearing nothing but underwear, in the middle of the night."

"Really?" Jorie is suddenly engaged. "Like was he listening to you guys in the bedroom, listening to, you know?"

"Huh, maybe that wasn't the most appropriate story to tell." Mona's cheeks flush burgundy. "I guess he could have been. It was such an awkward thing, we never talked about it again. God, he must have been just about your age, Jorie."

Jorie thinks about her father at her age, sitting outside his brother's bedroom, straining to hear the sounds of love, and she wants to ask her aunt more. But bratty Ryan, hair red as his mother's, pulls on Mona's sleeve, tells her that he's using chopsticks to eat the sushi, and she should come watch.

"Excuse me." Mona smiles and backs into the dining room.

Keelie rolls her eyes at Jorie, and for a severed second they're sisters, united by the fact that their cousin is infinitely more spoiled and awful than either of them. Then Keelie puts her hand lightly on Brandon's chest.

"May I get you another drink?" The affected grown-up voice again. "It looks as though my sister finished yours."

"Are you always this sweet?" Brandon asks. "Maybe you could teach Jor a thing or two."

Jorie starts walking away, and Brandon abandons Keelie to follow. Jorie looks at him flatly and tells him to get a bottle of something, so he goes back the bar in the family room for a bottle of Grey Goose. He reaches for her hand, and she lets him take it . . . for now.

Watching an overindulged child rattle off the names of the state capitals isn't something Jack would have thought he'd ever enjoy, but he and Mona stand around in his ex-sister-in-law's new place encouraging Ryan and actually clapping. And even though it isn't, it somehow feels familiar.

The whole discussion with Kathy had ended up being much easier than he'd envisioned. She has a court date the Monday after the party. True, Jack hadn't mentioned the event until after he'd checked her docket, but when he finally did, he hadn't even lied about Mona. He'd simply told Kathy that his ex-wife would be there too and waited for her to say something.

"Of course," Kathy had said. "She and Conn have always been close."

It had been a Sunday night and Kathy was wearing glasses on the end of her nose, her pale hair held back with a scrunchie. He'd felt more for her then than he ever had, so much that his heart actually seemed to swell and press against his ribs. "I'll miss you," he said, knowing it was true, but also knowing that he was taking Mona to Boston.

And he did. At seven this morning he kissed Kathy good-bye and picked Mona and Ryan up from the condo, where they'd never really lived together as a family. It was raining and Mona was wearing a fitted yellow slicker. Even though she and Ryan were under the building's awning, she held a bright blue umbrella and she twirled it a tiny bit when he pulled the car around. It was something about that action, a simple flick of her wrist, that made him certain this was the right thing, maybe not for Mona or Kathy or even Ryan, but taking Mona to see his brother in Boston was the right thing for him.

When their plane shot into the air, he reached for the armrest but grabbed Mona's hand by mistake. She smiled and squeezed his fingers, bumped her knee against his, and he'd felt it again.

Ryan didn't seem to notice anything until they checked into a junior suite at the Harbor Hotel and started unpacking.

"Wait." Ryan looked up from his video game. "Are you and Dad staying in the same room?"

"Is that okay?" Mona asked Ryan, but she was looking at Jack.

For the first time it occurred to Jack that his son could report back to Kathy, but the idea wasn't frightening. He would have to talk to Kathy when he got back anyway. "What, you're so old you need your own room now?" he asked lightly.

"I'm not sleeping with you, Dad, you snore." Ryan shrugged and went back to his game.

Even when they showed up at Laine's apartment this afternoon to get ready, no one had said anything about Kathy. Instead, Laine took her twice-over ex-sister-in-law into her arms. "It's been too long," she said.

And in this room full of his brother's people in his brother's city he's stopped saying "ex" when he introduces Mona. She's not correcting everyone either. And now their son is doing parlor tricks, impressing people by his ability to list trivial things like state capitals and the names of world leaders—the fruits of the overpriced private school he attends.

Mona taps Jack's hip with hers and smiles. "Wonder who he gets it from?" she says, and Jack remembers the Cuyahoga County Geography Bee when he was nine. His father had brought stacks of xeroxed documents to go over; his mother had kept ducking out to check her calls at the pay phone. Both of them had been older and icier than the other parents, and yet they'd still been there. And Jack wonders if maybe that's what's really important, just showing up.

"We should get a picture of this," Mona says. "Did you bring a camera?"

"We left it at home," Jack says, realizing that he means the hotel room. But he doesn't correct himself, because the junior suite at the Harbor is the only home the three of them have ever lived in together.

Connor's interest in his grad-school tennis partner's diatribe about the benefits of hatha yoga wouldn't fill a thimble, but he sinks back in the cream-cheese leather sofa, sips a Corona, and pretends to care. He's glad when Keelie rests her butt on the edge of the couch and touches his forearm.

"I got you a present, Daddy," she says when the grad-school tennis player gets up for more mini crab cakes.

"You didn't have to—"

"*Daddy.*" Keelie smiles, more sophisticated than thirteen. "It's your birthday, of course I did. It's in my room."

She takes his hand and leads him down the hall to her girlie room, where everything is shabby chic linens and baby's breath. It's almost identical to the one she has in his apartment, only this one is twice as large. He sits on her bed and fiddles with the lace of the long canopy, while she brings out a large wrapped rectangle, obviously a framed poster or painting.

Expecting something thoughtless and haphazard, he is floored when he rips off the curled ribbons and red foil paper, revealing the framed black-and-white poster of John F. Kennedy, the exact print that hung over his desk in high school.

"Where—" He shakes his head at his daughter. She's already achingly beautiful, and will only become more beautiful.

"I remembered it in our basement." Keelie's grin is wide, her satiny cheeks dimpled. "And Mom was always saying it was the only thing you took with you from your house in Cleveland. So I went to the Kennedy Library, and they had the same one."

Then he's on his feet holding her small, soft body. "It's the most amazing thing anyone has ever given me."

"Really? It wasn't that big a deal, I just took the T to the Kennedy Libr—"

"No, Ke, I mean it," he says, and feels as though an anvil has been lifted from his back, because he knows that she will be okay. No matter what happens, Keelie will be fine, because she has the skills to negotiate the world and depth below the sparkly eye shadow and pinked lips.

"I love you so much," he says, and then she *is* only thirteen—shy, and short, saying she loves him, too. Then she just stands there.

"You better get back to your friends." He tilts his head in the direction of the door, and she retreats to the safe and superficial.

When she's gone, he holds the poster at arm's length and stares into the flat black eyes of the late president. Then he goes to find his brother.

In the room her mother keeps for her but Jorie rarely uses, she and Brandon sit on the bed someone else made and pass the bottle of vodka between them. He tells her about what she's missed at school, about a party they're invited to next Saturday. His hand is on her knee, and she lets it stay there, lets him slide the hand along her thigh, considers the possibility that she's wrong to hate him. She feels herself floating above his touch, until he runs fingers under her top and tweaks her nipple. She pushes him away.

"Get off me, I don't want to."

"Okay." Brandon strokes her hair. "Whatever you want."

"Why are you even here?" Jorie asks, and because she wants him to leave, adds, "Shouldn't you be off banging a cheerleader?"

"What are you talking about? I love you."

"Why?"

"Why what?"

"Why do you think you love me?"

"I don't know." Brandon shrugs. "Because you're beautiful and smart, and you know things."

She remembers his face hanging over hers during sex, twisted and stupid, the way he panted and moved with more urgency when he got close to orgasm.

"Can you just go?" she says, and looks at her black boots. "I really just want you to leave."

When she looks up he's gone, and she distracts herself with the mail her mother stacked on her desk. Letters and pamphlets from colleges that'd apparently gotten wind of her astronomical PSAT scores, far away schools like Cornell, Columbia, Penn, Chicago, Rice, Stanford, and Miami (though they might have been more interested in the results of the Girl You Want to Fuck poll). But then she thinks of her father alone in the city without her. Earlier in the parking lot he'd looked faded, and she'd seen defeat in his eyes she recognized from her childhood, when she was only allowed into his hospital room for a few minutes at a time. She remembers he took her finger in his hand, their secret gesture since she was a baby. Taking another sip of vodka, she reminds herself to be more vigilant in making him see doctors, eat vegetables, and go to the gym. One more sip, and she goes back to the party to check on him.

Even though the party is for grown-ups, it's morphed into the kind of event she goes to with Brandon and his friends. Her mother and the dweeb dance in the living room, people laugh and bump into the heavy stone coffee table, everyone lubricated by wine and spirits.

"Where's Brandon?" Keelie asks when Jorie stumbles back into the living room without him. Jorie has a fleeting imagine of Brandon wandering around the Back Bay streets, wondering what he did wrong, but she pushes it out of her mind. "I sent him to boink a cheerleader," she says, words muffled by a wad of gum to mask the vodka. "What difference does it make to you?"

Keelie shrugs.

"Did you dye your hair to look more like me?" Keelie asks.

And for the first time Jorie realizes her sister does have black hair. It's not as though Jorie forgot, it's simply that Jorie never thinks about Keelie—days go by at her father's house where Jorie doesn't remember she has a sister.

But that's not why. On Thursday Jorie had been studying at Café Paridisio, avoiding Brandon and the boys at Natick Senior High who wanted to fuck her, when a familiar-looking blond man asked if she was Laine Rosen's daughter. Jorie nodded, and the man told her to say hi from Mike Murphy. It was a solid hour before Jorie realized that the man was the same one in the decaying prom photos in her mother's old room at her grandmother's house. And Jorie had thought about her mother at her age, having sex, making As, and shuffling between the houses of her mother and father. Until one day, poof, a broken condom or a failed diaphragm, whatever it was, then a wedding in January and Jorie's birthday the next month. It had made Jorie's stomach bunch into her spine, and she stopped by CVS for the Clairol on the T ride home.

"Did you dye your hair to look like me?" Keelie asks again.

"You mean fat?" Jorie says.

Keelie's dark eyes darken. "You're just saying that."

"If that's what you want to believe." Jorie turns away from her sister, starts looking through the old CDs alphabetized on built-in wall shelving.

"So I heard you were voted Girl You Most Want to Fuck," Keelie says. "That's the kind of thing that makes Mom and Dad really proud."

"Well at least people want to fuck me," Jorie says without turning around. "You know, because I'm not fat."

Taking down Bruce Springsteen's *Born to Run* album, she checks the playlist on the case. A few seconds later she hears Keelie walk away.

To be fair, Jorie has almost forgotten "Thunder Road" was her parents' song, almost blotted out memories of driving around strapped in her child seat in the back of the Jetta while her parents sang in the front. She *does*, however, experience a momentary happiness when the harmonica's whine starts, and her mother stiffens in the dweeb's arms. But then her mother breaks away from Steve, gray eyes circling the room for the source of the music. Jorie is surprised that she can't look at her and bows her head. Her mother excuses herself, scurrying down the hall so no one will see her fall apart. From across the room, Steve squints at Jorie. She shrugs and goes back to her room.

Holding the poster at arm's length, Jack feels himself becoming misty-eyed and philosophical.

"Amazing, isn't it?" Connor asks.

"Didn't Dad get this for me originally?" Jack asks. "On like the one family vacation the four of us ever took. New York or something?"

"Not New York, D.C. I was five." Connor says, and Jack is surprised, both because his brother is right and because Connor rarely talks about their father. "Dad had to work and Mom thought it would be nice if we all went. But then she had a headache, so he had to take us around, and you kept sneaking off to call Anna Fram."

"That's right. It was like a hundred degrees, and Dad almost punched the paddleboat guy at the Lincoln Memorial."

For the second time in as many hours, Jack finds himself thinking of his father and mother. About how when he had been an orphan at twenty-five, his brother fifteen, people always assumed their parents must have died together in some sort of accident, car wreck, plane crash, fire. How else could you be careless enough to lose both parents so early? But now he's at the age where most people he knows have lost one if not both of their parents, where no one makes those assumptions anymore. And he wants to say something, feels that uneasiness he did on the phone with his niece last month.

"It all comes back around." Jack shakes his head, because that's not quite right. "Everything is just so fucking fluid, you know?"

"Is that why Mona's here?" Connor raises his eyebrows. "Are you guys back together again?"

"Yeah." Jack nods. "I think so."

"What about Kathy? I thought you were engaged."

"We were; we are. I don't know." Jack sighs. "But Mo and I have Ryan, a fucking barrel of history. That stuff's important."

Connor just looks at him.

"It's something you should probably think about with Laine." Jack's not entirely sure but adds, "That guy with her is a total putz."

"Steve's a good man."

"Maybe." Jack shoos Connor's words away. "But she's still crazy about you—"

"Jack, she's happy or almost happy, a lot happier than before."

"She still loves you," Jack says, and Connor shakes his head, says that's not always enough. But Jack wants to say more, in truth more for himself than for his brother. "All I'm saying is that these things are more fluid than you might think."

"Is 'fluid' like some new word you just learned?" Connor asks, and Jack tries to remember where he did pick it up, why it's suddenly become his mantra.

"Eh, I think some guy used it in a *New Yorker* cartoon," he says. "I've been trying it out."

• • •

Jack is in the middle of a sentence, something about Ryan and an L train and the Lincoln Park Zoo, when it hits Connor, something akin to being thrown an object too heavy to catch. He's not just tired anymore but exhausted, the bedroom and the skyline through the window, a series of spinning floating colors, bleeding out of their lines.

". . . And the judge is standing next to me, right there at the lion cage," Jack is saying, but Connor holds up his hand to cut him off.

Jack's eyes slim, and he sets his diet soda on the nightstand. All the humor is gone from his voice, he asks, "You okay, kid?"

In the months when Connor had been sickest, Jack had flown back and forth from Chicago to Boston to yell at doctors and demand answers when Connor was too weak, Laine too frazzled. And Jack would be there again if Connor asked. Be there to get Connor into the office of every specialist in the Western world, to throw money around, to threaten lawsuits. But things are different now. Jack has his own son, his estranged wife, and a fiancée back in Chicago. And Connor is no longer a kid.

"I'm just really tired," Connor says. "I'm going to go to the bathroom, splash some water on my face."

Jack nods, says he should find Mona.

Someone is in the bathroom in the hall, so Connor goes to the one in the master suite. It's unlocked and dark, but when he pushes open the door and flips the light switch, Laine is sitting on the edge of the tub, long legs out in front of her, head droopy. She's not an emotional woman, but he can see she's upset, a crumpled piece of toilet paper in her hand. Immediately on her feet, she sniffles back whatever it is she is sniffling and smoothes the seams of her long black skirt.

"I'm sorry." Connor starts to back away, unsure what's appropriate anymore. "Are you okay?"

"I'm fine." Laine waves the hand with the crumpled tissue.

"What's wrong?"

Laine shrugs with open palms. "Listen."

And he does. Springsteen's raspy voice floating through the condo, so faint it's almost imagined. Seventeen years ago, driving around with Laine in the rusting Nissan Sentra. Both of them young and pretty, Laine's stomach growing with Jorie. Even then he wasn't sure he loved her, knew only that he should because she was smart and capable and he was lucky to have her.

"Jorie put the song on."

"I'm sorry," he says, and she looks down again. "I don't know why she does these things to you."

"Well, whatcha gonna do?" she asks. "Are you okay? You look a little piqued."

Telling her would be so simple, would make things better. If he told her any of it, she would take charge, make him better through her platinum will alone.

"Conn?" Eyebrows pitched in tents of worry, she looks so much like Jorie, or at least how Jorie used to look before her run-in with Clairol. It would be easy to tell Laine, but he won't. He's not her responsibility anymore. It's not her job to help him die, because he doesn't want the burden of loving her if he lives.

"I'm groovy sweet like a peppermint stick," he says, and she smiles, perhaps the saddest smile he's ever seen.

"I miss you saying that." She's saying she still loves him. And it makes everything in his body throb that he's still hurting her, after all these years of hurting her, after she's married to the kind of guy she should have married in the first place. She puts her hand on his shoulder, steps closer than Steve Humboldt would probably like. "Do you ever miss me?"

He knows she's really asking if he still loves her.

"Lainey, I don't—" he stops. He doesn't what? Doesn't love her? Isn't it some kind of love that makes him not want to hurt her so badly that he can't finish the sentence? "Of course I miss you."

Neither one of them says anything, and they're once again aware of Springsteen, so faint it's almost gone. Her fingers are still on his shoulder, and she's close enough that he can smell the chocolate on her breath from the fondue. Taking her hand off his shoulder, he holds it, slides his other arm around the back of her waist and starts swaying to the music.

At first she looks confused, but then she laughs, a laugh that is sad, but also not sad. So they dance, on the marble of the bathroom floor, their image reflected in the mirrors over the double sink and the clean black porcelain of the Jacuzzi and the shower.

And he thinks that maybe Jack is right, maybe things are in flux, changing direction on a whim. Isn't it true that everything in his life is the way it is because of a series of glitches, because his mom got pregnant when she thought she couldn't? Because his parents died? Had his father lived five, maybe ten more years, Connor might have gotten to know him like Jack did, may have gone to law school, too. Had his mother not kicked the bucket when he was fifteen, would he have known Jack at all, or would his brother have remained a holiday cameo in Connor's life? Had Laine not gotten knocked up in grad school, would Jorie have been born at all? And Keelie? Or would he and Laine simply have parted ways after a few months of hot sex in public places? So maybe he'll find his way back to Laine, even though she's married to Steve Humboldt, such an aww-shucks good guy for a banker. Perhaps Connor and Laine have forty more years in them, or maybe he's sick and *that* glitch will stitch up the gap between his girls.

There's no way to know. So they dance in the bathroom until they think the song ends, but the music is so soft it's hard to say exactly when that is.

•   •   •

Her aunt and uncle are fucking in Keelie's bedroom.

Jorie watches from the floor of the Jack-and-Jill bathroom separating her bedroom from Keelie's. She's on her hands and knees by the toilet, contemplating puking, and can see everything through the gap in the door. Mona is bent over at the waist, her hands on the lacy white bedspread while Jack presses himself into her from behind. He moans, his face like Brandon's when he hovered over Jorie on Wednesday.

She knows she should leave, that it's not right to stare, but she wants to see, so she crawls across the tile for a better look.

"Jack," her aunt moans, reaches behind her for his hips and ass, squeezes them.

"Oh God." Her uncle's words are choked and broken. "I love you, Mona."

Her aunt quivers and falls forward onto the bed, her uncle after. He kisses her neck, covers her in his weight, his body draped across hers. Then Jorie can't watch anymore, feels everything in her digestive system definitively working in reverse. She makes her way back to the toilet and stares into the bowel, listening to the sounds of her aunt and uncle zipping, giggling, and buttoning in the next room.

Before she can actually vomit, the door is thrown all the way open.

"Jorie?" her uncle asks, and she catches a glimpse of his square-toed shoes and the cuffs of his trousers, then whips her head around to puke up vodka and more vodka and chewed crudités.

When she finishes, she sits on the floor, looks up at him.

"Do you want me to get your sister?" her uncle asks.

"No." Jorie shakes her head, feels heat on her cheeks.

He squats next to her, elbows on his knees, hands hanging between his legs. It makes her think of his penis, then of Brandon's penis swollen and purple.

"Can I get you a soda or crackers?"

"Mmmmmnnnn." Jorie shakes her head again. "I'm okay."

"You just had a little too much to drink?" he asks gently. When Jorie hesitates, he adds, "I won't tell your parents."

She nods and mumbles a thank-you.

"Yeah, it'll be our secret. And between you and me, your father has had plenty of secrets." Her uncle's eyes are her father's eyes, his hands her father's hands, and she realizes this might be the only conversation she's ever had with him.

"Uncle Jack?" she says.

"Yeah?" he looks at her and nods. Even in her alcohol haze, the moment seems an important opportunity to ask about her father or her childhood or something.

"I slept with Brandon," she says.

It takes Jack a minute to realize that Brandon must be the pretty boy who had been loitering around the bar. It takes significantly longer to figure out what he wants to say to his niece. Almost a quarter century has passed since he screwed up this conversation with his brother, and if genetics do the job, he'll probably be dead before his own son exchanges his games for girls. This might be his only shot to pass on any wisdom.

"Didn't you used to be a blonde?" he says, and she looks at the floor. He tries again. "Did you enjoy it? The sex, I mean."

She shrugs.

"Do you love him?"

"He loves me." Jorie shrugs again. "Or he thinks he does."

"Well, there's your problem." Jack relaxes back on his heels. "It'll be better when you love the person, I promise."

Eyes wide and wet, she looks at him, and he feels as though he's said something of value. Then Jorie's body shudders and she lunges toward the toilet again.

The door to the hall swings open, and Connor is there looking from Jack to Jorie and then back. Palms on his thighs, Jack pushes himself to his feet.

"I think the shrimp salad was bad, your kid and I aren't feeling so great," he says.

"Thanks," Connor says. "I think I can handle it from here."

As he's walking out of the bathroom, Jack notices that his brother looks dimmed, and he starts to wonder if there are things Connor isn't telling him.

"Kid," Jack starts. Now, more than ever, he wants to say what he's been trying to say all night, before he wanders out of this bathroom and into the party, before he takes a plane a thousand miles back to his complicated life by the lake. But he can't get it out. So Jack claps his brother's shoulder, nods, opens his mouth but then closes it.

"Fluid?" Connor asks.

Jack squeezes his brother's arm tighter, feels the muscle and bone under his shirt. "Something like that," he says.

Using the edge of the bathtub, Jorie props herself into a sitting position. Her father runs a washcloth under the chrome faucet and hands it to her.

"Shrimp salad?" he rubs her back. "Yeah, right."

"I'm sorry," she says, and he tells her it's okay, sits on the floor next to her.

Even before Keelie appears in the doorway, Jorie is aware of her pink smell, feels stuff spin-cycle in her guts again.

"Ohmygod." Keelie says. "Daddy, she's totally trashed. At your birthday party."

"Shut up!" Jorie hisses, twisting around, clawing at Keelie's shapely calves.

"Totally trashed," Keelie says.

"I'm aware of that," her father says to no one in particular.

"She gets drunk a lot, Daddy," Keelie says. "You should probably know that. And she was voted Girl You Most Want to Fuck."

"You're fat," Jorie says. "Tomorrow I'll be sober."

Lower lip trembling, Keelie runs out.

"Ke, wait—" Connor calls after her, but she's already out of the room; then to Jorie, "That was a really mean thing to say. Why do you do that?"

"It was funny though, wasn't it? It's kind of like Churchill—"

Her father sits back on the edge of the tub. His head is down and his jaw shifts, just like Keelie's does when she might cry.

"Daddy?"

Her father says nothing, stares aggressively at the hardwood floor. Instantly she's sober.

"What is it?" she asks.

"My brother was always there for me. It would just be really nice if the two of you got along."

"Daddy."

"Maybe helped each other out every once in a while, especially now."

The toilet bowl becomes a crystal ball and she can see all of her father's people clearly. Her redheaded aunt and her father's brother, back at the party, naughty smiles on their faces. Jack squeezing Mona's hand as they dote over their spoiled son stabbing tuna rolls with chopsticks. She can see Keelie staring at the full-length mirror in her bedroom, pinching flesh from the swells of her hips, sucking in her breath until her ribs poke through, too worried she's not thin enough to notice her bedsheets have been rumpled. Jorie sees her mother curled into a ball on her bed, probably crying because Jorie forced her to remember what she loves. Her father is giving her these people, they are her legacy, but she has to ask anyway.

"Why does it matter more now, Daddy?"

His hands resting on his knees ball into fists. "You know."

Two words, and she ages three decades.

This is her entrance into adulthood—not sex with Brandon, not the driver's license she'll get on her second try, not the acceptance letter from Harvard next year, nor the birth of her son in a decade and half. Her father is leaving her his people, bequeathing them to her when he goes, be it in thirty years, five months, or next week.

And because she knows that the minute she walks out of the bathroom door nothing in her life will be the same, she does the thing she did as a child, she reaches for her father's index finger and wraps her hand around it.

acknowledgments

I tell my students that everything we are is somehow a product of family, and I lucked out in that department. Thank you to my parents, Nancy and Michael Goldhagen; my sister, Jackie; and my grandparents, Fran and Irv Victor and Marcia Chesley.

I also tell my students they should check the acknowledgments page to see if a writer is satisfied with her agent. I dig mine. Alex Glass—you're my own little Jerry Maguire without Scientology. Likewise, I have nothing but good things to say about my editor, Kendra Harpster, and all the nice people at Doubleday.

Thank you also to Michelle Herman, my thesis director at OSU, whose support is always above and beyond. Some other fabulous folks I met at Ohio State: Lee K. Abbott, Erin McGraw, Stephanie Grant, and Bill Roorbach.

To all the scattered people in my life, who make me proud of my life: Lauren Asquith, Sheri Barrette, Andrea "AC" Baron, Mandy Beisel, Erin Brereton, Jim Bush, Rachel Kramer Bussel, Kae Denino, Matt Krass, Chris Coake, Terri Goveia, Alex Marcus, Andrea Mason, Julie

O'Connell, Brian Romick, Jeremy Staadeker, Brett Stern, Jennifer Stevens, Ben Timberlake, Ryan Tracy, and David Victor.

Lastly, to Will Leitch, for making me want to be a better writer and a better person, and for helping me realize that the better person thing is of far greater importance.

reading group companion

1. What do you imagine the relationship between Connor and Jack was like when both of their parents were alive? What about when only their mother was alive?

2. What does this title mean? What "accidents" happen, and do you agree that they are accidents? Or are Jack and Connor fully in control of their destinies regardless of their pasts?

3. Where do you think the climax of the novel occurs and why? Do Jack and Connor ever reach any understandings about each other? If so, what might some of those understandings be?

4. What motivates Jack's and Connor's infidelities? Are those motivations the same or different?

5. What effect does the irregular passage of time between chapters have on the plot? Why did the author write it this way instead of in a straightforward, linear way? Similiarly, what effect do the multiple narrators have on the movement of the plot?

6. Jack and Connor view themselves as very different people, but in what ways are they more similar than they think? In what ways are they truly different?

7. By the end of the novel, Jack and Connor have one son and two daughters, respectively. In what ways does the next generation of Reeds carry on the family traditions and the characteristics of their parents?

8. The author gives Mona, Laine, and Kathy the opportunity to narrate chapters and give their perspectives. How do the narrative, plot, and perspectives differ from Jack's and Connor's when the women are given the narrative power?

9. How do you think that Mona and Laine feel about each other? About the other's marriage?

10. What changes Jorie's perspective at the end of the novel? Is it just fear or a genuine maturing? Can you speculate on what happens in each of the other characters' lives after the last page of the novel?